I0598795

# WINTER'S
# CHALLENGE

Don't miss the other books

in the Rise of Fall Series

DECHARLATHAN
PUBLISHING

# WINTER'S
# CHALLENGE

*The Rise of Fall – Book 2*

WRITTEN BY

**Jeremy Graves**

Winter's Challenge

ISBN: 978-1-954298-02-6

Cover design by Chiara N. Monaco

Special thanks to:

Teresa Wheeler – Proofreading & Main Editing

Charlotte Graves – Alpha Reading & Development

Nicole Young – Developmental Editing

Catherine Graves – Line Editing

Lacey C – Beta reading & Development

Gabe Wheeler – Beta Reading

Jess Loftus – Beta Reading


First Printing Edition, 2021

Join us on the web site to browse upcoming volumes and receive our newsletter. Enjoy full color maps and sign up to receive a free e-book of the first short story in the series at…

www.decharlathan.com

*For Jonathan,*

*The Demon Prince you have to love.*

# CHAPTER 1

The mist rose early this close to the Loch. It seeped up from the murky waters and swirled thick in the air. Moisture clung to everything, leaving it damp and vulnerable to the chill wind. The tall man had finished his meal some time ago, long enough that his clothes were now dry.

He wore a heavy coat over a greasy tunic, trousers thick and insulated against the bitter wind blowing in from the north. A large mug of ale sat untouched next to the plate. The patron had wanted to avoid seeming out of place and so had ordered it with the food. Tonight's negotiations were best conducted with a clear head.

The man leaned back in his chair, positioned in the tavern to allow him to both see the door and prevent anyone from getting behind him. He ran his hand slowly through the thick, wiry beard. Black whiskers covered much of his dark-skinned face except where it met a long, jagged scar that almost reached his neck. From a distance you might almost think the man asleep. You'd be wrong.

Next to his worn muddy boots, and half under the table, sat a rather mangy-looking warg. The canine packs that roamed the Winter tundra were vicious hunters with long front claws and sharp teeth. This one seemed out of place among men. Matted grey fur covered a rangy body that hadn't spent much time overeating. From a distance you might almost think the warg asleep. You'd be right.

The tavern cowered amongst the old buildings on the seedier side of South Harbor. Neither side was upstanding, but the most recent ruler had put forth some effort into making it better. Despite the name, the town lay at the northeastern tip of the kingdom of Autumn. Most people in South Harbor made a living from the waters of the Loch since they were on the southern end of the large body of water.

The man was here on business. The kind that's best kept out of earshot of the wandering do-gooder or an overzealous off-duty guard. Mind you there were few of the first and probably none of the latter, but people who traded in slaves tended to be cautious in Autumn.

His contact was late. Not a good sign. He'd arrived only a few minutes early, ordered food and ale, and sat to wait. The food was long gone, his ale flat and room temperature.

Over an hour past the agreed-upon time, his guest walked through the tavern door. The greasy-looking oaf was only a bit shorter than the big man at the table. He wore travel leathers, the oilskins often seen this close to the Loch.

The brown clay that made up the side roads, and stuck to everything, also caked his heavy boots. He had a severe limp that caused his long oily hair to wave forward and back with each step. He yelled for an ale and pointed at the table as he limped over.

"You're late," gruffed the early man, brow furrowed as he glanced to the sunlight through the nearest window. At the sound of his voice, the warg stirred slightly, shifted, and was soon out again.

"Twernt easy to get ere," the newcomer grunted.

"Can I expect a pattern of failure from your supplier?"

"I is da surplier," barked the limping man, a deep frown on his scarred face.

The big man eyed this oaf. He'd been told the man was a former member of the Wyld Hunt. Either it was a boast or the standards of membership were much lower than rumor would indicate. Either way, there was no doubt that this man was a lackey. Deals don't get made with lackeys. He set a foot gently on the side of the warg and rocked it back and forth as he sighed.

"You're lucky demand is so high at the moment. The Winter mines are shorthanded and strong backs are at a premium. I'll take all you have if your employer meets to discuss future dealings."

"I told yas I is dah—" His words cut off in a gasp as a blade point dug into his gut. His eyes widened, and he quickly adjusted his answer. "I mean, dat is, we all got a boss, ain't we."

"Yes…. I'd like to meet yours. *Now*," the big man growled.

"I'm ter meet meh lady afder we finish ar deelins."

"Until I meet your 'lady' our dealings are quite finished."

It only took a moment to settle up with the barkeep. The oaf never did get to drink his ale and looked crestfallen to see two full mugs on the table that hadn't been touched.

As they made it to the street, the mist began to work back into their clothes and beaded up on exposed skin. The fog swirled and chilled as Winter winds whisked into the dark streets.

Twice the oaf started to get 'lost,' but the warg kept him right next to the larger man with nips and growls of encouragement. After nearly an hour of working through the twisting streets and winding alleyways, they came to a spot where a house almost met the city wall.

The oaf pulled on a length of cut branch sticking out of the log barrier. A section began to rise at an angle. Enough room for a man to slip through. The warg went first, its dark eyes searching for an ambush, nose sniffing the air. After a moment, the oaf was allowed through and then the larger man followed. The opening led out to the north side of town.

The Loch stretched out to their left and before them sat the fording rafts that had hauled the cargo to this spot. They were just a few dozen paces from the border to the Winter kingdom.

The large man gave the oaf a shove as they neared the other slavers. They were of varied races, everything from a small brownie to a towering ogre. Maybe a dozen or so individuals.

The large man looked around at the faces. A long moment passed as they eyed him. Finally, a slender woman stepped from the shadows behind him. A slim copper spike touched the back of his neck and a voice came almost musically into his ear.

"I hear you were looking for me."

The large man smiled widely, the bright white of his teeth in stark contrast to the dark tone of his face and beard. He held up both his hands but showed no sign of distress.

"I was looking for a rumor; it seems I've found something else."

Her smile wasn't pleasant, almost conveying pain. It would seem she wasn't happy he'd pushed for this meeting.

"We had ears in the tavern. I don't often show up for these meetings. Why do you feel the need to insist on dealing directly with me?"

He rubbed his beard. "Well now, for starters, have you ever tried to talk numbers with him?" A nod to the oaf made it plain that the large man was sick of underlings.

She sighed. "I suppose I cannot fault you there. I sincerely hope you make this worth my while."

His eyes moved to the cages. "Looking at the haul tonight, you're short of my previous order. Not to mention three hours late."

"Somehow several sprites and brownies escaped. The bars to the cage were cut. We still haven't found who was responsible."

He lifted an eyebrow. "Cut? Don't you use bronze in your cells?"

"Something melted them. When I find out who, I'll deal with them. For now, we'll deliver what's here and add the rest to your next order."

He waved a hand toward the cages with a deep growl. "My next order is to be five times this many. I've two more mines wanting laborers and I'm already short. Can you both fill that and make up your deficit?"

The woman paused for a moment, her voice lowered to a snarl as she answered.

"I can get half that in one moon, the other in one more."

"I need more! Do you know anyone who can make up the difference? If not, I can look to other... more *established* providers."

Her pause was longer, greed pushing her to claim all the business, yet she was afraid to lose all she could handle due to lack of inventory.

"If you can get to Grimfield, enter the tavern called the Swaying Pixie and ask for a merchant named Lazuli. He'll pick up the inventory we cannot provide."

The woman finally lowered the dagger and the large man turned and looked at her. She wore fitted oilskin that was dyed a deep blue, high black boots, gloves, and a matching black belt. Her hair was a reddish blonde and was in a tight bun on the top of her head. Long pointed ears were the same pale brown as her skin.

She was a wood elf. Light reddish freckles covered her face and nose. She was striking if not outright beautiful. He'd have thought her attractive if she wasn't a slaver. He HATED slavers.

"Well, Rychell, you match your description perfectly." Gray turned to the slave carts and yelled.

"Did you hear all that?"

***

The words flowed through the air to the cages resting just down the hill. A man looked up and started to stand, his build thin and wiry. His hair was completely white and his lean body was covered in scars. He really looked like a slave.

Perhaps he'd escaped at some point in the past or been given freedom. Either way, the raiders had grabbed him up from the refugee camp where he'd been staying. He had put up somewhat of a fight, but in the end, he was captured.

He'd witnessed all the beatings, indignities, and the conditions the slavers had put these people through. Jack had experienced them himself.

The prince almost blew his cover when that sprite got sick. He couldn't think of a way to free just her, and she'd need help anyway, so he just opened the whole cage and gave instructions on where to find aid.

Now he waited. The warg almost gave him away when it scented him in the air and started to come over to say hi, but a hand signal stopped her. Then he heard the words they'd been waiting on. Lazuli was the name, and they had instructions on how to get to him.

Good, he was sick of this. These people deserved to have wounds treated, a hot bath, and a place to stay. He'd see to it that they got all those things. But first he needed to save his friend.

"Did you hear all that?" the large man yelled.

Jack slid a knife of fire into the lock on his cell door. It sputtered as the mist's moisture was boiled off the metal. Then it heated, made a popping noise, and fell away.

As he kicked the door out, it smacked the hand of the limping oaf that had led his ally to the meeting place. Both of the man's teeth parted as the lackey howled, the bronze cage door breaking the bones of his wrist.

The Prince of Autumn had already given the other slaves instructions to stay down until he was ready to free them. Most would've been too terrified to move anyway.

After he slid out, Jack felt a painful slap across his back. The knotted leather of the tongs had bits of copper woven in, and the whip tore small bits of flesh away as it lashed across his skin. He rolled forward, away from the next swing.

He turned to face the ogre. The brute had an excellent swing and the prince could feel a trickle of warm blood running down his back. Jack arched his shoulders as he winced and readied himself. The ogre wasn't looking at him now though. His eyes were entirely on the mangy-looking warg that had come with the big man.

At first, the slavers had paid little attention to the thing. It looked starved and sick enough to just drop dead. Sure, maybe keep your fingers away from those sharp teeth, but they were confident they could put it down if it came to that. Now they had doubts. As soon as Jack had opened the door, the warg had started to shift, a hand sign telling her that trouble was coming. When the whip hit her master, she lost it.

Maeve rushed at the huge ogre. Every time her paws touched the ground, the hound took more earth, rock, and soil. It only took four bounds to reach the massive thug. When she hit the mass of muscle and fat, she was as big as he was. Jack had told her not to kill; the ogre would wish she had.

The prince was worse for wear, but once he'd touched the ground of this realm, he'd felt the familiar great spirit of his home. Power pushed through the surface of Autumn and into the prince she'd missed for months. He had no trouble channeling his anger.

The slavers looked on in horror as the boy they'd whipped, starved, and spat upon transformed. The boy gained the visage, the mark of the Demon Prince of Autumn. A blazing orange skull of bright light and heat surrounded his face. Only glowing yellow eyes showed through.

Maybe just a hint of a glowing smile.

***

Gray had no trouble telling if Jack was free. No sooner had he yelled than he began to hear the screams of terror. Also, by the sound of it, Maeve was doing something horrible to an ogre.

He, on the other hand, had his hands full. They had learned that Rychell Balcan had been trading in the area. She was a rogue wood elf who'd been capturing refugees and selling them into service in Summer and Winter. Both routes were shortened by cutting through Autumn.

Despite clear laws to the contrary, many traded within the kingdom's borders. The problem was catching them. Now that he had the elf right in front of him, Gray wondered if he hadn't bitten off more than he could chew.

She had a copper dagger that was shaped like a needle and was using it in combination with an earth aspect that kept altering the ground under his feet. The taller man felt like he was constantly tripping as the dirt under him shifted and moved. It was like every step was trying to strain his ankles. The sword of air he'd conjured was blocking her shots, but she'd drawn blood from him twice.

Finally, he decided that he'd have to get creative. Rychell had leaned back to pull up dust and rock and had slung the debris toward his eyes. Gray hardened the air around him into a shield. Then he pulled a disk of air under his feet, stable and flat despite the contortions of the soil below.

Now he pushed his attack, using similar tactics against her. Hardened air formed and moved around her knees and ankles, tripping her and throwing her off balance. She realized that he'd win if the fight carried on, so the elf lunged at him, dagger pointed at his throat.

Gray shifted his grip and poured power into his own conjured sword. The air began to hum as a tiny line of teeth formed on the edge of the blade and moved so fast that the sword would cut through most anything. His blade caught the dagger just above the hilt, the metal cut so cleanly that Rychell thought she'd done him in, her knife handle pushing just below his chin.

The look of disappointment as he cuffed her wrists with bands of air and forced the handle away from his uninjured throat was priceless. Gray shook his head once more. How could such a lovely creature be so cruel? He wouldn't mourn her punishment, or the fate of the other slavers. He startled out of his moment of introspection as a slow clap came from the cage carts.

Jack was sitting calmly in the driver's seat of one of the wagons. A brownie rubbed salve on his mangled back. Maeve was prancing around with a sizeable muscled arm in her mouth. The prince needed to talk to her about overdoing it, but Gray had to admit the ogre was alive, and it wouldn't be whipping anyone ever again.

They quickly secured the slavers. As luck would have it, there were several cages available to move them. They were getting all the freed slaves out and settled when they heard the horns. Jack looked up from the apple he'd found, his mouth chewing as he jerked his head toward the ominous sound. Maeve tossed the grisly arm aside and ran to see what was happening.

Gray gave the order for the former slaves to stay near the wagons as he and Jack ran after the hound. The horns sounded again, this time closer. They moved all the way over to the Winter border, holding where the great realm spirit of Autumn's reach stopped.

A large distant form was running toward them, heading for Autumn's border. Things were fuzzy to Gray's eyes. He'd been working on shaping air into a lens to work like a spyglass, but he wasn't there yet. In the dim light, Jack's eyes took on an orange glow as he described what he could see with his enhanced vision.

"It's big... and running toward us. There's an army chasing it. Maybe hundreds, some mounted." Jack swore and Gray could guess why. This many Winter soldiers crossing the border would be an act of war.

"It's a yeti. It's carrying someone... I think." Jack swore again.

Grey saw shapes and they were growing more substantial and clearer, but he still couldn't make out what had Jack angry. He didn't have to ask.

"They're shooting it with arrows.... It has more than a few in its back. That army is dead set on making sure whatever it's carrying doesn't reach the border."

Then they had to wait. Jack was a prince and if he crossed into Winter to interfere, he'd be the one to incite a war. Anything that happened in Autumn was another story. Gray could see his friend was furious. If the army crossed over, he didn't doubt that there would be blood.

The yeti continued to run but now had over a dozen arrows bleeding it and slowing its stride. Finally, it staggered, still thirty long paces from the line. The creature made eye contact with Gray and then tried to toss the bundle across the kingdom border. More arrows sprang out of its white fur as the bundle flew.

Yeti are extremely strong, but even if this one hadn't taken enough arrows to kill twenty men, it couldn't have made the throw. A shout of triumph left the troops chasing the mighty creature, but then the sound shifted to one of anger and frustration.

Somehow an unseen force had accelerated the throw as it reached its apex. The girl, who was wrapped in furs and bleeding from a wound in her side, flew the distance and almost seemed to slow as she landed gently in the big man's arms.

Gray had learned a term in his first year of college. *Plausible deniability*. It's a fancy lawyer way of playing stupid. It's tough to prove someone knows something if they won't admit it.

He might not have pushed a cushion of air under the girl that the yeti died for, trying to get to the border. It's possible he didn't blow a strong wind behind her that carried the limp form far further than a yeti could have thrown her. It wasn't certain that he used that same air to soften her landing, which was a good five paces over the border into Autumn.

Perhaps this yeti played sports.

***

As the girl flew over the border and into Gray's arms, Jack was on her in an instant. His eyes widened as his jaw dropped. He knew that pale face.

"Raine! Raine, speak to me. I need you to say it. Say it and you'll be safe. Raine, please say it!" The girl stirred slightly into consciousness and looked into the face above her own. It was a stranger, unfamiliar features staring down at her. She started to drift, but the voice. It was Jack's voice. She opened glassy eyes and whispered.

"Hosp.... Hospitality." Then she slumped.

Jack smiled. "I grant your request; you're *my* guest now."

Now, they had a chance. The prince gave his orders.

"We won't have time to travel the roads. Get your portal and get back here. It looks like a stab wound and she won't make it much longer."

Gray didn't argue. For the most part, Jack treated him like an equal. When the young man acted the prince, it was best to obey. He was already running toward town.

Jack knew that some of the old laws still held the magic to enforce themselves over the more modern traditions. Hospitality was one of those. If someone came into your home and asked for Hospitality, you could grant it. If anyone tried to interfere with your duties as a host, then they lost all other protections under the law. Realm spirits like this law to be obeyed. The young man was betting on it.

He was a prince and could claim any location within the kingdom of Autumn was his home. Right now, his home was a patch of dirt just across the Winter border, next to the cold, forbidding waters of Loch Mozeg. The girl had asked for Hospitality and he'd granted her request.

Winter had sent an army to get this girl. If they crossed over the line into his home, they'd need to start shopping for new soldiers.

Jack looked down at the girl. Her white hair almost matched his, though it was in stark contrast to his standard shade. He put himself protectively between the girl and the horde of soldiers. A hand signal switched Maeve from digging a random hole to a crouched, ready position.

The lone prince of Autumn and his faithful hound stared down a legion of Winter soldiers.

\*\*\*

Gray was running hard and was glad he hadn't neglected his exercise. The mission to bring down one of the groups that ran slaves through Autumn was a hard-won battle with Claire. She hated the idea of slaves being captured and moved across her land, but she had few people that were both trustworthy and powerful enough to do something about it.

The queen had insisted they have a portable portal on hand in case things went poorly. While it wasn't overly large to carry, it was unwieldy and might have drawn suspicion, so he'd left it in his room at the tavern. Now he was glad they had it.

Sliding back through the hidden entrance into the city and running toward the inn, he spotted a guard. Pulling out the seal that was under his shirt, he began to speak. The guard panicked and drew a sad-looking short sword of bronze. Gray had no time for that; he whipped air around the man and thickened it around everything below the guard's neck. Gray thrust the seal into his face and gave quick orders.

"By order of the queen, granting authority under the seal of her will, I order you." Gray paused only a moment to catch his breath before continuing.

"There's a caravan on the north wall, just up from the Loch. Locked inside are prisoners of the kingdom; near it will be slaves freed by the queen's agents. All will be brought into the city walls and cared for. Tell me you understand."

The guard was near shock, but he nodded, seemingly glad that this man wasn't going to kill him. Gray pulled the air away and let him go, continuing his run, a gust of wind pushing him forward.

The large man slammed through the tavern door and turned heads as he ran in and tore up the steps to the lodging above. Smashing into the door to his room, he shouldered it open, not bothering with the key.

He had run into town because he didn't want to risk the well-being of the slaves or the escape of the slavers. He needed to run into a guard. Now his only concern was getting back to the border where Jack would need him.

His satchel was packed and ready; he grabbed it and moved to the window. The brown tinted glass was fogged with moisture and looked over the clay roof to the stables.

The big man pulled it open and rolled out into the night. He concentrated for only a moment before the air under him became compacted and the winds pushed him up and forward. Eyes from the street moved to the spectacle and his cover was blown, but that was no longer of concern. He didn't have time to lay low.

As he went over the outer walls, an arrow stuck into the thick air under his feet. It seemed one of the guards thought him a threat. The air around him thickened into a basic shield. Not his best work, but he was multitasking. Ignoring the guard, he flew on. In moments he saw the Prince of Autumn staring down hundreds of charging Winter soldiers.

\*\*\*

Jack showed no fear. It was now clear the approaching riders were mounted on kelpies, water spirits that could take a physical form near to that of horses. They were fast and were all but immune to the cold, good attributes for a Winter steed. The riders halted just paces from the border.

A tall soldier with various frills and such on his armor strode to stand right on the line, obviously a leader of some sort. As he spoke, Jack was instantly aware he didn't like this man.

"You're interfering in the business of Winter, urchin. You will bring the girl to me, and we'll leave your border unscathed," the man yelled, staring at Jack expectantly.

Jack cared little for the accolades of being a royal. He never understood taking pride in something you didn't earn. It was unusual for him to use his station to get anything; he liked to earn what he had.

But Claire's words echoed through his mind, *'Diplomacy saves lives.'* He'd better give it a try. Even if he could hold the soldiers off if they rushed, they'd likely be able to hurt Raine. He took a deep breath and did his best to choose his words.

"You speak to the Prince of Autumn. The lady has asked for Hospitality. I'm standing on the soil of my home and have granted her request. If you cross the line into my kingdom, I'll send you home in pieces."

Jack meant it, though he hoped it wouldn't come to that. Most of these men were under orders and he hated killing without reason.

The leader laughed. Just looked him right in the eye and laughed. They didn't believe him. Jack remembered his disguise.

Claire had eventually given in to granting both him and Gray a new appearance. She now wielded Transmutation and could alter the physical shape and look of things. Gray was too clean-cut to play his role as a slave buyer for Winter, and Jack was likely to be recognized, even this far from the Blood Keep.

His face had been altered and scarred, his hair made nearly white. His body was mostly the same with the open wounds from the ogre's lash still on his back. He had to concede that he really did look like an urchin.

The Winter soldiers were loathe to step foot across the border, but they weren't going to leave without their prize. The leader once again addressed him.

"I understand you might be hesitant to meet our request; perhaps we could come to an understanding." Reaching into his belt, he pulled out a satchel of coins. The amount would have fed a small family for a year. Jack didn't really care about money and responded with his typical diplomacy.

"If you step across my border, you'll need help getting those out of where I'll put them."

The false smile faded from the man. All pretense of patience was gone. He waved to a soldier who brought the leader a long spear, polished bronze covering a sturdy wooden core. The point came out to a needle tip. The leader glared daggers into the prince who didn't look at all like royalty.

"You should've taken the coin, peasant." He launched the spear, his aim true and practiced.

Jack never moved while the throw was pulled back and aimed. Right as the man released, Jack snapped the fingers of his right hand and said, "Fetch."

The hound threw soil into the air as she lunged toward the leader and then turned, catching the spear in her mouth. Maeve was still in her small formed size, but her jaws stopped the projectile as if it had hit a boulder. The little hound returned the spear, setting it on the ground in front of the Winter army.

She may or may not have chewed on it some, but it was still technically in one piece. Her tail wagged so hard that the back half of her body moved with the motion. She was ready for more play.

Jack kept his eye locked on the man who'd just tried to kill him. A slight smile appeared on the young prince's altered face.

The leader gave a command and three of his men pulled long bronze swords and began to move toward the line into Autumn. Jack whistled, and Maeve returned to his side. He used the last of his diplomacy.

"He orders you to your death. Don't enter my home looking for violence. You *will* find it."

Jack was happy to see that two of the men hesitated and looked to the leader, perhaps afraid of the prince, or maybe of his strange companion. One of them was a bit more obedient and stepped into Jack's home with sword drawn. He was two steps into Autumn when Jack gave a slow underhanded toss, a bright orb of orange flame soaring in an arc toward the lone soldier. The man caught it in a gauntleted hand. His instincts had won out over his better sense.

The globe didn't explode; it flared. The heat coming off of it would have turned cold stone to liquid. The soldier didn't have time to scream. The spot where he'd just stood was quickly turning into a puddle of melted armor, the steam of his fluids jetting up into the air.

The other two men looked on in horror as their fellow soldier was reduced to a pool of bronze and ash. They both looked to the leader, whose mouth was agape.

Jack didn't envy this commander. Clearly, he was under orders to bring the girl back. Failure in Winter was often fatal. They wouldn't have sent so many if they were going to be willing to let Raine go. The leader had to decide whether to risk ordering an army into another kingdom or going home empty-handed.

Jack wasn't sure how the fight would go, but he only needed to stall. Gray would come back and they'd be gone. Time was on his side, even if the math was pretty terrible. He was outnumbered several hundred to one, but he was sitting on the powerhouse of his homeland. Also, he had a Maeve, who was currently digging another random hole. She didn't like to hurt people, but if he gave the signal, she'd tear through them.

The leader looked enraged, and Jack could predict his next order. The prince readied the power in his core, envisioning a wall of flames, ten feet high and a hundred paces across. By setting it two paces on his side of the border, the scorched earth would be evidence of his defense in the encounter.

He pulled the energy together, weaving the spell. As the charge came, the soldiers began to pile up only a single pace over the border. They were mounted, and the kelpies and soldiers heaped up against one another, a full-speed charge into a barrier of dense air.

Jack turned to see Gray standing just behind him. He'd been so focused on the Winter army he hadn't noticed his friend land beside him. Maeve wouldn't bother to alert him to an ally.

The man's face was already red with the strain, and sweat was forming on his brow. The stress had Gray at his limit in seconds. Jack walked over and set his hand over the man's thick wrist. The flow of the realm spirit's power flowed into the larger man, his energy restored. The wall of thick air was now powered not by one caster, but by an entire realm.

Jack dug through Gray's satchel with his other hand; the familiar shape of the orb cluster came into view. The prince activated the portal between them and the army, blocking the view of him and his small party from the direction of the enemy. The door opened into a private room inside the Blood Keep, just between the royal quarters and the newly built dragon sanctum.

A whistle sent Maeve through the door. Gray dropped the shield and scooped up the injured girl. Jack couldn't help himself; he poked his head around the portal and made eye contact with the Winter leader. The big soldier was nearly crushed but slowly coming to his feet.

Jack's eyes lit into bright yellow orbs. As the leader looked on in horror, one yellow eye winked at him before disappearing. Both Jack and Gray could hear a cry of anger and frustration as the pop and hiss of the closing portal ended the sound.

They were home.

# CHAPTER 2

Gray's return to the Blood Keep felt rushed and the wound on the pale girl's side was life-threatening. He'd guessed what Jack had in mind, even if he didn't know who the girl was or why she'd arrived in Autumn under such circumstances.

He didn't wait for Jack to follow through; the tall man ran toward the dragon sanctum as fast as possible. In the halls to the royal quarters, a guard came upon him. The man readied himself to fight. It was understandable.

Gray was wearing a rough and unfamiliar face while running near the queen's apartments, all while carrying a young woman in noble Winter garb who was near death. It was an honest mistake, but he didn't have the time. The guard now tossed and held against the wall of the hallway by bands of opaque air, Gray stopped to give him instructions.

"I need you to have Joobel summon Bloom to the sanctum and alert the queen." He set the guard down, the man torn between going for his sword or following orders. He needed the man to obey.

"RUN!"

The guard took off down the hall. Gray continued plowing on in the other direction, through the breezeway they'd set up to the large dome. The dragon sanctum. It had a couple of regular entrances and one large opening in the south wall. The sun would warm the room some during the day and the dark stone held in the heat. His own design.

Harvest stretched out, having completed his patrols of the kingdom's borders. He looked up and growled at the sight of an unfamiliar face and the smell of the girl's blood. Maeve came in behind him in her standard form, and that more than anything told the huge death dragon that this wasn't a time for battle. Gray looked up and paled a bit. He'd forgotten he still wore a different face.

"Harvest, it's me. She's hurt badly and connected to Jack and Claire somehow. Joobel will summon Bloom, but she needs to get here ready to help. Can you meet her and explain?"

Dragons could speak over vast distances using the mind-to-mind connection they called dragon-speak. These vast distances expanded exponentially if other dragons relayed the messages for them. The man saw Harvest close his eyes, and then his words appeared in Gray's mind.

"There's no need. I've spoken to my sister just now. She is only a couple of minutes away and will be ready to act when she arrives."

Gray nodded at the ebony giant. He was as large as the wood wyrms of Summer now. The Naming had made him huge and Bloom was only slightly smaller. The two of them went a long way to keeping Autumn safe from the greed of the other kingdoms.

He began arranging the girl where Bloom could reach her. Jack came down the steps only seconds after Gray. Norim, Claire, and Joobel all arrived only moments after the prince. The guard had done his job.

Gray had pulled the blood-soaked furs back and was cutting the fabric of the elegant dress around the wound. A stab from a dagger, if he wasn't mistaken. A fine blade of air was sticking out from his index finger, deftly cutting a rough circle in the cloth around the injury.

He picked the bits of fabric and dried blood from the area, then felt her pulse just as Norim and Claire started to take over first aid. Joobel quickly went and pulled the girl's head onto her lap. The gnome's hand on the girl's pale forehead pulled the pain away so she could breathe easy.

Jack was standing protectively over them. Gray still didn't know how the prince knew this girl. He was about to ask when a solid thump sounded from just outside the sanctum.

A mighty green dragon took two steps inside and released a blast of fog. The glowing mist covered everyone present. Bloom was also Named and didn't lack for power. She didn't need to conserve her energy like others of her kind might. Her healing fog soon filled the sanctum.

Gray looked at the still shirtless Jack, whose torn back was filling in. Dried blood flaked away as the flesh came together. The lightest of scars was soon the only evidence of the ogre's whip. He also felt healing at work as aches and pains of his hard living over the past few weeks reduced, and the cuts and bruises left over from his fight with the elven slaver faded.

The Winter girl had been so close to death only moments before. Now she was sputtering, weak yet whole. The injury and the battle to survive had drained her. Claire pulled her cloak over the girl, as her dress was now torn wide open. Gray could see that the days-old wound left only a circular folded scar.

Jack laid a hand on the girl's arm. Her eyes opened wide as she felt energy rush into her. As weak as she'd been, she now looked ready to fight, body healed and spirit charged. Jack looked up, first to Gray, and then to Joobel.

"I'd like to introduce our cousin. May I present Raine Anahita...." His eyes flared with anger.

"The Winter Maiden."

***

Claire had been resting in the royal bedrooms when the guard reached them. He only had to move down two halls to reach the queen, who had retired to chambers. She shared them with her adopted sister, royal advisor, and emissary to the Sept of Fallen Leaves. Joobel was stretched out on a sofa and complaining that Jack had been away too long.

Norim and Claire were sipping tea and trying to figure out a way to stretch the ever-thin army to patrol the Summer border more efficiently. Norim had remained in service to the Keep, serving both as advisor for the queen and caretaker for several young boys who were given a home a couple of years previous. The naiad provided a calming presence that helped offset that of the more excitable advisor.

Claire missed Jack as well, but Joobel was getting on her nerves. The queen arguably missed Gray even more, but didn't want to lock him into the politics that mired her life. Not to mention the prophecy; he didn't deserve to bear that burden.

The knock on the door was somehow both soft and urgent. Claire started to get up, but a loud hum preceded the opening door by only a second. Joobel was the only one who could hear the soft whispered tone of a guard who seemed afraid he'd done something wrong. The hum filled the air again as Joobel began flying through the room and talking in excited tones.

"There's a big man with a beard running through the halls with an injured girl! He said we're supposed to meet him in the sanctum and for me to get Bloom but she isn't far away and the girl didn't look good. We need to hurry!"

Claire had gotten better at interpreting excited-Joobel-speak and started to move for the healer's kit she kept in the next room. The queen looked down to see it was already in her hand, her long brown hair still blowing from the passing gnome.

The queen looked to Norim, who only nodded, and they both left the room to head to the sanctum. They arrived shortly after Joobel, more because it wasn't a long walk than the compared speed of travel. Claire looked to the gnome, who gave a silver-haired nod.

"She's close."

Joobel meant Bloom; the dragon was the best bet this girl had to survive. Claire looked down to the young woman whose stomach was open from a deep wound. The slender build and pale skin. The long white hair. A sudden realization rushed over the young queen. This was Raine, her cousin from Winter.

Why would she be away from home, and why was she near death? It made no sense; she was one of the most well-protected people in Fairie! Why would she be wounded and lying in the dragon sanctum of a smaller kingdom?

As she looked around the room, she saw Jack standing protectively over his cousin. Gray was working quickly to prep the wound for Bloom.

Now she and Norim began helping just as the green drake arrived and the mist poured over them. Jack beat her to the introduction. What in the world was Raine doing in Autumn?

Claire wanted answers, but this wasn't the place. She went over and hugged Harvest's leg. The top of his head gently brushed her in greeting. Through her bond, she used dragon-speak to let him know she'd share all with him later. Joobel did much the same with Bloom, giving thanks for the collateral healing.

Jack had taken over helping Raine, who now walked on her own, with one arm over his neck to help steady her. Claire could see the mixed look of joy and jealousy on Joobel's face. Jack was now home safe, but also currently helping the lovely girl walk back up to the Keep.

The queen rolled her eyes. The gnome was insanely jealous; it might have been what turned Bloom green. The girl was his cousin. Besides that, Joobel was intensely lovely.

Claire had often been tempted to change her appearance to one that would rival the gnome, but then she remembered the perfect face of Wenette and the darkness inside her. No, she must never use that power for vanity's sake. Her hand went unconsciously to the three lines marring her left cheek. Perhaps she might make some subtle changes someday.

She looked to the people gathered around her.

"Raine will stay with me tonight. It's late and she needs rest. We can speak in the morning."

"Oh, Claire, I'll be back soon, but I want to spend some time with Jack before going to bed. It's been so long and I have so many stories to hear."

She nodded to the gnome and turned until her eyes met Gray's. His face was a mess, scarred and covered in that thick beard. He clearly wanted to have time with her as well.

"I'm glad you made it back safe. I...." She bit her lower lip. "I'll fix your appearance in the morning."

The words felt wrong in her mouth. Why did he just stare at her with those big eyes? She held his gaze and he finally nodded and walked down the hall.

Claire entered her apartments with Norim in tow. She felt tempted to get Raine's story right then, but whatever had brought her a stab wound, and a possible exile, would be a story she should only have to tell once.

Norim helped get the girl into a tub. Wood burners would normally heat the water but it was late, and they had already cooled from Claire's bath earlier. Norim had thought of this, and Joobel padded in holding Jack by the hand. Claire had done a great job disguising him and she wouldn't know the young man if she hadn't given him the scarred face he was wearing.

Jack reached under the tub and a moment later, steam began to rise. He took his leave with Joobel following along.

The queen rolled her eyes at them. Part of her was jealous and part was tired of the lovesick gnome. Claire forced it out of her mind as she left the bathroom. Norim would help Raine get in and see to her needs. The naiad felt the need to mother anyone who would let her.

Claire got extra pillows and set them on her large bed. It had once been her mother's. At first, she'd wanted to keep her old room. It was Torg who'd talked her out of that. The captain of the guard pointed out that anything she did that belittled her claim would also limit her ability to serve the people.

She slept in one corner of the huge mattress. Raine would sleep in the royal room with her tonight. It was the most well-protected location in the castle, with guards patrolling both the inner halls and outer wall.

Also, Jack was just across the hall, Gray was two doors down, and Joobel was in the smaller bedroom that was part of her chamber. Even with all that, the queen suspected that it would be wise to be extra cautious. She'd asked a favor of Jack, one that he granted without blinking an eye.

Maeve normally slept on a special stone pad that sat next to Jack's bed. He'd gone through three beds before he gave in and had it installed. While she looked small, the construct that held the soul of a family dog from another world weighed more than Gray. A cushion sat on the pillar, though no one doubted that

Maeve liked it for the memory more than comfort. Tonight, the hound slept on a pillow next to the window of the royal bedchamber, her little tail wagging anytime someone looked in her direction.

Raine came in shortly after. Norim had dressed her in one of Joobel's nightgowns. The Winter Maiden was younger than Claire and her size was in agreement with the fact. She was a couple of moons older than Jack and he'd only celebrated his fifteenth autumn just recently.

Her cousin had grown since the last time Claire had seen her. That had been years ago. Though the Winter Citadel was only a couple hours away by dragon flight, she dared not take Harvest into another kingdom.

The two girls had once been close; now as women of power, both had drifted apart. Claire's last letter had been to inform her family in Winter of her mother's death and her own coronation. The northern kingdom had sent an emissary, but no one of note.

Now they'd have a slumber party of sorts under these terrible circumstances. Raine still looked quite traumatized, her eyes red and bloodshot. No doubt she'd done her crying in the tub so as to blame it on the hot water. Claire had used that excuse herself many times.

"I want to thank you, cousin, for your kindness. It's only proper that...."

Claire shook her head. "Hush, you're tired and a guest. Rest tonight, and in the morning we can discuss the future."

Raine began to sob, the convulsions subtly shaking her narrow shoulders. The young woman put her pale hands over her face.

Norim stepped in to let Claire know she was going to bed for the night. The naiad laid a hand on Raine's shoulder, calming her frayed nerves and putting her at peace for a time. Norim's skill was common among her race and not seen as powerful, but it was often a boon to the kingdom in soothing the royal family of various stresses. The tall woman stepped away, her light blue dress flowing behind her as she swiftly left and shut the door.

Claire looked at her cousin, thinking through the odd chain of events that had led to Raine being named Winter Maiden. She wasn't the choice many had assumed.

The Queen of Winter had two daughters, Raine being the youngest. Myrin, the older sister, had been passed up. The queen had deemed her too quick to anger and lacking the forethought of the consequences of decisions.

The fact that this was all true had Claire's older cousin in fits. She blamed Raine and had attacked her in the middle of the throne room. That too was a difficult thing.

Myrin was a rare user of Frost Fire, the cold flame that was breathed by the frost drakes, Winter's dragons. It was a powerful weapon, with Myrin the only living person to possess the skill.

Raine's power was also of the water aspect, but her spirit was Purification. It was also uncommon, but not much of a weapon for battle. In a contest between the two, there was no doubt that Raine would lose. The queen had interceded with a blast of ice and Myrin had been sent away.

Claire knew that the bad blood had affected Raine. She was good-natured and hadn't sought her position. She loved her sister and hated that she no longer got to see her.

Though Norim had calmed her, the Winter Maiden still seemed stunned. Claire led her to the bed and helped her under the blankets. Instead of going around to the other side, Claire crawled next to Raine and held her, both women soothed by the closeness even after years apart. Soon the soft sounds of even breathing filled the royal bedchamber.

\*\*\*

Maeve missed Her Boy. Her Boy sent Maeve to sleep on floor. Maeve doesn't like floor sleeping. Floor sleeping is for bad girls.

The hound didn't really sleep, at least not in the same way living things did. Sleep served to repair the body and mind; her body had no such need, but the little hound's mind still benefited from rest. She was content to sit while others slept and play happy memories in her thoughts.

The mind of a dog was simple. Once basic needs were met, such as food, water, and warmth, then she only wished to be with family, and to play, of course. When others were resting, she'd remember. After the Naming, her memories had gone from vague recollections to firm and comforting recalls.

Now she was thinking of the time she'd gone on a hike with Her First Boy and a chipmunk had attacked. The lean brown hound had bravely barked it away before it could eat him. All memories are seasoned with perspective.

It was as she was mentally doing battle with the vicious evil chipmunk, that her outer senses began to seep into her mental skirmish. A clicking sound, the smell of leather, a cool breeze on her simulated fur. Maeve came out of her memory. Someone is here. Someone comes through window. Someone is sneaky. Like a chipmunk.

An evil creature that attacks family.

\*\*\*

The assassin hadn't seen the stone hound. In his left hand was an orb of a magical liquid. When turned, the fluid would mix with powder inside the sphere and would start to put out a gas, a mist designed to work much like the miasma of a death dragon.

The contract had been for the water spirit user, a Winter Princess. While not opposed to killing to get at his mark, no one wished to be hunted for the murder of a queen. More so one with a monster of a dragon.

The killer slowly began to turn the mechanism; he wasn't worried about the gas. He held a spirit of change and so was immune to the weapon, as would be the Autumn Queen who was of the same aspect. The mark would die quietly, her chokes so subtle that she wouldn't even wake the other girl lying next to her.

The security here was decent. He'd had to subdue three guards and scale a smooth five-story wall to get into this room. The lock on the window was well made, gnomish probably. It had taken him several minutes to pick through the mechanism.

The bounty for this contract was ludicrous, more money than he'd made in the past five years. The Winter sprite who'd brought word of the job had only been dispatched earlier that night, and most assassins would've had to plan and use a team.

Not him. His spirit was a form of maker magic, rare and powerful. He'd set the orb under the bed and the gas would very slowly fill the room. The queen would wake to find the Winter girl dead beside her.

He leaned down to position the orb and found himself face to snout. It was a little brown hound.

***

Man is still sneaking. Man might be bad. Maeve might chew on him a little just to be sure. Man is making a clicking sound. Holding something. Someth— BALL!

Maeve zeroed in on the toy. It smelled funny, but all the best toys have exciting smells. The man is surprised to see Maeve. Maeve likes surprise. Maeve get ball.

The assassin was shocked to find a hound here, more shocked that it seemed to want to play. In his surprise, he jumped back and hid the carefully prepared contraption behind his back.

Maeve want ball! Man playing game. Have to get ball! Give Maeve ball!

Realizing that the orb was what she wanted, he tossed it away and ran for the window.

BALL! Maeve get ball. Maeve has ball. Maeve bring ball back to man. Man can throw again!

The assassin had carefully scouted the room on his way in. He hadn't seen the cushion Maeve had moved while getting up. Stumbling over it, he flopped over the window sill. He'd dealt with this before and confidently reached to his back and slung the grapple. The hook expertly caught hold of a portcullis on the wall of the Keep. He began to use gloved hands to slow his fall.

Unfortunately, he hadn't prepared for a deceptively heavy dog leaping out the window after him. She landed right on his chest, still holding the orb he'd tossed in the room. The added weight caused the gloves to smoke as he failed to slow his decent enough.

He landed on his back with a Maeve on top of him. The hound was the only one around to hear the crunching sound his ribcage made as they slammed into the cool ground below.

\*\*\*

Maeve was upset now. Not only had the man stopped playing, but she'd swallowed a ball again. The deadly mist was steaming from her nose and ears as she looked up at the still open window. Brown paws moved in a trot to the entrance at the base of the east tower. The dark mist stopped before she ever got to the door.

It wasn't the first time the prince's hound had to scratch to get back inside the Blood Keep.

# CHAPTER 3

Jack was awake early as a guard brought Maeve back to his room. Not everyone knew about Maeve's peculiar history. The fact that she kept jumping after birds from a five-story window and coming back unharmed had more than a few people suspicious. It was probably just a bird again, but Maeve was in his sister's room for a reason. He wouldn't get back to sleep until he checked on both her and Raine.

As he approached the royal chambers, both guards lowered short spears at him. He'd almost forgotten he still looked like a slave from the Wylds. He lit his eyes a bright yellow as he went straight for the door. All of the guards were well aware of the rumors and songs about the Demon Prince of Autumn. They had no doubt who was entering the queen's chambers. Both men also recognized the hound they'd thought was inside the room.

As Jack closed the door behind him, one guard looked to the other and asked, "Bird?"

The other guard agreed with the theory, nodding with his reply. "Bird."

Despite being nervous, Jack wasn't keen to wake the young women. He had no doubt Norim would chastise him for entering ladies' sleeping quarters without notice or permission.

But his need to check on their safety outweighed those mental chastisements.

His bare feet padded on the floor as he crept into Claire's room. Both women were breathing slow and even. Raine even had a light snore. He scouted the chamber with dimly glowing eyes. Everything seemed in place except the open window.

That bothered him. He often left his wide open, enjoying the night air. After all, he didn't get cold. Claire, on the other hand, was usually wrapped up and still chilled. She'd asked for Maeve as extra security and would've locked the window.

Jack looked down, eyes flaring brighter as he spotted the figure in black lying on the grass. He thought for a moment and then closed the window. The prince locked it again and fixed Maeve's cushion. The hound lay back down and Jack poured heat into the chill air before he slipped back out of the room.

The door was no sooner closed than he had a long slender dagger at his throat. It would seem Joobel had heard an intruder. Jack lit his eyes enough that she'd recognize him. Her brow furrowed but he just waved her to walk with him. In the hall, the prince gave orders to the guards.

"Go search for any patrols that haven't checked in and have any injured brought to Bloom." He sighed, remembering Harvest. "Make sure and announce yourselves."

"Of course, my prince, but what of security here?"

"Send up guards for the door. I'll be patrolling outside."

Joobel was hearing this for the first time. She waited till they were alone before asking her own questions.

"Did something happen? It's weird to sneak around at night and I thought you were there to hurt someone. Or worse! Why were you walking around in the dark?"

"The window was open, and Maeve came through the lower halls. I think someone opened the window and she tossed them back out. We'll know soon enough."

Joobel was silent for once. The idea someone had broken into the room next to her clearly upset the gnome. Jack was in a similar mood.

The pair made their way down to the lower levels and into the inner garden courtyard. It had become quite lush in the past few months. Bloom had been spraying it down as a gift to Claire.

The flowers and trees bloomed to rival the Beryl Gardens of Spring and the fragrance was delightful. The beauty and life the garden showed were in stark contrast to the dead man lying just below Claire's window.

Joobel was near to being sick as Jack started digging through the man's pockets. After a gruesome moment of searching, he found what worried him. The prince swore in a loud whisper.

"You'd better not let Norim hear you speak like that," Joobel muttered.

Jack handed her the paper; Joobel read it and swore. The note was a contract notice. A queen's ransom for proof of death of the former Winter Maiden, Raine Anahita. The coin sum was huge and the reward included a title and lands. The crime she was convicted of was the murder of Queen Eria. Raine's own mother.

"Could it be true?" the gnome asked.

Jack forgave her doubt. She'd never met Raine and only knew of her from passing comments on occasion. They had grown apart over the years, something Jack was now regretting.

What must Raine have gone through? Jack had always liked her. She was kind and brilliant. It had been good news to him when word came that Raine was chosen as heir to the Winter throne.

Her older sister Myrin was scary to most. Jack had made a point of putting her in her place when they were much younger. Myrin liked to push Claire around, no doubt due to the fact that she saw herself as heir to a much larger and stronger kingdom. She'd tried to do the same to him but her words did nothing, and even back then, he'd frightened her too much to try a physical form of bullying.

He sighed and looked at the woman he'd grown to love. "Anything is possible, but I don't think so. She had nothing to gain from killing her mother. Aunt Eria was fair to her daughters and Raine was already in a position of power. She loved her family and I can't think of a situation where she would hurt anyone for selfish reasons. Her power isn't even useful in a fight. Joobel... I think she's a victim in all this."

Jack looked around. With the bounty on her head, Raine would be under constant assault. The notice could only be a few hours old and this assassin had hoped to strike before they were aware of the threat.

He began to move the body, sliding it to the side and under some bushes. He'd deal with it in the morning. He waved Joobel to another set of bushes opposite Claire's window. As he settled down, he reached out and held her hand. With his other he pushed heat into the gnome, warding the night chill from her.

Joobel lifted an eyebrow. "What are we doing?"

"That was the first attack; there will be more."

He was right, more so than he cared to be. The next attack came only half an hour later. It was still a while till sunrise when three figures crept through the garden and began to set up to scale the wall.

Jack had no intention of making Joobel fight, but he liked the company. He had his eyes glowing a faint orange, dim and hidden in the shrub. Once sure of his target, he built the weave on one finger. It was a trick he used to hunt, a flash of heat so hot that it no longer gave off light. He could kill silently, the disruption of the air the only sound, and that was like a bug flying by.

The first two killers never knew what hit them; the third noticed an ally fall but turned just in time for his own demise. The prince moved to hide the bodies with the first.

One more assassin tried to use stealth that night to remove Raine from the picture. This one was a lean woman with pale skin. She dressed in leathers that were dyed black and grey with some streaks of red. The disguise blended in with the shadows on the wall so well that Jack missed her. It was Joobel who saw her approach.

Since the gnome's bonding with Bloom and Naming by Claire, she'd been full of surprises. Not the least of which was her size, several times taller than any other gnome. She had other gifts as well, such as the ability to take pain away as she had for Raine. Jack hadn't been aware that she could see the flows of life.

The faintest green glowing in her eyes was the only clue that the woman was able to detect living things in any light. Here in the garden, all the grass and trees lit up her sight so much that she didn't make out the woman until she was starting to move on the dead stone of the Keep's wall. She pointed the shape out to Jack and he had to significantly brighten his eyes to make her out.

Unfortunately, that gave him away. The woman jumped to the side and threw several copper disks at him, the faint glint of the metal from the light in his own eyes the only warning. He pushed Joobel over, the sounds of impact ringing against the wall behind them. The gnome's sight saw the dimming of vitality from where one hit the branch of a bush.

"Jack, they're poisoned!"

He nodded and took off. Depending on how good the poison was, he could burn it out of his blood. He'd practiced that trick since the incident with the former pale goblins. Best not to test it here though, and he had to get away from Joobel. She had no such defense, and his eyes were targets.

He ran to the side, hearing the little discs hit around him. Since he was already detected, there was no reason to use stealth. Jack formed a ball. The earlier projectiles were pure heat; this was pure light. He slung the orb into the sky above and it flashed brightly, a five-second burst of daylight in the dim garden.

The woman's cry was confirmation that she'd adjusted her eyes to the dim night; she'd be blind for a moment now. Jack wasted no time closing the distance. His projectiles were more dangerous this close to innocents, his favorite gnome being chief among them.

Jack dashed in, wielding a dagger of conjured flame. The woman jumped from the wall and began using cover as the prince closed the distance. He waved one hand, swatting the bushes with an eruption of searing heat. The green branches crackled and popped, moisture boiling away before bursting into flames. Jack ran right through the small inferno and slashed his flaming blade at her throat.

Her own hand came up and he slowed as if hitting invisible mud. The prince grinned; he was familiar with this tactic. Gray used something similar when they sparred.

Jack loved hand to hand combat. Just over two years earlier, when he and Claire had left to find their mother, he could only get a good fight from Torg. Now Jack had surpassed his teacher.

Joobel had been learning how to fight and often would try and take him. But despite her incredible speed and ability to use three dimensions thanks to her wings, he held back most of his skill with her.

Now his matches with Gray, those had become epic. Jack had far more power and his fire was deadly, but every time he fought, the larger man would have some new trick to win. Gray still only defeated him in maybe one out of five matches. When word got out that they would be sparring, crowds formed in the training yards. All wanted to see how the insane battle would play out.

This woman had an air aspect like Gray. Jack was both excited at a real match and saddened that such a gift would soon be lost to the world. She was good, but she wasn't Gray.

As the woman pushed the shield to buy herself some distance, she lashed out with a whip of hardened air. Jack flashed a bright light in her eyes and went in low, heat flowing from his leg as he swept at her feet. She lifted up off the ground, then flew back, landing gracefully.

Jack slung his right hand out; not one projectile, but over a dozen flew forward. Each one was a more robust version of the 'pops' he'd made as a child. They hit trees, bushes, and the ground in massive blasts of light and sound.

The woman covered her ears and squinted just as she saw Jack form the point of heat and launch it at her. It was invisible, so grace was out of the question; she flopped down on her back and began to roll. The maneuver never completed.

Brown paws held down her arms with amazing strength and sharp white teeth were wrapped around her throat. In a final act of defiance, she whipped the ring on her finger and flicked the gem; a needle dripped poison. The woman stabbed it into the leg holding her left hand. The hound didn't seem to notice.

Jack came over and put his hand to the woman's forehead. He would've killed her had Maeve not shown up. The prince might not like killing, but it would be far from the first time it had needed to be done. Now with the enemy subdued and Joobel walking over, he wouldn't take another life. He did take almost all of her energy; the woman's eyes lost focus as she stared at the side of Maeve's head. Then all she saw was darkness.

Jack assumed that this would be the last attempt on Raine of the night, with the sun already peeking over the horizon. He was wrong. As the assassin went unconscious, Jack heard a scream. The prince looked up, his stomach dropping down.

The last assassin was unexpected.

*** 

It wasn't often that Harvest got to do his real job. He knew the wisdom of deterrence and understood why his queen asked him to patrol the kingdom each day. He brought hope to many and was a reminder of his bond-mate's power. Making sure he was seen along Autumn's borders was a message to the other kingdoms that Autumn had defenders.

He might be the only death dragon in the kingdom, as Bloom was something else entirely, but he'd been Named. Spirit Names came with both cost and benefit and his bond-mate gifted him first of any. He was magically bonded through his hatching, the realm, and his Name.

Harvest wasn't just what he was called, it was his spirit Name. With it came immense power. He absorbed energy from the air and the ground. Pulled it from his food and water, even from the air he breathed. He was a creature of magic, and so with the added energy, he grew.

A mighty sea dragon named Depth had been teaching him not only how to do battle, but how to serve his queen and realm. One of the many skills he'd been learning was how to use his dragon-speak, not only to talk to other dragons, but to know where they were. He and Bloom practiced on each other, each locating their sibling from across the kingdom.

Gray had once told him it was like a form of radar, bouncing signals around to locate others. He liked the tall man who was so smitten with his queen. The black drake could identify Claire and Joobel using the ability, pinging the skill around him and picking up others who had the talent.

Harvest hadn't been put on alert that night. Claire had seemed agitated but didn't indicate danger to him. When he heard a series of explosions, he was roused from his slumber. Dragons only need a couple of hours of sleep a day, but he enjoyed more if able.

He was about to take a quick flight to check on things around the Keep when he pinged his bond-mate. He'd done so hours ago. She was sound asleep and doing well.

Others showed up in his mind. His sister was next to him and her gnomish bond-mate was awake in the courtyard. The four were the only ones in Autumn who were normally in range. He did this so often that as he began to take to the air, he was surprised to get another hit. Another user of dragon-speak was nearby.

Harvest pinged again and the user was still present, now much closer. Large yellow eyes widened in horror as the death drake realized what this meant. The Blood Keep was under attack.

By a dragon.

***

Claire had been in a deep sleep when she heard the glass breaking. She faintly remembered explosions and had a rather terrible flashback to the night her mother was taken.

She shook away the fog and came back to herself. The window was broken, but no one was in the room, only her, and—oh yes, Raine was with her. She'd been worried someone might try to hurt the Winter girl.

She ran to the window; her eyes lit to the ghost world. Jack and Joobel were below and Maeve had someone pinned. She started to let out a sigh of relief as her dragon's words thundered through her mind.

"Claire, get down; he's going to freeze you!"

She looked up into the sky, wondering what was going on, when she saw it. A large blue shape was flying straight toward her window. She only hesitated a moment as she saw the great mouth open and a dark blue weave begin to form.

Claire leaped for the bed. Raine was just coming awake and shrieked as Claire grabbed the side of the large mattress and rolled over her cousin, wrapping them both in the thick pad. The bundle containing the Autumn Queen and Winter Maiden pushed against the far wall as a blast of arctic cold slammed into the room. The wood of the bedposts creaked, rock walls and floors cracked, and bits of stone shattered as the intense cold pervaded everything inside.

Claire hugged Raine close. They wouldn't survive a second blast, as she was already chilled to the point of losing consciousness.

The young queen regretted many things as she waited to die, not the least of which was failing to protect the future queen wrapped up with her. She could feel puffs of mist with each breath Raine took.

Instead of a second blast, there was a thunderous roar. She'd heard that war cry before. Claire loved him; she had Named him. Harvest was awake. Her protector was enraged.

A moment later, the booming crash of dragon hitting dragon shook the whole Keep. She could feel Raine shiver against her. A single tear left her right eye.

It froze against her reddened cheek.

\*\*\*

Joobel looked up as she heard the sound of great wing beats. At first, she thought that the commotion must have woken Harvest. She'd know if Bloom was in flight. The gnome reached out and spoke in the mental language of her bond-mate.

"It's ok. We have the assassin under control." It was Harvest whom she heard next, but he wasn't talking to her.

"Claire, get down; he's going to freeze you!"

Then she saw the frost drake over the other wall to the garden. To her horror, the beast lined up and shot a torrent of frost fire into the broken window of Claire's room. She heard a scream.

As Joobel took to the air, she saw Jack was ready. She grabbed his wrists and powered the paper-thin wings on her back. The pair of them moved upward.

At one point, she was going to hide her wings and try to fit in here as one of Jack's race. He convinced her not to; she was unique and was a source of prestige to her people. She was still going to argue until the young man told her that he liked her wings and was proud of who she was. In her mind that settled it. It was, of course, what she wanted, but she loved him for saying it. Now they were both glad she had the ability to fly.

Jack would have had trouble with a dragon. In the air, he'd have less contact with the realm, and therefore less fire. Also, Joobel would have to try and maneuver with nearly as much weight as she could carry. It turned out that it wasn't an issue.

Harvest came from the direction of the sanctum and hit the drake at full speed. Both dragons tumbled high over the north gate and the crushing sound of battle woke most of the capital.

Joobel was fond of Harvest. She was, in many ways, his first teacher. When Claire was away in the land of death, Joobel stayed and was able to talk to him through the dragon-speak she'd gained through her bond with Bloom. She wasn't worried about him. He wouldn't lose. She was concerned about her sister.

The path was clear as she lifted Jack to the window. The floor hissed as his bare feet crossed the frozen stone. Joobel looked around in a panic. She couldn't imagine anyone surviving. The gnome lit her eyes to life and could see Jack and nothing else.

Wait! The faintest light flickered at the edge of the room.

"Jack, there inside the mattress!"

The prince nodded. He didn't try to move them yet. Both his hands touched the edge of the thick pad. He released waves of warmth, slowly at first, and then more and more. Finally, there came a voice.

"Ok... that's enough."

Then another voice; it was Raine this time. She was upset and near panic, but her words didn't seem to be for herself.

"Don't kill him! Please, he's sick.... Just don't kill him!"

Jack was at a loss, and Claire was still too angry and hurt to respond. Joobel was the one who interceded. Her words weren't for the ears of those in the frozen bed chamber but for the minds of the dragons of Autumn.

"Harvest, please don't kill the frost drake. Raine says he's sick. I think she wants to try to help him."

"This creature attacked my queen. He *will* die."

"Did you not once attack me before you knew how to serve your realm?"

Harvest was silent for a moment. Joobel had never played that card before, mostly because she held no ill will toward the death drake. When he was less than a day old, Harvest had attacked Bloom. In doing so he'd nearly killed Joobel.

She knew it was a low blow, but Raine was insistent that the frost drake was sick in his mind. Harvest could and would kill anyone who threatened Claire. It would hurt while he was doing it.

"The drake was after Raine; Claire is fine. You need to stop him from hurting anyone but do *not* kill him. If I'm wrong in this, then you can always finish him later."

"I'll await the word of my queen." A moment of pause and then, "I'm sorry for hurting you when I was young."

"I forgave you the day it happened. I only wished to give you perspective."

Joobel saw Bloom flash by the window, no doubt heading to stop the imminent death the frost drake would face without her aid. The gnome looked back to the others in the room, now that she'd dealt with dragon business.

Both Claire and Raine were in bad shape. They had red and purple welts on their feet and ears from the cold. Jack had warmed them, but the pain of thawing must be terrible. Joobel moved forward to ease the pain until Bloom could undo the damage. As she worked, the gnome spoke to Raine.

"The dragons have subdued the frost drake. We had better waste no time in getting down there because Harvest is in quite a mood. Also, we need to have Bloom fix you both quickly before the damage becomes permanent."

Claire nodded and moved to change. Jack didn't leave the room but went and looked out the window while the others dressed. The bounty on Raine was still quite high and he wasn't going to leave them alone.

Joobel moved to her room; she also needed clothing for the day. She had Raine follow her. Her clothes would fit their guest better.

In only a couple of minutes, they were moving through the halls. Jack was scouting the way ahead, looking for danger. They met several guards, but he had them leave a wide gap. Assassins had tried that disguise before.

Soon the group was just past the north gate. The ground outside looked as if a war had been fought. Large chunks of earth, broken trees, and scattered wooden limbs lay all around.

The frost drake was on his side. One wing was nearly torn off, while the other was crumpled under him. One strong black claw had his body pinned to the ground and the terrible black jaws of Harvest were locked around his throat just under his head. Clouds of frost fire repeatedly erupted from the blue dragon, harmlessly hitting the already frozen grass and brush.

He'd gone mad. Jack and Raine were walking calmly to the spectacle, but Joobel and Claire struggled. The shrieks coming through dragon-speak were a horrible din of insanity. Joobel screamed as the madness assaulted her mind. Jack saw the women he cared for in such pain and his rage flared.

"Drain him!" Claire screamed.

***

Jack barely heard Claire's order, but it confirmed what he was going to do anyhow. The Autumn dragons would find the drake's mental assault annoying, but it might really hurt Claire and Joobel.

He reached the top of the drake's head, unbothered by the horrible scene of Harvest's teeth at work. The prince knew that if Joobel hadn't stepped in, the frost drake would be long dead. Jack began to pull power from the Winter dragon.

Something was wrong; the energy wasn't as it should be. It felt oily and rancid. Frost drakes were creatures of water; normally when he drew on the water aspect it tasted of things like salt and mist. This wasn't right.

Now Raine was beside him. Her words were nearly a shout. Jack hadn't listened to her as they were walking out; he'd been focused on danger. Now he began to understand.

"My home has been corrupted; the great spirit of Winter has gone mad. All who draw on her power are tainted. I could help him if I had more power, but last time I tried—"

Jack remembered that Raine's spirit was Purification. His own skill could draw out the power and change or move it, but in the end the corruption would remain, possibly doing the same to him in the process. Raine could do something else, could save the dragon if she had enough energy. Energy was his domain.

Raine didn't know of his real power, his spirit of Transition. Only a handful of people knew that fire was a borrowed ability. His real spirit was one of energy manipulation.

She seemed surprised when he laid a hand on her shoulder and began to pour the stolen drake's magic into the young woman. Raine gasped as the magic welled up. Understanding what he wanted, she laid her hand on the drake. She pushed her purifying magic through the aura of the mad beast; rope-like tendrils of her power swept the taint away. Jack pulled the energy and poured it into Raine, who used the power to seek out the tainted magic and cleanse it.

The process took only a few minutes, and the drake stopped his thrashing and screaming. Joobel and Claire were able to join them, still shaken from the mental assault.

"How did you...?" Raine gasped.

She seemed shocked at what had been done. Jack had just pulled the entire magic store of a dragon through her. She didn't seem tired or even low on power.

Jack pulled the ladies away, Bloom moved over, and Harvest reluctantly let go. The prince guessed Claire had ordered him.

The frost drake didn't move; the exertions and blood loss had all but done it in. Bloom's green mist began to flow. A nearly severed wing began to stitch back together; the crumpled one popped and clicked as bones snapped into place. Significant scratches and the spot where Harvest almost tore out his throat were coming back together, lightly scarred but whole. The drake would live.

Raine put a hand on the head of the dragon. Frost drakes were usually larger than death dragons and this one was large by any measure, but Harvest was something altogether different. The Winter girl slowly stroked the head of the drake, gently biting her lip, her face dark with worry. She turned and spoke to those around her.

"This is Sleet, the royal drake of the Queen of Winter. He was my mother's." Raine pushed moisture from her cheek with one palm.

"Before I killed her."

***

Claire had stopped her cousin from speaking and made arrangements for Sleet so they could discuss things in private. Both Bloom and Harvest had responsibilities and couldn't change habits without raising questions. Maeve was to be the frost drake's new guard.

Sleet thought that a joke until Harvest said something mind-to-mind. Then the great blue dragon nodded with wide eyes. The drake had come back to himself but stated that even then, he could feel the corruption seeping back inside of him. It was another issue to discuss.

Claire had called this meeting and made sure that it was private. Those present were sitting in a secluded meeting hall, far outside the Blood Keep. It wasn't in Autumn, or even in Fairie. Issabol had set it up at her request.

It was a war room of sorts where time moved faster than in their home world. Claire had gotten the idea from Heluvot, where time moved slowly. They had been able to take a good deal of time to prepare for that quest without losing much by doing so.

This land they simply called the world of fast time. Outside was a rather pleasant landscape that was alive and well. Though no great spirits lived in the land and the magic was weak, it gave them time. They could spend over an hour here for every few minutes that passed at home.

Now they were all gathered. Around the table sat Claire and Jack, Raine, Joobel, Gray, Issabol, and Norim. They must figure out a way to either save Winter or defeat it.

The madness that Claire had seen in that dragon wasn't unfamiliar. Autumn's Queen had witnessed it once before. It was the same madness that had consumed Wenette.

She was terrified.

# CHAPTER 4

It took a few minutes to introduce her to everyone. Her cousin Claire gave a brief rundown of the events that took place in the night. As the Autumn Queen finished speaking, she gestured to her and sat. Raine stood and began to pace as she told the story of how she came to Autumn's border.

"About three moons ago, I started to notice something wrong. First with my mother, and then with several others in the court. They became agitated and paranoid. Accusations were made and duels fought."

Raine wiped her eyes and continued. "It went on for weeks before I began to figure out why. The great spirit of water, Winter's realm spirit, has been corrupted. The tainted power would spread whenever someone drew on the energy of our realm."

The revelation was a shock to all those present. Life in Fairie was based on the great spirits of the various aspects. Most realms had a kingdom that shared its borders. Life was easier that way.

Even the Wylds had great spirits; both fire and air had realms, if not an organized ruler over them. Some like Gray had a power that wasn't of their chosen home, but if the great air spirit were corrupted, then even he would feel it eventually.

Norim looked up at the revelation. Her face had grown pale and she fought a tremor in her shoulders.

Claire looked to her. "Have you felt it, Mistress?"

The naiad nodded. "I have. I thought it might be stress. My sisters have noticed, as well. We're from Autumn, but our water magics have been... different."

Raine sniffed. "That's how it starts. I would've figured it out earlier, but I'm also of the water aspect. Winter is a land of much battle and injury. While I cannot heal like Bloom, I can cure infection, poison, and some kinds of sickness. It's a power I constantly use, more than many others of the court. Yet I felt unaffected."

Claire tapped a finger to her bottom lip. "Your power protected you?"

Raine shrugged. "I believe so. This was why I tried to help in the only way I knew how. I tried to take the tainted magic from my mother. I told you I killed her, and I did. It wasn't murder, though. Mother was harsh and often cruel, but she loved her people. I...." A pale hand wiped her cheek. "I loved her."

Joobel stood and took Raine's hand, her power holding down the emotional pain of a story that had to be traumatic. The young woman continued.

"Two days ago, though it feels like so much longer, I got her alone. Only my retainer Sroto was present with me. Sleet had left mother on an errand and wasn't there. She trusted me and so had no other guards."

The girl pushed long white hair behind one ear with a trembling hand and paused a moment.

"Yeti are of both water and air. Sroto was lucky and had an aspect of air. She wasn't affected by the corruption, though many of her kind are. She came with me and I spoke to mother of her wishes for the Loch to the south; strange things had been happening there. When we finished, I went to hug her, as I often did."

Joobel was pushing down harder on the pain. Raine took a deep breath and continued.

"I used my power.... I tried to tear the corruption from her spirit. It was working, but I wasn't strong enough. I still could've gotten it all, but when it felt me cleaning it away, it started tearing at her. She screamed and stabbed me with a blade of ice."

Her fingers went to the spot at her stomach, the wound that would've killed her had Jack and Gray not gotten her to safety and the healing of Bloom.

"Then her core was torn apart. The tainted magic just attacked her life force.... There was nothing I could do."

Raine began to cry, the memories overwhelming her. Pulling herself together, she looked around at her distant family and those who served with them. Many had risked their lives for her in some way or another. She had to hold on to hope. Her sister was still influenced and her people were suffering.

"I need to free Winter from this sickness. Whatever has been said, I'm now the rightful Queen of Winter. I *need* to find a way to reclaim my throne and free my people."

***

Raine's words had staggered Claire. Of those present, she could truly relate. She'd also killed her mother in a way. It would always haunt her, though she'd made a level of peace.

This was where she'd earn her right to rule. Claire would come up with a plan; she already partially had.

"Raine, are you familiar with the Bitter Challenge?"

The Winter girl nodded. "I am, but that would only apply to an outsider. I'm the Winter Maiden."

Claire shook her head. "You, my dear cousin, are a wanted murderer and an enemy of the state. If you show up to claim your throne, Myrin will have you killed. She'll be queen now. The woman was unstable before and might have done so even if she hadn't been driven mad by the great spirit's corruption. Your best hope is to show beyond doubt that the great spirit of Winter has chosen you as her ruler."

Raine threw her hands up. "The great spirit is the problem; the whole of the realm is corrupted!"

Claire sighed, looking around the room. "I know. I think Winter is going to need a new great spirit and you're going to have to help us switch them."

The room went silent. The endeavor was more than they could hope to pull off. Only one other great spirit of water was known to exist. It was Gray who spoke first.

"Claire, Fluvial is little more than a powerful water spirit now. What you're proposing would take—"

Autumn's Queen raised a hand. "It would take someone who could drain a massive amount of power from the old realm spirit, purify the corruption, feed it back into Fluvial's heart-dew stone, and do all of this while the entirety of the Winter army is trying to kill both the rightful queen and us."

"Well, yeah, it would take all that...." Gray decided to let her work.

Claire tapped one finger on her bottom lip. "I'm aware of the risk and the difficulty... but let us look at what's at stake. That dragon had Wenette's madness." Claire paused to let that sink in. Raine wouldn't understand the significance but would catch on soon enough. The queen sighed; this had been eating at her for the better part of two years.

"I don't think Wenette was building an army to conquer Fairie. I think she was preparing to face something else. Issabol said the prophecy drove her crazy, but she wasn't mad with power. She was losing her mind trying to find a way to survive the thing that killed Heluvot. The Autumn Crone was corrupted."

Jack saw where she was going. "You think that the Black March is already here? That the attack on Winter is part of it?"

Raine looked up, confusion on her face. "What is the Black March?"

Claire nodded, looking first to Raine and then back to her brother. "The Black March is what one of the survivors called the creatures that consumed his world. I believe this is the same threat. He said that two of the spirits there resisted the corruption. Most others were consumed and one great spirit of change went mad. If you wanted to conquer Fairie, what would be the best way to defeat the numerous types of magic our world has?"

Joobel said the words slowly to herself, in horror. "You would take our magic. It's our best weapon, our best defense. Our most powerful creatures are infused with it. Take it away...."

Gray frowned; his jaw clenched. "We'd all be helpless."

Claire took a deep breath. The responsibility hung heavy on her. She loved these people and feared to lose them, but the stakes were too high. A true queen would risk friend and family to save all.

"Raine, as of today, you'll become someone else. Your face will have every assassin in our world after your head. I'll change your appearance and you can go back to Winter and prepare for the Bitter Challenge."

Claire sighed, looking to Gray for a moment.

"Autumn will help you win back your kingdom, but we won't do it for free. If we're able to get you the throne, you will sign a nonaggression treaty with Autumn, form a military alliance, and outlaw the use of slaves within the borders of Winter."

The Winter girl's eyes widened. "The treaty I would've done anyway. The alliance is wise with the threat of a common enemy... but half of Winter's economy comes out of the mines. If I try to—"

Claire slammed a hand against the table. "I'll not bring aid to a land that trades people as property. This isn't a negotiation. When the time comes to enforce your law, you will find you're able."

Raine took a deep breath. Claire knew she already hated the practice of slavery but feared half the nation starving from the economic impact. Without the help of Autumn, Winter was doomed anyway. Finally, the girl nodded in agreement.

Claire gave a slight shake of her head. "Say it, cousin. I need your word."

The Winter girl pushed her hair behind one ear as she sighed. "I, Raine Anahita, rightful Queen of Winter, do swear to sign the treaty, to form an alliance... and to outlaw slavery in my kingdom."

Claire smiled at the younger girl. "We both know it's what is right. You'll understand in time."

Autumn's Queen turned to those gathered.

"Norim, I'll not order it, but I'd like for you to take on the appearance of Raine after she leaves. Her disappearance will have people looking and some might figure out that she's in disguise. If she seems to remain here under our protection, then we can direct the attacks to a place we're ready for them. Also, most would assume that I'd keep family close, so I would still have my advisor."

Norim nodded without consideration. Someone would have to do it, and clearly the naiad would rather it be her than another. "I'll do as you ask."

Claire looked to Gray and then to Joobel. "I need both of you to start working with Issabol. We need to make a weapon against the Black March. They went through a good deal of trouble to remove the threat of magic. If they were immune to all of it, they needn't bother. I want to know what hurts them. When the attack on this world begins, I need us to be ready."

Finally, Claire looked to her brother. She'd sent him on dangerous tasks many times now. He was so much stronger than when they'd left to find their mother. But this was different; she wouldn't be with him. Her place was on the throne, keeping her kingdom safe. It hurt to do it, but he was crucial to her plan.

"Jack, you'll go with Raine. The Bitter Challenge has some requirements that we're going to have to alter some to make work. Without your specific skills, there would be no way to make this happen."

Jack simply nodded and looked at Joobel, his eyes saying sorry. The gnome only smiled at him. She loved him for who he was, even if it took him away sometimes.

Claire turned back to her cousin. "Raine, you must enter Winter, gain a loyal dragon, forge a great weapon of the realm, and have a champion of water back your claim." Claire paused for a moment, then finished. "Then you must fight your sister to the death. Can you do this?"

Raine pushed her hair back. Her hands trembled and for a moment it seemed she might break down. Her pale blue eyes misted up, but her jaw tightened.

"I have no choice but to try."

The planning continued for some time, mostly Claire answering questions about details of strategy. The real challenge was that most of this had to be done in secret. Neither Claire nor the dragons could cross into Winter without drawing attention. Autumn couldn't be seen interfering in the matters of the north.

***

The meeting had gone on for hours. Now Raine was walking the streets of the capital escorted by the big man who had helped save her the previous night. Gray was a friendly sort, both competent and reflective. She liked him and was glad her cousin had such people around her.

Claire hadn't waited to alter Raine's features, and now her face felt... wrong. Her long white hair was now reddish brown and was shortened to her shoulders. Her cheekbones were higher, and her nose was slightly widened and covered with light freckles.

Her frame was mostly unchanged; Claire had said that she couldn't alter a person's size without creating magical flesh and refused to do so. More practically, a change in proportion would mean relearning to move an unfamiliar body.

The Bitter Challenge hung over her like a dark cloud. Raine knew the requirements. She'd learned them long ago, though it had been centuries since anyone had been able to put forth all of the three. The weapon was possible, as a few of the artifacts of Winter still existed.

The frost drakes were loyal to the royal family and really made the challenge almost impossible. Sleet might try to serve her, but he'd quickly succumb to the corruption and would be no help. All of Winter's other dragons were compromised now. This was on top of the fact that any champion powerful enough to back her claim was sure to be so corrupt as to be more enemy than ally.

She tried to put it out of her mind for now. Gray had promised a tour of the changes in Autumn.

She looked up to the tall man. "So... what's all the fuss about? Claire said you've been busy."

Gray smiled with a shrug. "Yes, well, when Claire asked me to help come up with ideas... I kind of cheated."

Raine chuckled. "I don't understand, how could you cheat?"

"In my previous home, we have centuries of learning how the world works. Things that make life better for everyone. I took those ideas and adapted them to this place. I'm trying to accomplish with magic what my people did with technology."

She eyed him with curiosity. Her light brown hand moved to push her shorter reddish hair behind an unfamiliar ear. Despite all the pain of the past few days, she smiled.

"It's a good theory, but I wonder if it really works. What changes have you made?"

He smiled back and led her to a small pavilion. It sat right off the main street and seemed to open into a large building that wasn't visible from the sides. She gasped as she walked around it, staring at the strange sight.

"This is one of the entrances to the main hub. We're connecting the kingdom through doorways just like it all over Autumn. We could be in the southern city of Thera in seconds, and then move to the western town of Quagmore only minutes later."

He waved a hand toward a row of doorways. "You could eat dinner in Grimfield and dessert in South Harbor. Trade will be more efficient and aid can be distributed in moments. It's one of the ways we're trying to rebuild the economy here."

Raine was torn between jealousy of the travel network and amazement at the possibilities.

"Do you think Claire would sell these strange doorways to us? Travel in the north is hard and we could do so much—"

Gray chuckled, holding both hands up. "I make no binding comments for my queen, but I'm sure she'd be willing to help you serve your people. Hold up, I need to use a restroom."

He moved to a small building that had two doors. One was marked with the shape of a woman in a dress and the other the broader shape of a man. Both the structure and his words confused her.

"What is this strange place?" She watched as a woman left one side and gave a smile and nod as she went on her way.

Gray laughed. "This is one idea I had little trouble selling my queen on. It's called indoor plumbing. If you can make sure no other ladies are in there, I'll come in and explain."

The girl cocked an eyebrow but moved to look inside. The room was empty and she waved him over. Gray moved to a stall and pushed open the door. An odd chair of smooth stone sat inside, the round outer edge sitting above a small pool of water.

"You sit here, and... do your business. When you're finished you clean up with the soft paper and then pull this lever."

He tugged the little handle and the water disappeared. Raine watched the whole thing with rapt fascination. "Where does it go?"

"There's a facility set up to the west. The portal below the bowl transports it. The waste is treated and converted to fertilizer. We get a valuable resource, less illness, and things smell much better in the cities."

Now she was floored. It was one thing to have to use an outhouse or deal with chamber pots. Winter was cold; no one wanted to get up in the night and wade through snow to relieve themselves. Her people would pay nearly anything for this strange contraption.

"How much to sell these to us?" she pleaded.

Gray shook his head. "I serve my queen; you'd need to talk to her. Feel free to use this side, I wasn't joking about needing to go. I'll meet you out front shortly."

Raine did try out the strange room and confirmed that she was sold on the idea. As she washed her hands and moved back into the street, she could see he wasn't done with the tour.

"Are you ready to see our newest project?"

Gray was grinning. His mood was infectious and helped take her mind off her troubles and the recent death of her mother. She nodded, a similar smile creeping across her face.

"I can say I'm curious. Lead on."

They moved back to one of the street portals and through it to the main hub with lots of other doors. He moved to a larger opening with a sign above it that said, 'Future home of Autumn's School.'

He stepped through and walked out to what appeared to be a small city. Workers were setting up foundations for large buildings.

Raine's blue-grey eyes focused on a group of people arranging equipment. There were training yards being set up and she could see a large room being enclosed through the side of an unfinished wall.

Gray followed her gaze and grinned. "This is going to be our secret weapon. Here is where all of the young people of this kingdom will be brought to learn."

Raine looked to the man. He seemed animated, as if the idea of giving the whole of the kingdom a tutor was some ground-breaking idea.

"It's an interesting idea... but what good will it do?"

Gray waved his hand, eyes sparkling. "My queen will choose from the best talent for her important positions. Every child will learn trades and share information. The young will be educated.

They will learn how to use their spirits, how to fill the needs of the kingdom. Discoveries will grow our collective knowledge and the next generation will change the world. They're our most valuable resource."

Raine shook her head. "I don't see the difference between a poor farmer and an educated poor farmer. Will this not just show people their own hardships?"

He frowned. "The idea is to limit the amount of hardship. No one should have to go hungry or go without a home. By teaching the young people of today, we'll build a better tomorrow."

She sighed, looking at all the wasted expense of it. "Yes... but what's the point in the end? It seems like you're just paying for an uprising down the road. There will always be those who struggle."

Now she could see he was getting upset, but the whole idea seemed off. He rubbed his cheek for a moment and then waved her to follow.

They once more weaved through the doorways and came to a barracks. He moved inside and she followed along. There were children everywhere. Dozens of young people were running and playing. A couple of older children were learning to read at a table in the corner.

Gray waded through the small bodies. "These children are all orphans, either abandoned or left behind at a parent's death. They're destined to suffer all throughout their lives. Let me ask you, when you look at them... do you see opportunity or burden?"

It was a painful barb. It was easier to look at people as numbers, yet these were very real. Each child had hopes and dreams just like she did. What if she wasn't the daughter of a queen? What if she was one of these little ones?

A boy nearly her own age walked over and stood at attention. He gave her tall companion a nod.

"Wind Walker, it's good to see you. We're short beds in the eastern hall; new arrivals came with the last batch of refugees from the east. I put in a request with the guards.... Perhaps you might be able to move things along?"

Gray rolled his eyes at the nickname, then scratched his chin as he looked over the conditions of the hall.

"Thank you, Bayu, I'll look into it. Have some of the smaller ones share for now. The dorms are on the way."

Raine watched as the boy moved to help a small girl get down from a table she'd climbed onto. A flick of his wrist wrapped the girl in dense air and set her gently on the floor. She turned to Gray once more.

"He seems competent."

"Yes, and he'll be much stronger than I am. Claire found him trying to rob travelers on the road outside the capital. He was a young man who would've been a drain on the kingdom, but now he'll serve it well. He's one of Norim's wards, adopted by the Keep. Do you see why it's so important to create opportunity?"

She pushed her short hair back as she took in the whole of the man's idea. Those who had no opportunity would try and create their own, stealing what they needed and forcing the kingdom to pay for others to keep them in check. It was starting to make sense.

They moved back to walking through the streets as the big man filled her in on the state of Claire's rule. Gray also spoke of moving water through the portals, providing ample irrigation for crops and clean drinking water for all. Taxes had gone up, but most of the merchants were so happy to have a stable business environment that they didn't complain much.

The tall man also explained that Harvest wasn't used as an enforcer within the kingdom. The drake was now a symbol of hope and spent a few hours a day flying over the various towns of the kingdom. His patrols were once a cause of fear, but soon the citizens cheered when their great protector flew over.

Bloom had a different route. She made it to each village or town about once every two weeks. Her job was pretty much to breathe on people. At first people found her weird. Eventually the sick and injured came to look forward to the visits of the strange dragon who showed up and healed a bunch of citizens. She was even more popular than Harvest.

Claire had taken both Joobel and Norim as advisors. Norim had a good deal of wisdom and was born among the people. Joobel had boundless compassion and was able to counter some of Claire's increasingly harsh judgments.

Gray told Raine about the power Claire had taken from the former Queen Wenette, and of his worry about the madness starting to form in Claire. The two spent the rest of the afternoon walking the streets.

Raine made a note to herself to get Winter someone like Gray. Even if many of his ideas seemed insane and some of the words made no sense. Autumn was clearly better now; she could see it in the people's faces. She could learn some things from Claire and this strange man.

She looked at the tall dark fellow next to her; he was rather handsome. If she couldn't find someone *like* Gray....

Well, the aspect of air was welcome in Winter.

\*\*\*

Joobel was beginning to get frustrated with her queen. She'd made five failed attempts to explain why she should go with Jack into Winter. Claire told her repeatedly that she would stand out and draw unwanted attention. Her third attempt had her dressed in lovely Winter garb, her wings hidden away. Claire hugged her but said no.

The gnome was now out of excuses. Claire was right from the start, of course, but she'd gotten Jack for less than a day. Now Joobel was pacing on the ceiling, bare feet padding across the red stone. Her wings blew papers off the tables and made a general mess.

The gnome knew she was petulant, but she also knew that her outbursts made Claire smile and her queen needed that. Soon they would both prepare for a meeting near Loch Mozeg. She'd been there several times now.

Issabol had set up a large portal there that both Bloom and Harvest used to meet and train with Depth. They were both much larger than any death dragon had been in living memory, but they were still young. Depth had become a tutor to them.

Tonight, they wouldn't be meeting with only the huge sea dragon, but with another immigrant from another world. One that had survived the Black March in Heluvot. They sought counsel with Fluvial, the great water spirit that had crossed over with the mighty sea dragon.

The spirit was now a pale shadow of her former power. Claire's plan to save Winter was dependent on her help and cooperation. This could go very well, or quite poorly.

Norim, disguised as Raine, walked into the chamber and rolled her eyes. Claire had done a masterful job of altering the naiad's face into Raine's original look. Gray had gotten his old face back and Jack had gotten an entirely new one, close to the reddish hair and features of his cousin.

Joobel knew Jack wasn't interested in Raine, but she was pretty and he was protective of her. Gnomes had no traditions or restrictions against coupling other than with siblings, so in her mind, the young Winter Queen was competition. She fought her impulses, but it was difficult.

Norim began picking up the papers. Feeling guilty, the gnome flew down and helped her. Claire walked in with her nose in a book, no doubt checking the legality of the Bitter Challenge and Raine's ability to contest Myrin's claim to the throne.

Claire was wearing her standard gold and brown garb. She now had the robes of the queen re-imagined to something more functional. After trying to ride Harvest in something that was blowing everywhere, the long robes were now a part of Autumn's history.

The tunic the queen wore buttoned up in the front and draped just past the waist. A matching skirt came down just above the knees with thick leggings sewn in. High boots buckled in gold trim came up her calves and she wore a thin circlet of gold woven with silver leaves. She looked important, if not entirely royal. Norim was in one of Joobel's stylish dresses and she looked quite charming as Raine's twin.

Claire had made Joobel start wearing her skirts with the leggings sewn in as well. The last time she walked on the ceiling and a guard walked in, he had a fit. The poor man was sure he'd be executed. The gnome forgave him and reminded him about knocking.

Joobel had thought the whole thing funny, but now her clothes allowed her to fly around without causing people to faint. 'Til this day she'd kept that story from Jack.

Norim would be staying in the Keep, specifically in the apartment that had been constructed inside the dragon sanctum.

Maeve would be going with Jack, but no assassin would challenge Harvest.

Joobel helped Claire carry her papers and preparations. They moved to the door and down the hall where they met the prince and his hound. Jack took Joobel's free hand as they walked to the portal to Issabol's home. Gray and Raine were already in place.

Claire briefly went over the plan again while Maeve wiggled against Raine to reaffirm that she was a good dog and Raine should pet her. All were wearing garb to protect them from the cold air and penetrating mist of the shore of Loch Mozeg. For Jack, this meant a sleeveless tunic and a pair of short trousers.

They walked through to the hall of portals and Issabol greeted them. She wouldn't be going; instead, she held a list of things she needed for Claire's newest commissions. Joobel and Claire used Issabol's workshop. The queen's new skill with Transmutation allowed her to make things that the ancient child couldn't create alone. Maker magics often worked well together.

Claire accepted the list and looked over the materials.

"Some of these will be difficult."

"You could always cancel your request," Issabol quipped.

Claire chuckled and hugged the ancient girl who looked about twelve autumns or so. Issabol was well over three thousand, the spiraling orbs in her irises the only hint of her true age.

Here inside Issabol's home was the portal that would carry them to the Loch. It was once used by growing dragons and was much larger than normal. The group moved into the chill air of northern Autumn.

Soon all of them were standing on the shore of the largest lake in Fairie. Only a small portion of the water stood over Autumn's realm spirit's control. Claire closed her eyes and spoke in the tongue of dragons.

"Hello, big fish. I ask that I might speak with you and our mutual friend."

Most of them knew the story of how Jack had once greeted that most colossal dragon ever known in his concise and irreverent way. It had become a favorite joke of the great sea dragon. His rumbling laughter echoed in the minds of all.

Depth would arrive in moments.

# CHAPTER 5

Portals still bothered Raine. It was mind-bending enough to move across a kingdom as quickly as walking into another room, but the shift in the air pressure! The moisture and light all changed faster than you could adjust.

Though it was disconcerting, she loved the thought of having these in Winter. If she survived the Bitter Challenge, she'd bargain hard for the services of the Portal Master. Those so called 'portal potties' would change lives.

Claire was looking out to the dark water of the Loch. Gray noticed Raine's confused expression and leaned over to whisper, "She's speaking with the great sea dragon."

"I thought we were to speak with a spirit," Raine said.

"Depth will bring the spirit with him."

Raine lifted an eyebrow. "I've heard that name. Surely a dragon living in the Loch would be rather small."

He shrugged, turning back to the murky surface. She followed his gaze, her eyes confirming she was right. A form a little smaller than Sleet moved across the water. It was only when the shape got closer that she realized what she saw was only the top of the creature's head. Depth wasn't big, he was massive.

The dragon's vast maw curved in a wide smile, showing triangle teeth that were as long as Raine was tall. A long thick neck pulled the face high in the air as its large round body awkwardly climbed onto the rocky shore. Where frost drakes or death dragons would have front legs that extended into wings, this dragon had huge flippers, with smaller paddles replacing the back legs. The tail disappeared into the water but would be nearly as long as the body and thickly muscled. It had a fin that sat along the top and bottom of its tail.

In the dim light, Raine could see that the top of the creature was dark like the water it swam in, but the bottom was as pure white as the snow of her home. Raine felt Gray put one finger under her unfamiliar chin, slowly pushing her mouth closed. She glanced up at him as he spoke.

"I did the same thing the first time I came out with Harvest to meet him."

Raine nodded and turned back. Now the colossal head was leaning in to stare into the face of Jack with one huge eye. The voice boomed so loud in her mind that it made her teeth hurt.

"I see you haven't found a way to kill yourself, little morsel."

"I've tried some stuff, but nothing as dangerous as a big fish," Jack replied with a wry grin. Another rumble shook all the small minds onshore. Claire stepped closer to the dragon, her words sliding into the minds of everyone present.

"I'm glad to see you well, Depth. How does our great sea dragon fare in my land?"

Depth grinned, his teeth gleaming even in the low light.

"I've made many friends among the waters of this place. I'm grateful to live among you. It has been too long since our last game. Perhaps there will be time?"

Claire shook her head. "You honor us with your friendship. I'm afraid our task is one of dire urgency. I find that a common enemy has found our world. The Black March has come to Winter."

Raine was shocked to see this great unstoppable creature show fear on a face that was mostly teeth. He glanced around and then looked back, his mighty voice lacking the restraint from before. The rumble in her head almost put her on her knees.

"They must not take this world; we will fight them!"

Claire stepped forward and laid a hand on his broad white chin.

"My friend, we'll fight with all we have. We wish to include our Lady in this conversation. She might be the key to saving the north."

Instantly the water alongside the huge tail of Depth began to rise and flow. In seconds, a tall woman was striding up the shore. Her light blue hair moved like a river's current. Her eyes glowed with power as she walked with fluid grace, a gown of shimmering dark blue shifting as if alive. She walked to Claire and, to Raine's utter bewilderment, kneeled.

Raine had seen so much already. The presence of a water spirit shouldn't have phased her as much as it did. She held the aspect of water and knew in her core what this being was. As everyone else stood on the shore, they showed respect, but none of them could truly feel the intensity of the being.

As Fluvial kneeled to Claire, queen of a kingdom that was not even water, Raine fell to the ground. The Winter girl felt like a gnat before a dragon.

Fluvial had been diminished from her former power before the Black March had conquered her home. The plague had destroyed the children of her vast seas on Heluvot. It wasn't her power that Raine felt. It was age. Wisdom and resolve. This spirit was likely older than Fairie.

Raine saw this ancient spirit kneel before a mortal woman. She'd pledged to serve this human woman, her own cousin. It was too much. She felt tears flow down her face. She was nothing before this being. Her water aspect, the spirit of Purification, cried out. Her heart was pounding, and she was having trouble drawing breath.

Then she felt a hand against her cheek. Calm flowed through her. It was like the power of Norim, but the naiad was back at the Keep. She began to stand, seeing the great spirit standing before her. Raine was further shocked as Fluvial drew her in and hugged her. The feeling of calm ran through her even more strongly.

Fluvial's face moved to her ear. "There's no time for such things, daughter. If the Black March is upon us, we must act."

"I'm not worthy to serve such as you."

"A good friend of mine once told me of a weak and frightened girl in a terrible land of death. She showed him that without equality, there would be no justice, no order, and no future worth fighting for. I want this land to have a future. Do you?"

Raine slowly nodded. "I do.... My people are suffering. But what if I'm—"

"Your great spirit is sick! It's your strength your people need." Fluvial turned her eyes to Claire.

"I'd like to help, but I cannot serve two masters."

***

Claire understood Fluvial's words to Raine. The exchange of loyalties was part of why they'd come. She stepped forward and cleared her throat.

"I, Clarissa Ashotok, Queen of Autumn, release you from my service, Lady Fluvial. While you will always be welcome in my Kingdom, the people of the water realm need you. May you serve them well."

Fluvial nodded and then, to Raine's horror, she knelt before her now.

"Raine Anahita. You are worthy of your kingdom. You're *my* queen now, and I will serve you until you leave for the next world."

Claire smiled at her cousin's reaction as Fluvial pledged to serve Winter and the rightful queen. She took out a kerchief and handed it to Raine. There was so much more to do. As of now, though, they had a queen with an uncorrupted great spirit. It was a start.

Raine needed more than a few moments to compose herself. When she was ready, Claire began to go over her plan. There were three further challenges of concern: the dragon, the champion, and the weapon. The task wouldn't be easy.

All of the Winter dragons were corrupted through the link with the corrupted great spirit. Sleet had been cleansed, but was already showing madness again and he was far from home.

"I shall serve as the morsel's dragon," Depth rumbled.

Claire shook her head. "I'm not sure they will recognize you as a dragon. Fairie only has drakes and wyrms."

"Bah, after I eat a few they will cooperate."

"You can't eat my people!" Raine gasped.

The dragon seemed ready to argue when Jack spoke for the first time since their arrival.

"Let's steal an egg."

Claire threw her hands up. "Brother, we need a dragon, not an egg. Only another dragon could hatch...."

She of all people knew that there was an exception to that rule. Harvest and Bloom had both been hatched by mortals, specifically Joobel and herself. The enormous amount of energy needed to do it was siphoned in by Jack, who could gift it if he had a source to draw on. He was right; if they could steal an egg from a frost drake, they could hatch it.

Claire began tapping her lower lip. "I think... that might actually work. Though the magic would need to come from Fluvial. To be a true dragon of Winter it would need to link with water. If we hatched one and it came out like Bloom, they would decide it's something else."

She didn't need to explain that Bloom was only a death dragon in name. The drake was much more a creature of life, thanks to Joobel's gifted energy during hatching.

"Ok, so we steal an egg. Assuming that works out, we still need a champion..." Claire said.

"I might not look like your other dragons, but I'm clearly of water. I am your Champion," Depth rumbled.

Gray looked way up. "You're pledged to Claire. Would you also need to be released?"

"He wouldn't. As long as I don't order him to stay out of it, he's free to act on his own. He will always be linked to Fluvial, regardless of what pledges are made."

Claire looked to her friends and continued.

"So, we have a champion that none can argue. We have plans for a dragon, so that just leaves the great weapon of water. I thought that Issabol and I could...."

Her words trailed off as Fluvial stood. The spirit reached one hand into her breast, the living water parting around her grip. She drew out a long slender sword. It looked for all the world like it was made of steel, containing the iron that would doom any who touched it.

Iron was hungry for magic; a world where it was present could never gather enough to have spirits form. A weapon of steel would be a crime for anyone in Fairie to wield. Yet if that were the case, the great spirit couldn't have stored it inside her. Whatever it appeared to be, the blade was something else entirely.

The great water spirit took the sword and effortlessly sliced a boulder in two on the shore. Then she turned it over and slammed the blade into the larger half of the rock as she spoke.

"This is Caledfwlch, a blade that was ancient when entrusted to me. It is sentient and chooses whom it will serve. Only those it deems worthy may wield it. It's one of the great treasures of my world and the only one I have in my care. My queen, if the blade deems you suitable, you'll have no trouble taking it."

Raine slowly walked over to the sword. The long edge was buried nearly to the hilt. If it had been positioned such, a regular sword would have broken, even if she were strong enough to rip it out. But this wasn't about strength.

The young woman didn't brace herself for a mighty heave; she only looked at the handle. After a moment, she put a slender hand on the hilt, running fingers through the unfamiliar symbols. It didn't look special other than the metal that wasn't iron.

As she touched it, the blade sank slightly further into the rock. Fluvial smiled as Raine reached and gripped the sword. She failed to pull it out straight, but that didn't matter. The stone was like water as the blade pushed free.

Raine spun the sword in her hand, lining up her form. She wasn't as good a fighter as many in Winter, but the weapon would go a long way to evening her odds. She turned to Fluvial.

"You honor me, my Lady."

The great spirit frowned. "The honor isn't mine to give. The sword does as it pleases. Anything you wish cut will be as water before the blade. There's a cost to keeping it longer than you need it. I suggest you remember that."

Raine nodded, looking at the unfamiliar face reflected in the blade. Jack asked to hold it and she held it out. The prince touched his finger to the weapon for a moment, a curious look in his eyes. He handed it back without trying to cut anything.

Claire was now feeling hopeful. They had two of the three requirements and plans for the third. With such a weapon, Raine would be quite respectable in a fight.

They continued planning into the night. Finally, she had one last favor to ask of Fluvial. She'd waited until the being was no longer pledged to her, not wanting to ask this while the great spirit would feel obligated.

"Lady Fluvial, both Jack and Raine will be traveling and likely fighting in a land of corrupted energies. Raine is immune to corruption, but the current great spirit may recognize her and seek to intervene. We request a piece of heart-dew so you may fuel their needs."

Before the Lady could answer, there was a shift in the ground. The grasses near the shore began to move and a small whirlwind pulled the vegetation into a form.

Just outside the circle of conversation stood a woman. She had skin darker than even Gray's. Long black hair flowed down her back, with a few strands swaying in her face. Her features were rounded and supple, not willowy or slender like Raine's or Joobel's, but muscular and curved.

Her teeth gleamed white in stark contrast to the skin of her lips, while dark and intelligent eyes moved around to take in those present. Claire had seen the wisdom in eyes like that. Fluvial had eyes like that. Autumn's Queen felt the pull of her spirit, the pull from her mother's spirit, and from Wenette's.

Jack stood, and before Claire could stop him, he smiled and spoke.

"Hello, Aunty Autumn, I was wondering if you were going to show up."

Claire was mortified. This woman was the avatar of the ancient spirit of her kingdom. The source of the power and life for her people. Standing before her was the great realm spirit of change. Autumn's Queen wasn't often speechless.

In this moment, she had no words.

\*\*\*

Jack had felt the alteration in the flows of power nearly a minute before the others noticed the shift in the grasses. He had spoken to great spirits before. Even now, he could feel the heart of the great spirit of fire in the Mountain Wyld. Fluvial was his friend.

The prince's tendency to treat everyone the same frustrated his sister, but the way he saw it, he had a good deal of power and didn't want people to bow and scrape in front of him. Why would anyone else? He'd rolled his eyes when Raine went all weak in the knees.

Now the great spirit of Autumn had shown up. Made sense. She had a stake in this as well. If Winter fell, then Autumn would be at war. If the Black March got a foothold in Fairie, it might be the end for everyone. Now that he could see the embodiment of Autumn, he felt like he'd known her all his life.

Claire got upset when he used the title 'Aunty' to tease Issabol, but the fact was, he knew that Issabol liked having a family. No one wanted to feel alone. Issabol needed to feel connected, to feel like a part of the team.

If his words threw Claire, she almost fainted at what her brother did next. The young man walked to the approaching great spirit of Autumn and hugged her. What's more, she hugged him back and kissed his dimpled cheek.

Out of the corner of his eye, he saw Gray push one finger under Claire's chin and slowly push her mouth shut. Jack's smile widened. Autumn whispered in his ear; he nodded and moved ahead of her.

"Everyone, let me introduce you to Lady Omisha, our benefactor... as it were."

To Jack's delight, Omisha went to Claire and hugged her. Then she did the same for all the people who called her land home. This seemed to normalize his behavior, and the look on Claire's face was priceless. Finally, she hugged Depth, who was still one of her children, even if he was adopted. She gave a deep nod to Fluvial, who returned it with a confused expression.

Omisha seemed unsure of how to greet Raine. Finally, she just hugged her too. Jack guessed it was good to err on the side of a hug. Plus, Raine was as shocked as Claire. Jack liked seeing the women in his life surprised. It took the edge off when he was the one surprising.

Finally, Omisha sat with the others. She looked around and smiled. Then she spoke to *her* queen.

"You didn't know what you asked when you requested the heart-dew from Fluvial. She'd no doubt say yes, but if she fed much power to Raine and Jack, she might not have enough to remain intact. She was true to her word when she came here, and hasn't adopted any other creatures in this land. Only the dragon is hers."

Omisha looked up at Depth, whistling before adding, "Aren't you just a big fella." She sighed, looking to the group.

"Fact is, Fluvial is much older than me. Possibly, she once had more power than all of the Fairie realms combined. Now she's respectfully staying small, and powering a hatching might be too much."

Claire's face paled, "I didn't realize, I—"

Omisha waved the words away. "My queen is right, of course; the power needs to come from Fluvial or Winter will know Raine is back. Also, the dragon egg might turn out... special." The great spirit looked at Joobel. The gnome looked terrified, but Omisha only laughed.

"Do not fret, my gnome, you're mine as much as the others. I've never had as good a time as I did watching you girls hatch those dragons. You gave me back my protectors. I can't say how good that felt. Also, Spring is more than a little upset that the first dragon ever to have healing breath serves Autumn."

The great spirit of Autumn chuckled at her own words. Jack wondered what it would be like to have her at parties. She would keep things lively. Omisha took a deep breath and continued.

"Understand, I mean no disrespect. Fluvial is older than I ever expect to be. Yet when power gets low, we can unravel. Like all spirits, we'd come back together and be stronger for doing so, but we don't have centuries to work with. So tonight, I'm going to gift her some of my own power."

Fluvial's jaw dropped open, her hand moving over her chest. Great spirits coveted power. To give any to another was unthinkable. Not to mention they were incompatible. She couldn't take the power of change and use it to fuel water. Omisha seemed to understand her confusion. She smiled and slapped her knee, then began to brag.

"Fluvial, my dear girl, you've met Jack many times. You know he throws fire around like he has more than enough to spare. That's because he does. He might smell like he belongs to fire, but he is wholly mine. Honest and true."

Omisha's face moved to a serious frown. "His power is old and unique. Only one other has ever wielded it. Mind you, keep this to yourself. The other realms wouldn't be happy if they knew what he is. Only one other great spirit knows of his true spirit. That must remain the case, at least for now."

Fluvial stood slowly. She walked over to Jack and lifted a flowing eyebrow.

"May I?"

Jack shrugged and nodded.

Fluvial held out her hand, a single finger touching his forehead. A moment passed, and the great spirit looked down with wide eyes.

"That's how these little ones hatched dragons! He fed them your power."

Omisha clapped and said, "Oh, did he ever! You should've seen it. He's how I'm going to gift you some energy."

Fluvial nodded and walked over to Depth. She communicated silently with him before turning back, sitting down next to Raine. The mighty sea dragon lumbered into the water and swam into the murky depths.

"If you only have one child, he seems like a sturdy choice," Omisha chuckled.

Fluvial nodded. "He is."

"I'm not as worried about power as I am my family. Hard times have passed within my borders. I lost my protectors and many of my children. I got some back."

She looked meaningfully at Joobel, who squeezed Jack's hand. "I also got some strange new ones." She nodded at Maeve, who was chewing on the rock Fluvial had cut with the sword Caledfwlch.

Autumn's spirit grinned. "The fact is, your queen promised mine an alliance and the Black March is a threat to us all. On top of that, Summer has been planning to invade our kingdom for some time now. It seems they're upset at the slaves that keep disappearing between the Wylds and Summer's border."

Jack chuckled. "We're just getting started there. We have the name of one of the chief traders. He won't be happy to see us."

"I admit I was concerned when Ornella first made that decision, but it was the right thing to do. I'll support your efforts as I'm able." She turned back to Fluvial. "If our children are successful, you'll inherit a realm twice the size of mine. When you come into that power, I want you to work with us in building something new."

Fluvial was negotiating from a position of weakness, a terrible situation, but this warm, strong spirit wasn't trying to take advantage of that fact. The water spirit remained cautious, biting her lower lip.

"Please explain what you mean."

Omisha lifted her hands to encompass all present. "I've many adopted children in my realm, but one seems to think he can make this world better. He has convinced my queen, and I admit he's winning me over as well. Do you know how many sick people I have in my realm?"

Fluvial remained silent, slowly shaking her head.

"Twelve! Within my borders I have *twelve* sick, out of nearly half a million. Those are scheduled to be healed late tomorrow morning. We currently have no one starving. All orphans are now housed in the capital, learning how to use skills that will help others. We have new crops, both hybrids and selected strains. Soon we will be growing more food than we need. We will be offering trade to Winter."

Fluvial remained speechless. Omisha didn't want power; she wanted to share the bounty her kingdom was experiencing. She nodded and let the Autumn spirit continue.

"For centuries Winter has survived by culling the weak, taking only the strongest. Those who cannot find food, starve; those who cannot fight, are killed. The blood of slaves fuels your mines. I once thought there was no other way."

Her dark eyes moved to Gray. "I was wrong. We can make both our kingdoms stronger. With us united, Summer will be slow to attack, and in time they will see ours is the better way. Our queens agreed to a simple treaty; I want something more. Will you accept?"

Fluvial stood. The Autumn spirit still confused her, so unlike most of her world. Not so long ago, she was waiting to die, the ruler of an empty sea. Then she had a chance to be less but live on in a new world with her last child.

Now she had a chance to have children again, spirits of water that would draw on her and grow. She could hardly imagine a world where the poor and weak could find a place to not only survive, but to flourish. She walked over and hugged Omisha.

"I agree."

***

Claire had given little thought that the great spirits would speak to one another. She suspected that the fact they did so in physical bodies now was for the benefit of herself and the others. Her kingdom and that of Winter would be bound together now. It would be all or nothing.

If they failed, then the Black March would consume Winter and would have the foothold it needed in their world. Now, as the young queen watched the two great spirits embrace, she felt her resolve grow even stronger.

The sound of splashing came. Depth returned carrying the large chunk of heart-dew. It was the manifest power of Fluvial. Her existence was tangled up in the strange shimmering blue stone. Depth waddled near to where they were standing and gently set the stone on the shore.

The sea dragon seemed amused at the embrace of the two spirits that held claim over him. Claire noticed the toothy grin had widened far more than was needed. For such an imposing sort, he sure had an odd sense of humor.

Omisha walked to the stone, stopping a few feet away. She placed a palm on the rocky earth of the shore. Her land, the realm she maintained for her children. The ground flowed, seeming to move like liquid.

Claire had seen heart-stone before. She had a piece of it in her ring. It also had a strange shimmering quality, though its color was brownish gold. Her ring allowed her to pull on the power of her realm even when she was far from home. Now she saw a much larger piece. It moved up out of the churning earth to sit right next to the heart-dew.

Jack moved to stand next to Omisha. The spirit nodded at him and the prince began to do what only he could. He put one hand on the smaller blue stone and another on the one of golden-brown.

At first, it looked as if nothing was happening. Sweat began to roll down his brow, his lean light brown arms starting to glow, each a color matching the stone it touched. Then she realized that he was changing the magic. He always described it as the 'taste' of spirits. He could take it in and change it to match the one he gifted.

Now Jack was moving a tremendous amount of power; his face reddened with the strain. Claire saw his muscles begin to tense, but then the tension evened out and he just sat there.

The blue stone begin to grow. Eventually, it doubled, then doubled again. In time the brown stone disappeared and the blue one was holding all the gifted power.

Omisha turned to her children. "I'll always stand with you, though you may not see me again."

Then the great spirit of Autumn was gone. Fluvial seemed to have gotten a bit taller with her increased power. She put her hand on the stone and seemed to be torn in the decision. Finally, she pulled her hand away and turned to Claire.

"She's right. This would have been a dangerous offering had not your Lady gifted me her power."

Fluvial held out a pearl of the precious blue stone.

***

Jack stood as Fluvial gave his sister the piece of heart-dew. It was likely worth more than any estate in Winter. Next the water spirit walked over to him. She took his hand and smiled.

"You've done much for me. Without the kindness you and your sister have shown, I'd be wasting away in a dead sea. My power will not work with hers, but this I can do for you." Jack's left hand began to glow, a bright and brilliant blue. Fluvial continued.

"The more specialized magics of water need a spirit. This is the most basic power of water, but I imagine you will wield it well. Much as you can use basic fire in huge quantities, so shall you have the same power over water."

Jack turned his hand, staring at the dimming point of light inside. This was no spirit, but more a borrowed power like the heart-fire in his right hand. The prince felt the power of water. He could channel his own energy through the stone and wield an aspect he had no birthright to. It was power, something he'd tried to avoid.

He could steal the spirits from others. He'd told Claire of what he'd done in dealing with Anwir, the rogue earth aspect who had helped Wenette. He'd taken the man's earth spirit to remove his control of the golems Jack feared might be used against them. The prince knew he could've possessed that spirit, but he was strong enough in his mind. Now his power had grown.

Jack pushed energy through the heart-dew, making a ball of crystal-clear moisture in his hand. The ball spun and swirled, then he heated it till it steamed away.

Thinking for a moment, he tried something else. He made a flame, then poured in the water magic as he pulled away the heat. The flame flickered to a bright blue-white. He pulled that energy into an orb, tossing it onto a nearby rock. The rock began to screech and frost as the moisture in the air condensed on its surface.

After a couple of seconds, the rock shattered. Frozen chunks of stone flew in all directions. Gray had enough time to throw up a shield to catch the projectiles and no one was hurt.

"Omisha wasn't wrong about you," Fluvial gasped.

Jack winked at her with a faintly glowing eye.

# CHAPTER 6

The arrangements made, Depth and Fluvial returned into the Loch. Gray was the last through the large portal. He noticed Raine staring down at the sword Fluvial had given her. He smiled and nodded to the weapon.

"That's quite a gift."

Raine pursed her lips. "I don't think that's the right word. It's more of a loan. Something about this blade feels.... It makes me nervous. When I've done what's needed, I'm giving it back. It feels like it's feeding off me."

Gray held his hand out and she handed him the blade. He felt the balance and looked at the edge. For all the world, it just looked and felt like a normal, well-made sword. The one he would often conjure from air wasn't much different in design. He waited to feel if the blade took power from him. Nothing. He resolved to ask Jack what he'd felt from it.

For now, he looked to Raine and said, "If it's draining you somehow, I have a room here. Would you like me to keep it there for now?"

Raine seemed to hesitate, but then nodded. She trusted him and the blade was making her feel... somehow not herself.

Gray took the sword and walked down the hall. He saw Issabol inspecting the pearl of heart-dew with reverence. Gray hated to interrupt, but he wanted to ask her about the sword.

As he approached, she looked up, her eyes jerking to the sword.

"Where did you get that?" Issabol growled.

He shrugged. "It's Raine's. She said it was making her feel odd. I was going to stow it for now."

Issabol held her hand out and Gray handed her the hilt. The ancient child held the weapon like a craftsman, inspecting without any inclination to wield it. She soon found an inscription; her brow furrowed but she didn't explain further.

She held out the sword to Raine. "Take the weapon and tell me what you feel."

Raine once more held the strange blade. A faint rhythmic music filled her head and she found herself wanting to cut things, or people. Issabol nodded as she watched the girl's reaction.

"I'd like for you to demonstrate its power."

Raine took the sword and slid it tip first into the stone wall. The ancient girl watched with a frown. Her gaze moved to Gray.

"Try to pull it out."

The big man tried but couldn't budge it. When Raine put her hand back onto the hilt, the blade flowed through the thick stone as if through the surface of a stream. She took the sword and shaved off a piece of stone. It was as if the old rock was warm butter.

Issabol let out a low whistle. "In your hands it's a dangerous item. The power it holds is old and quite powerful. It's a weapon of water and only one of your aspect could hope to wield it. Moreover, it has a mind and it chooses who it will serve."

The ancient girl sighed. "I'll make you a sheath for it, something it won't slice through on accident. Perhaps a barrier that will keep it from taking energy from you. For now, put it some-place safe."

Issabol turned back to the blue pearl. Claire moved over to describe how she wanted to craft the item for Raine. The ancient child nodded and let the queen work out the design. She seemed happy with how Claire was learning.

Gray took the sword and moved down the hall, setting it neatly in the wardrobe in his room. He turned and was surprised to see Raine had followed him, now standing just inside the door. Dark patches were forming under her eyes and she slumped against the frame.

"If you're tired, you're welcome to use my room here for the night. I wanted to go back to the workshop. The design they were discussing gave me an idea."

Raine moved inside and shut the door. Sitting in the chair, she nodded to the bed. He was confused by her behavior but sat down to face her.

"How do you handle all of this?"

Gray tilted his head. "Handle what? You mean the magic of the...."

Raine shook her head. "This world. You're not from here, yet you're mixed up in all of this." She held her hands out as if to encompass all of Fairie.

"I had no choice. When I was newly free, Claire and Jack saved my life. They gave me a home and a mission."

She pushed her hair behind one ear. Raine looked down for an instant, then back up to him. "Is there more?"

"I don't understand what you mean." Gray scratched at his chin, looking anxiously at the door.

Raine followed his gaze. "I love my cousins. They might soon be all the family I have left. I owe them much. I'd never betray them. So, I ask, is there something between you and Claire?"

Gray swallowed hard. "I... there is.... I care for her. I don't know that she feels the same."

She held his gaze, her own jaw tightening. "I felt you catch me as my dear Sroto died. I watched you stop an army. You saved my life. The aspect of air is welcome in Winter. If you aren't in love with Claire, I want you to consider coming north with me."

Gray felt his own mouth fall open. The pretty face he was looking into wasn't even hers. He thought back to her pale skin and long white hair. Raine was beautiful and an amazing young woman. Her youth was a consideration; he was at least five years older than her, and a crucial five years by his standards.

He wanted to give a good response but all he could choke out was, "I... do love Claire. I have since I saw her return from Heluvot. I was so afraid she was gone forever. When she came through... I held her back. Not just to save her, but because I couldn't lose her again."

Raine nodded at him and paused for a moment. "Are you familiar with the Mother, Maiden, and Crone?"

Gray thought for a moment; he knew some from speaking to Claire. "The Maiden is the heir to the throne, the Mother is the queen, and the Crone is a former queen."

Raine smiled at him. "All true. The Crone is a reference to having left power and one who is unable to bear children any longer. Tradition says that the maiden cannot bear a child and remain the heir."

She paused for a moment, face growing dark before she continued. "Mother isn't an empty title; a queen must provide a new heir to her realm. If we succeed and I can take back my throne... I'll need to bear children. It is my duty. If you learn that your love isn't returned, I want you to consider being my consort."

Gray paled. "A consort being...?" He swallowed hard, already knowing the answer.

"Husband. Though marriage isn't required; the spirits know Summer has many consorts. I had a good father. He was quick to anger, but he was good to my mother. Though he died years ago, she loved him and he loved her. I want that for my children."

Gray gasped, struggling with words. "So, wait…. Are you proposing to me?"

Raine sighed. "Do you know what happens in Winter when a royal child is born weak?"

He shook his head. "I have my guesses."

"If I'm queen, I'll need a strong husband who can father strong children. The security of the kingdom depends on it. Your aspect is welcome. You're a good choice."

Gray was flattered but could tell she held no love for him. She was impressed with his power. How could this girl love a man she'd met less than two days ago? He left the bed and knelt before her, taking both her hands in his.

"Raine, you're family to the most important people in this world to me. I consider myself your friend and will do everything I can to help you and your people. I told you where my heart is. Though I'm not sure where that will lead, I'll see it through until I know for sure. You're a wonderful person and I'm honored you asked, but I can't follow you into Winter."

Raine nodded slowly, wiping away a tear. She'd been through so much, and rejection always hurts. Gray pulled her into a hug and she cried into his shoulder.

Just as he was about to let go, the door swung open. Claire was holding a small basket and took one step into the room. She saw the two in an embrace and without a word turned away. As the queen stomped down the hall, Joobel poked her head in, looked around, rolled her eyes, and followed Claire.

Gray wasn't sure what had happened, but he was confident that he was in trouble. The damage was done and Raine still needed rest. He helped her up and gave her the room.

He went to see how complicated his life had gotten.

***

Joobel wasn't a subtle being. Gnomes tended to say what they mean and mean what they say. The odd dynamic between Claire and Gray was getting old, this back and forth of sort of saying how they felt and then recoiling when the other wasn't in perfect sync.

The gnome knew it was different for her. She'd imprinted on Jack the first time she saw him, though only Claire knew that. As soon as possible, she'd told Jack how she felt in no uncertain terms. The spirits knew how long she'd have had to wait for him to say something.

Now Claire had made up a silly story in her head of how the man she cared for had fallen for another. Joobel could tell at a glance that Gray was only comforting the Winter girl. It was even more apparent when she thought about all the times he just stared at Claire with those forlorn eyes. They kind of looked like Maeve when she wanted something. This was all a colossal waste of time.

As the gnome walked into Claire's room, she saw the woman sitting on the bed, her hands covering her face. She was crying but still trying to hold back her emotions.

Joobel closed the door slowly behind her. Walking over to Claire, she tenderly lifted her chin, looking into the light brown of her eyes. The color of falling maple leaves. Then the gnome slapped the Queen of Autumn hard across the face.

Claire jumped up at the shock of anger and pain.

"How dare you strike—"

The gnome threw her hands up. "Oh, do shut up, sister. For so long, you've skulked around pitying yourself. All the burdens of the crown and the prophecy. You wallow in your loneliness and sneak jealous glances at any who would choose happiness instead. It breaks my heart to see a good man who adores you, try and fail time and time again to earn your attention."

The gnome began pacing as she continued her tirade.

"He tries to help you build a better world. He seeks to provide justice in your kingdom. He has risked his life countless times. Do you know how many I've seen turn away in disgust from your powers? Death, Entropy, and Transmutation. I of all people know what evils they can bring about! I have never once... not *once*... seen him ever look at you with anything other than admiration. He has been in love with you since I met him."

Claire was losing the composure the slap had given her. The words wore away at her resolve, and she began to weep once more. Joobel slapped her again. Claire was starting to tear up from the pain in her face as much as her broken heart. The gnome wasn't done.

"He's a nice man, and so when a person with as much pain and loss as Raine sought a shoulder to cry on, she chose a kind and caring one. Now you're going to dry your tears, pinch your cheeks, and go have a real conversation with the man who has been pining for you all this time. Do you understand?"

Claire started to sniffle. "I don't think I can—"

Joobel slapped her a third time.

"Will you stop that? I'm not like you. I can't walk around half-dressed and driving every guard in the Keep crazy. I cannot say how I feel because I don't know! I'm cursed! My whole life will be terrible decisions and horrible results. I'm going to destroy a world—"

Joobel stomped a foot, stone cracking under the force. "And *save* another. Don't forget that the prophecy is our hope as well as a curse. Many have pledged themselves to your cause. Their fates are already bound to yours. Why is it wrong to seek some measure of happiness amidst the terror and fear? Why not tell him how you feel?"

"Because... I'm afraid. What if he doesn't want me?"

"I'm perfectly willing to slap you again!"

The queen shook her head. "Please don't.... I can't feel my cheek."

Joobel hugged her adopted sister. Neither noticed that the gnome shouldn't have been able to strike her queen. Not because of station or the oath of service. Joobel was a Named creature of magic and bonded to serve Claire. Yet when Claire had agreed to do so, she'd added the condition that Joobel never let her make a bad decision without stepping in. This didn't just give Joobel the ability to confront Claire; it required it.

Soon the two had talked more openly. The tension was gone and Claire opened up about her fears. Joobel had helped her clean up and was about to step out when there was a knock at the door. The gnome answered it and happily greeted Gray, pulling him subtly into the room. She flitted her wings and closed the door as she disappeared into the hallway.

Claire looked up at Gray, who seemed confused and upset. He was there with her. He *chose* to come to speak to her. She stood slowly, the composure of a queen regained.

"We need to talk."

\*\*\*

Jack had been a bit thrown when Joobel followed Claire into the hall. They wouldn't have much time to spend together and it wasn't like her to spend any of it off doing something else. It probably had something to do with emotions and stuff.

His gnome was very in tune with such things and the prince assumed she'd make things work out. For now, he was watching his great, great, great—well, a good deal of greats—Aunt Issabol work her craft. Jack wasn't a man of feelings, but he had a good deal of curiosity.

Issabol was working on a masterpiece of portals with the most valuable substance in Fairie. The pearl of heart-dew was held in a small clamp. Five tiny orbs were arranged around the blue stone. The ancient girl had long since accepted that if she didn't explain her task, Jack would flood her with questions. She was fusing an orb to one side as she spoke.

"Each orb cluster works just as a larger portal. Though instead of opening a door through space, it connects the stone to its whole. The linked heart-dew gives the user a link to the greater mass of energy. As long as you have skin contact with the jewel, you can access the energy of the connected realm."

"Will the larger piece give more power?"

Issabol smiled slightly. "The total power you can access is dependent on the main source. A larger piece would speed up the rate that you can draw it in, though."

Jack looked down at his ring, the band connected to a small orb. Inside was a piece of heart-stone, linking him to the great spirit of Autumn. He thought for a moment.

"Would the amount of skin touching it affect the rate you can draw?"

Issabol paused. "I guess it could. I mean—"

Jack was already concentrating on his ring, pulling power through, then he placed his other hand atop the band. He nodded. "Yup, it seems it does. If that's the case, why don't we put the orb inside me?"

Issabol lifted an eyebrow and frowned. Jack could see he'd been too vague. He set the ring against his breastbone.

"Claire could just put the orb right into my chest. Then I couldn't lose it, it couldn't be taken away, and I'd be able to draw the maximum amount of power."

Issabol bit her lower lip, trying to think of a reason it wouldn't work. It would make her task easier if she didn't need to disguise the item like jewelry and his thoughts on skin contact were right enough. He had a point.

If Claire could transmute the orb right into the skin, then it would be impossible to know it was there. It was a remarkably good idea. She looked at the prince, surprised he would have thought of something so intuitive.

He shrugged. "Yeah, I know... I'm smarter than I look."

Issabol chuckled. "It would be impossible not to be."

Jack continued watching as the orbs were all affixed, and Issabol pulled power into her hand. She held it over a cauldron of thick purple liquid. The liquid flowed up and toward her fingers. She moved the substance over to the heart-dew outfitted with the tiny portal orbs, wrapping it around the blue pearl. She pulled the clamp away as the liquid evened and hardened. The ancient girl then concentrated, little forehead creasing with effort, and the hard-purple surface began to glow with power.

Once finished, she took the small gem in between two fingers. It began to pulse with energy. She handed her creation to Jack, who closed his left hand around it. He tasted the power, like cool saltwater. He tried to draw energy from the gem, but it was closed to him. He could have taken the animating weaves from the orb, but the heart-dew was of the water aspect and wasn't his to take.

He nodded and handed the construct back to Issabol. She thought for a second, before holding out her hand.

"Let me see your ring."

Jack gave her the jewelry. He didn't like wearing the thing but couldn't deny the usefulness of having backup power. He had to swallow it once back in the Wyld when slavers almost found it. He didn't tell her about how he'd retrieved it.

Now Issabol set the item in another clamp. In a few seconds, the tiny orb pulled away from the band. She channeled more liquid from the cauldron and made the surface wider. The once-perfect orb was larger now and flattened. She set the flat surface to the center of Jack's chest and held it in place with a piece of cloth that was sticky on one side.

Issabol stuck her tongue out slightly, focused on positioning it correctly. "Try it now."

Jack pulled magic through the object. It was still a pale comparison to having his feet on Autumn soil, but it was an improvement over the previous model. He gave her a curt nod.

"Better."

"Always so descriptive. I agree that if Claire will place it just under the skin, it's a better solution."

Jack nodded and pulled the cloth away, wincing as it plucked hairs from his chest. The prince handed the disk to Issabol, who set it aside near the water jewel. The girl frowned; her forehead furrowed again.

"Did you touch the sword that Raine was given?"

"I did. It's alive... and hungry. The power within tastes of blood and ash."

Issabol nodded in agreement. She frowned, remembering holding the weapon.

"It's not good or evil, but it wants to be used. A weapon can be used for good, to protect and defend. I fear that when there is no one to protect and nothing to defend against, it will still want to be wielded. I don't need to tell you what that will leave."

"The sword will want her to kill."

Issabol set a hand on his arm. "You'll be the one with her. You will be the only one who can stop her. The purest hearts are the ones easiest to warp. They see no evil in themselves or others. She won't know what's happening until it's done. Raine is kind; you mustn't let her lose herself."

"Like a child burning ants," Jack muttered.

His wasn't a pure heart. The prince knew what evil was. He nodded to confirm he'd watch over his cousin. Jack looked up as Joobel entered the workshop. She looked pleased with herself.

"What have you done?" the prince sighed.

The gnome gave him a dazzling smile. "Oh me? I haven't the faintest idea what you're talking about."

Then Joobel looked at the young man she adored. She took a pose and in a perfect impression of him, winked one glowing green eye. He couldn't help but laugh.

Jack did enjoy a challenge.

# CHAPTER 7

It took almost three days for her to craft a scabbard for the sword Caledfwlch. Issabol was able to measure and touch the blade as she would have a standard weapon. Only in Raine's hand did the edge gain its unearthly sharpness.

The sheath was crafted as a masterpiece of the ages. Issabol had asked Joobel to see if Bloom would donate a shed skin and her breath for the construction. The green drake was more than willing. If Joobel had asked, she might have donated her massive beating heart.

The dragonhide was hardened and infused with water aspect supplied by Jack through the heart-dew stone in his left hand. Then Issabol weaved the same purple liquid into the material and Bloom breathed her healing mist onto the item before it hardened. Finally, the ancient child added a tiny scraping of heart-dew taken from the pearl Fluvial had given to Claire.

The Portal Master pulled all the magics together, then hardened the soft material around the blade. The process had been exhausting and she'd need several days to rest, but it was a fantastic accomplishment. Raine came in to receive her gifts as the others gathered around.

First the sword was handed to her inside of its scabbard. Raine belted on the sheath and then drew the blade. Issabol nodded in satisfaction as she pulled the scabbard up on one side and had the Winter girl try to cut through it. The blade stopped as it touched the infused dragon skin. There was a slight hum, but it didn't cut through.

Issabol sighed. "Sheath the blade and hold out your hand."

Raine did so, the light brown skin so different from her normal pale shade. Issabol took a small copper knife and ran it across her palm. The Winter girl jerked her hand back in surprise. The cut was deep, the muscle inside her hand visible, but there was no blood. Both of them could see it pulsing inside the wound, but not a drop spilled out. Raine looked up in shock, only partially because the ancient girl had cut her.

"That really hurt!"

"As long as the scabbard is touching you, no wound will bleed. With a blade as dangerous as that, this offers some hope of undoing a mistake. It will also help protect you in the trials ahead. There are few things that sword will not cut. This scabbard is now one of them."

Issabol's swirling eyes narrowed. "Be careful, and when the blade is done serving you, I implore you to return it to the great spirit of water. Sorry about the cut; Bloom will fix it up for you shortly."

Raine held her other hand over the wound, a low mutter leaving her lips. "You could've just said so; it's not like I wouldn't have believed you."

Issabol ignored her grumbling as she walked over and took the slightly bulging disk she'd reworked for Jack. She had made sure Claire was willing, but Issabol wanted to show the group how the new artifact would work.

"Jack, remove your tunic."

The young man flipped the shirt off and stood bare-chested as Issabol handed the coin to Claire. The queen took the jewel and set it in the center of her brother's chest. She concentrated as she focused Transmutation into his flesh. The item sank into his skin to sit just above the breastbone.

As Claire pulled her hand away, the wound closed around it. There wasn't so much as a scar, the slight bulge of the coin-shaped construct the only evidence it was there.

Jack stood and pulled energy through the disk. A flickering orb of fire appeared in his hand. The prince smiled, nodding in satisfaction.

Issabol picked up the larger coin that was for Raine and the re-worked ring from Claire. She handed both objects to Autumn's Queen, who put them in her pocket. She could take care of that in private; modesty need not be compromised. The two women walked out of the room, taking only a few moments to install the gifts. Soon they both returned.

Issabol looked to Raine. "Pull on Fluvial's power."

The Winter girl closed her eyes and focused. A smile crossed her face as the crisp energy flowed.

"I didn't realize how much I missed my home," Raine whispered.

"It is time," Issabol said.

Raine nodded to Jack and they both stepped over to Claire. Jack met her gaze with an apologetic stare.

"Sister, you said Wenette was mad. Her spirit was corrupted. You now hold that spirit. We can't take chances."

Raine put both of her hands on Claire's face and concentration came over the Winter girl's features. Claire started to pull away, then lashed out, but her hands were caught. Gray was standing behind her, holding her arms. Claire's eyes bulged and her Banshee Wail rang out, Jack pushing the attack into the ceiling before putting a hand on Raine's neck. He fueled her power.

Joobel hadn't been in on the secret. She was a Named creature of Claire's and the queen gave her order.

"Stop them! Kill them!" The words carried ancient power in an otherworldly tone.

Joobel's bond was unique and she followed the order she knew Claire would give if the corruption weren't inside her. The gnome laid her hand on Claire's forehead and the Autumn Queen's pain faded.

The tainted magic was subtle. The corruption had been waiting and growing. Those of the aspect of change were resistant and Claire was strong. Once it discovered it couldn't defeat her other spirits, the taint retreated.

Raine's magic was pulling out the slime, dissolving the ooze. Jack's power boosted her ability many times over. The corruption was subtle and had deep roots in the other spirits of the queen. Those roots were ripped out, the taint fading until all of them were pure once again.

It had taken several minutes to cleanse the queen of the infecting magics. Raine was tired. She'd sensed corruption but hadn't expected so much, so deep and thick in Claire's core. It was a tribute to how hard Autumn's Queen must have been fighting its influence.

Issabol had feared this was possible, but she hadn't been sure how to cure it. Raine's spirit of Purification was fortunate indeed.

Claire looked around, eyes still wild with confusion. She pulled an arm free and swung a fist outward. Her blow caught Gray in the side of the face just as the woman started to faint from the strain. The tall man caught her and carried Claire to her room. Joobel followed along, her face a mask of concern.

Jack stood trembling. He hadn't truly expected there to be an issue. If the madness had completely taken Claire over, there would have been little anyone could do. Harvest wouldn't have been able to refuse the command as Joobel had. He'd have killed everyone present.

The prince looked to Issabol. "Seems we dodged a blade today."

The ancient girl looked at the prince and shook her head.

"How many more are aimed at our throats?"

***

Gray lay awake. He'd humored Jack when he'd said that Raine had sensed a hint of the tainted magics in Claire. It seemed safer to test it just in case.

Claire herself had said that the frost drake's madness was like that of Wenette. The Autumn Crone had kidnapped Ornella, Claire and Jack's mom. She'd sought power, but Claire thought her motives might have been more complicated than just taking control over Fairie. Was it possible that she wanted to unite this world against a common enemy?

He'd finally had a real talk with Claire. She cared for him, might even love him. Was that the corruption? Was the tainted power the reason she took so long to tell him? Would she even remember the conversation he'd waited so long for? Sleep was far away. The big man decided to take a walk.

Jack had said Claire was tainted. That was an odd way to think of it. He'd visualized the corruption as a poison. Now he began to picture it like a disease.

Gray knew well that the chief reasons his own world had conquered many of the diseases that plagued the population were clean water sources, waste management, and vaccines. He had taken steps to help the people of Autumn with the first two.

Indoor plumbing had been set up in many facilities of the capital, waste was being treated, and many illnesses were greatly reduced. He'd been working on a way to get water to everyone, but filtration was difficult with the materials he had available. Raine might be able to help with that if they could get things under control in the north.

Now he considered vaccines. The tainted magic was affecting those who were drawing magic from a corrupted spirit. Raine was seemingly immune; her magic was purifying her spirit as she used it.

They knew the source of infection and had an immune patient. Gray had never studied medicine; he preferred technology. He wouldn't have the equipment or expertise to combat this if it were an infection, but there were those in his world who could.

The big man had accepted that he could never go home. Truth be told, despite missing family and friends, he was happy here. He was making a difference. But none of it would matter if the Black March got a foothold in this world. He'd looked through the doorway to Heluvot. He'd seen what this world would become if they lost this fight.

Gray needed to get home. Not to visit the land of his birth, though he'd love to see his family. He needed help. Magic might not be the solution to all of this. It might be technology. He needed an expert in infectious disease.

There was an idea he'd been considering for some time. When he had been brought to this world, he'd been inhabited by a powerful spirit of air. His skills, like Jack's, were the vanilla version of his element. He still loved how versatile his abilities were with the air aspect.

Gray had a good deal of control and power. Yet he couldn't visit his home world. Those who could had a spirit of renewal.

His home had faint levels of that type of power. Some could draw on it and survive, even if they weren't quite as strong.

For him to do so, he'd need a source of energy linking him to the realm of air. One that could pull the power from a distant world. He required an item like the disks the others had to visit his home.

Gray passed by the workshop. Issabol was still up, fine-tuning the portal she'd send with Jack and Raine. He walked in and sighed.

"Lady Issabol, may I speak with you?"

The girl looked up. The headpiece that let her see delicate details made her eyes look large and bulbous. She set down her instruments and pulled the magnifying eyepiece away.

"Of course, Gray. How are you holding up after Claire's... cleansing? Is your face hurting?"

He rubbed his jaw. Claire was powerful in many ways, but she had a weak right hook.

"I'm fine, but it got me thinking. What if we're looking at this wrong? What if we're treating this like a poison, or contamination, but it isn't? What if it's something else?"

Issabol was generally annoyed at interruptions, but this man was clever and curious. He'd surprised her before. She got up and waved for him to follow.

In the next room she placed a copper kettle filled with water on the stove. From a cabinet she pulled out two teacups and a tin of leaves. A plate with jam and bread rested on the counter nearby. They continued their discussion as she engaged in her task. Her hands flowed from item to item, a ritual of preparation she'd performed millions of times.

"You're talking about the tiny creatures that can make people sick?"

"Yes. Where I'm from, there are a few kinds. Viruses, bacteria, and others."

Issabol turned to lift one eyebrow. "You think that the corruption that Claire had, which has gripped the great spirit of Winter, is one such as this?"

"If it was a poison, say, then the more it was spread, the less potent it would become. Like spreading jam over bread."

The big man took a small spoon and spread some of the preserves across the surface of a slice of bread. Then he took another piece and rubbed the jam onto it. The jam covered both parts but was thinner. He went for another slice.

Issabol lifted a finger. "I understand. Please don't waste my bread."

Gray put one piece in his mouth and continued. "Bacteria don't work that way. They turn the body against itself. The number increases as they spread. That matches the description Depth gave us of how the Black March went through his world."

Issabol was pouring hot water and adding herbs as she nodded.

"If you're correct, do you know a way to fight them?"

Gray accepted a cup and blew on the hot liquid. "I have a basic understanding of such things, more than most, just from being curious. We'd need a disease expert to understand how to proceed."

Issabol bit her lip as she sat across from him. "I assume those are common in your world."

"Well... no. Many people in my world specialize in something. We'd need to find someone who has been studying these things for years."

The ancient girl shook her head. "Among our people of Autumn, only Joobel could travel to your world and stay for any amount of time. Your magic would fade in minutes. You would die."

Gray shook his head and grinned. "Could Jack go with the artifact you made him? Could Claire? What if you made one for me?"

Issabol frowned as she took a sip. His gift, and his curse, was air. All the other aspects had a bedrock of their land. The heart of each great spirit's power. Renewal in Spring, Water in Winter, Earth in Summer, and of course, Change in Autumn. Even the Mountain Wyld sat on the realm of Fire.

The air realm was limited to a mountain top, the base resting at the point where the Wyld, Winter, and Spring met. Issabol hadn't heard of a bedrock for air.

"I'm afraid that without the stone that matches your aspect, I cannot make you what you need."

Gray swallowed the bread and sipped the tea. "What if I could find some of it?"

Issabol tilted her head, brows furrowed. "You intend to quest for something that I've never heard spoken of? I've been around quite a while, you know."

"Oh really? You don't look a day over two thousand."

She rolled her eyes as he continued.

"I know that if the Black March is using a disease to corrupt our world, then we're as equipped as my world was a couple of hundred years ago. A disease called smallpox killed hundreds of millions of people. My world defeated it. The last infection was decades ago. Help me go there so I can bring something like that back to this world."

"Perhaps you could tell Joobel what is needed and we could send her. She could go as she is now and be fine. Well, perhaps a bit less energetic." Issabol smiled at the thought of a sedate gnome.

Gray shook his head. "My world is complex and messy. Even I will have trouble doing this. Without guidance, she might be discovered. With her wings she would be instantly noticed."

Issabol sighed, sipping more of her tea. The orbs in her eyes seemed to speed up as she stared at the strange man. Finally, she seemed to deflate.

"I see. We need all the help we can get. I'm not equipped to battle this threat. I don't even know how to begin. I suggest you travel to the mountain top. Some call it the realm of Dawn. It is past the Mountain Wyld, but has no ruler that I know of."

"I'll depart after Jack and Raine leave."

"You should take Joobel with you."

"Do you think she'll be of help there?" Gray asked.

She didn't. Honestly, she thought the whole attempt wouldn't be of help. But the thought of Joobel wandering around and pining for Jack was already hurting her head. Add the constant requests to have her make a viewing portal to check on him.... Issabol shuddered slightly.

"I think it's imperative that she join you."

Gray considered her request before nodding. In a land of air, a winged ally might be a good idea. The tall man stood, giving his hostess a bow.

"Thank you for your counsel and the snack. I should get some sleep."

He moved back into his rooms, a plan taking form. This time he was able to fade into slumber.

\*\*\*

The next day was to be a later start. Issabol worked into the night to provide a portal that Jack and Raine could use to come home. Gray kept the same portal from before.

The series of projects had worn her thin. She'd been tired yesterday, and after last night, Issabol was simply exhausted. So many things weighed heavy on her mind: the corruption in Claire, the hungry blade called Caledfwlch, and the discussion with Gray. What if the Black March was using disease as a weapon? What if it was the disease?

There was so much to consider, and events were moving quickly. She'd always had the luxury of time. Her work to manipulate space had an odd side effect of altering the way she experienced time. The years had little impact on her.

Issabol had aged so slowly that even at over three thousand autumns she appeared to be younger than Jack. She'd wondered if her body would ever grow old enough to marry and have a family of her own. The whole of her long life had been spent as a child.

The strange thing was, in many ways she still had the desires of a child. She held little interest in marriage or children yet. She might someday, but not now. She missed her own parents and her little sister, who grew to have a family of her own, children and grandchildren.

Issabol had once involved herself with those nephews and nieces. Time was kind to her, but cruel to those she loved. It seemed one day she held a newborn baby, and the next, buried an old man. Her heart began to harden.

People became like the leaves of the trees or the fruit of the vine. Enjoy the company, she learned, but don't grow attached. They would fade quickly.

Part of her wished that Claire would use her Transmutation like Wenette. She could stay forever young. The queen could rule for many lifetimes.

Such power used selfishly could change the wielder. Claire already had so much potential, the extent of which she was far from understanding.

Raine had also been on the ancient girl's mind. She was a kind and generous person. She'd struggle in the cruel north, but with the right support, she might change it instead. There was more to the young woman than her pretty face and kind actions revealed. It was hard to describe, but events would come to show her as more than a scared girl on the run.

Raine's sword was an enigma. Issabol had made many artifacts. Maker magic was rare and hard to master. Her power gave both the benefit of time to learn the skills and the long-worked connections that could provide the unique and valuable materials required.

She had held the blade, but its power wouldn't serve her. Only water could wield it, and then only those chosen. She had made many powerful items and yet had never seen anything like it.

Issabol was old, but Fluvial was ancient. The spirit had claimed the sword was old when she'd received it. Wherever it came from, it wasn't to be trusted. The weapon would test Raine. As Issabol thought her name, the Winter girl walked into the hall of portals.

Four satchels sat on the ground. Areena had helped put together the clothing and food stores before running off again. Issabol had made more of the little cakes that would allow them all to both travel light and have plenty to eat. One would sustain an average person for a day.

Two parties would depart. Jack and Raine would leave for the frozen tundra of Winter, while Gray and Joobel would seek the mountain peak of the realm of Dawn. It was the only place any of them could think to look for the bedrock of the great spirit of air.

No one would see them off besides Issabol herself. Claire had left to attend to the matters of rule, having said her goodbyes the previous night. The queen was still recovering from the purification that had taken place; the revelation that she was infected was a sore spot for the already introspective woman.

Raine was the first to arrive. The young Winter Queen approached the ancient girl and seemed to struggle with her words.

"You've done me a great service. I hope to return your generosity someday."

Issabol shook her head. "I seek to protect my kingdom and home; the fall of Winter would doom us all. You owe me nothing."

Raine stroked the raised surface of the scabbard, not used to being in someone's debt. Now it seemed she owed many people. More than she could hope to pay.

"The scabbard alone is worth more than I can say. I wish to—"

Issabol held up a hand. "If you're smart, you'll give the sword and scabbard back to the great spirit the second you finish with it!"

The words had snapped out before she could stop them. The sword made her nervous and she wasn't quite sure why. The ancient child sighed, biting her lower lip.

"The scabbard offers some protection, but I don't trust that blade. When you've regained your throne, please don't give in to the temptation to keep it."

Raine looked at the hilt of Caledfwlch. If she were to touch the grip, it would sing to her with its strange power. The song was almost lovely. She shook her head, remembering Issabol was watching.

"I'll return it when the job is done."

Issabol gave one curt nod. "See that you do."

Jack and Joobel entered the hall of portals, hand in hand. The gnome was soaking up their time together before they would depart. Jack's face wasn't his own. He now looked like the twin brother to Raine's new face.

His hair was the same length but had lightened to a reddish-brown. His features were sharp and lean; high cheekbones and a freckled nose would confirm to anyone that they were brother and sister. Some might suspect they were twins, being so close in age. Jack smiled to Issabol.

"Good morning, Aunty. Were you able to rest?"

Issabol rolled her eyes. "I'll rest when you're all out of my home."

The young prince ignored the quip and hugged his tiny ancestor. Joobel did the same and began to strap on her pack. Gray entered just after and all quickly began getting ready to depart. Joobel hugged Jack and kissed his dimpled cheek; he was resigned to her affection and promised he'd miss her. Raine hugged Gray, to his surprise, whispering in his ear.

"My offer stands. I thank you for my life."

The big man reddened at her words. "I... um.... Have a safe journey."

He made a show of pulling his pack over one shoulder. A portal sprung to life against the wall near where they stood. The landscape beyond its threshold was harsh and rocky.

Issabol refused to open a portal in the land beyond Autumn's borders unless the circumstances were truly dire. Each party would step out to the edge of the change realm nearest their destination. Joobel gave Jack another hug and walked through after Gray.

Another portal opened next to the previous one, the view falling upon tundra. A range of snow-capped mountains rose in the far distance. Tall pine trees covered in a layer of white stood tall to the west. Jack nodded to Issabol as he followed Raine into the kingdom of Winter, a happy brown hound trailing behind him. Under her breath, Issabol whispered only to herself.

"Safe journey, my friends."

***

Bright light shone through the wide window of the queen's sitting room. It was early afternoon, the beams not quite reaching the legs of her low table. Claire was addressing the various concerns of the people of her realm. Norim, wearing Raine's likeness, was sitting nearby reading some scrolls and texts.

Occasionally she looked up to view her surroundings. Every couple of hours, Claire would get up to stretch her legs and retreat to her chambers. Norim would follow and they would discuss her handling of various situations.

Ruling a kingdom wasn't glamorous or songworthy most days. It was politics and putting out the numerous fires the people would inevitably start. Most of her morning passed hearing how many couldn't do without the labor of the children, even though many others complained about a lack of work.

The young of the kingdom would soon be attending school. Farmers with large families tended to rely on the children to earn their keep. She'd set up a fund to help with the transition, hiring help for those who truly needed it.

Several blacksmiths were complaining about the new market of gnomish-made goods that were of outstanding quality. Trade hadn't caught up with fresh supplies and the prices had been driven down. A temporary issue, but it still required her attention.

Claire looked out the window of her sitting room. With the sun stretching toward the west, her brother and friends would be traveling out of her kingdom. She'd wanted to see them off, but with so much going on, a queen had to keep a firm hand on the reins of her kingdom. At least, that's what she kept telling herself.

A knock at the door pulled her mind from her worries.

"You may enter," Claire said, voice raised.

A guard opened the door and stepped inside. With him was a messenger sprite. Many of the creatures of Fairie could fly, and with the portals in all the towns and villages, she could get news within the hour, a far cry from the days or weeks it used to take.

The sprite flew in against protocol, the guard starting to protest. The messenger was on the table and bowing before anyone could complain. Her words came out squeaky from such a small throat.

"I was sent from South Harbor, my queen. A Winter legion is approaching the border! Our scouts on the lookout towers of South Harbor estimate they will cross in just over two hours."

"What?" Claire screeched, papers hitting the floor as she stood.

The standing army of Autumn was only a small portion of the size that Winter could put on the march. Jack claimed he'd faced down around one hundred soldiers. She believed him; her brother never bragged. Such a number could be stalled easily enough. She needed details to make an informed decision.

"How many make the approach? I need an estimate. Also, move closer, I can barely hear you."

The sprite hopped and buzzed onto the desk next to Claire's couch. Her voice was easier to make out but no less squeaky.

"The lookout didn't give a good estimate, but he did say it was thousands. I'm sorry I don't know more. More messengers will come as information is available."

Claire's eyes went wide. "Thank you. Let South Harbor know that help is coming from the Keep."

She waited for the sprite to leave before giving the guard his orders.

"Let the rest of my appointments know that I've kingdom business and will be out the rest of the day. Send a few guards to the sanctum with Raine; Bloom will be there shortly and our guest will be safe in her presence."

The guard nodded. "Yes, my queen. Anything else?"

"Report what you have heard to Torg. Make sure he knows to ready our troops in case they are needed," Claire said, tapping her lower lip.

"As you wish.... My queen... is there a reason they might *not* be needed?"

The queen waved him off and the guard departed. His light chain mail clinked as he left the room and closed the door. Soon they'd be here for Norim, who looked so much like Raine that Claire even forgot sometimes. As long as Winter thought she was here, they wouldn't be looking for her anywhere else.

The woman who looked like Raine stood and moved to stand next to her. A calming hand rested on the queen's arm.

"What do you plan to do?"

Claire grabbed gloves from her desk. "I hope to stall them. The number of troops won't matter if they don't cross our border."

Norim frowned. "And if they attack Autumn?"

"Then, they will die," the Banshee growled as she pulled on her coat and hat.

The ones she wore when riding Harvest.

*** 

Joobel was excited and sad all at once. Knowing Jack would be away grated on her and she still felt jealous of Raine. At the same time, she was often cooped up in the Keep on business. The gnome was honored to be on a quest.

Gray was walking next to her, his long stride making her almost run to keep up. She would flit her wings some to help her eat the distance. The large man had mostly mastered his flight some time ago and they would be aloft for a good deal of the journey. For now, they wanted to cross the border on foot.

The Mountain Wyld was the quickest route to the realm of Dawn. Despite the roads they could take through both Summer and Winter, neither kingdom seemed like a smart place for the odd couple to be traveling.

Gray had once been a slave in Summer. They were grooming him to be a consort to the Summer Queen before he'd learned enough of his spirit of air to make the rather long and dangerous flight that carried him into Autumn's Twilight Vale.

He'd escaped the Summer guards only to almost die to some exiled wargs. His introduction to Autumn's royal family was a story Joobel had heard from Claire in detail. Jack's shorter version she'd gotten him to tell only once.

Gray was there at the border when Raine escaped Winter. He was mixed up in the dealings between Autumn and the two largest kingdoms in Fairie. The tall man seemed to be far more concerned with their current quest.

She looked over at him; the travel leathers mostly hid his dark skin. As he often did when traveling outside Autumn, he wore clothes that were well made but worn. He made an effort not to stand out. The brown of the leathers blended well with the colors of the stone they now walked upon.

Gray carried no weapon, but in Fairie that often meant that the person was even more dangerous. Only those with strong spirits carried no weapons. They *were* the weapon.

He'd convinced her to dress likewise. Her handmade travel clothing was dark green dyed leather, trimmed in sedate browns and greys. Her dress was also well made, of gnomish construction. In fact, she'd made most of Claire's clothing as well.

Gnomes were well known for craftsmanship. Through Claire's Naming, and perhaps her bond with Bloom, Joobel was many times larger than any other gnome, but she'd lost none of her skill. She'd gone through pains to create the appearance, at least from a distance, of wearing worn and used attire. Still, a close inspection would reveal that her garments were crafted with both excellent materials and unique skill.

She'd given in and tied back her silver hair, strips of leather matching her garb weaved in to hang down her back. The top of her head was capped in a similar attire. She did carry weapons.

Two slim copper daggers were strapped to her belt. She had some skill with them, Jack insisting she learn, but they were more of a deterrent. If it came to fighting, Gray would have to do most of it.

The biggest issue with laying low was her wings. She was unique among the gnomes in having them and making clothes that could both hide and allow her to use them was a challenge. She enjoyed designing them just the same.

It was said that a long-ago ancestor had sought refuge among the Sept of Fallen Leaves, Joobel's tribe in Blood Mountain. The bloodlines produced rare offspring and it was considered a blessing to have a winged child born.

The gnome used her skills in crafting clothing to hide the paper-thin extensions ingeniously. The coat she wore had slits in the back that covered wide strips of soft leather. When she wanted to fly, she need only pull her shoulders forward and the covering would part enough for her wings to push out of their hiding place. Though they appeared transparent and weak, they were incredibly strong and had no trouble working around the garment.

As Joobel looked to the big man walking next to her, she sensed the anxiety he was feeling. Jack sometimes joked that her real power was knowing how everyone felt and getting them to work through things. It had always been a talent. Perhaps the magic that made her grow had increased her empathy as well.

The gnome had spent little time with Gray recently and was curious to get him to open up. Every time she tried to get a conversation going, he answered with sparse words. Finally, she gave up her pretense at subtlety. Gnomes were bad at it anyhow.

"Why won't you talk to me?"

He didn't respond right away. Several steps passed before he formed words. Joobel knew well that Gray liked to think before he spoke.

"I'm afraid."

Joobel was often scared of the powers of their world. Usually she was scared for others, as her nature tended to lean toward compassion and self-sacrifice. This tendency had nearly gotten her killed more than once.

The gnome could understand why he was afraid, but not the scope of it. She'd heard him speak of the idea of the Black March using a plague to attack them, but the concept of very tiny creatures living and eating them from the inside seemed a bit far-fetched. Regardless of whether he was right or wrong, she knew he needed to discuss his fears.

"Only fools and madmen know no fear. How do you intend to overcome yours?"

"I seem to recall a young prince that must lean toward one or the other."

"Jack is a special case." Her eyes went dreamy for a moment. "He's also afraid of the battles ahead."

Gray rolled his eyes. "Could have fooled me. You weren't there when he was facing down that army."

"He had you there," she countered.

Gray's laugh caught her off guard. It was a bark of genuine mirth from a man who'd spent the whole walk brooding. Joobel cocked an eyebrow at him. He wiped one eye and looked down to her.

"You have it wrong. I didn't save Jack from them, I saved Winter's army from Jack. Don't forget that I'm the one who spars with him. I know his techniques. If I'd let them cross into Autumn, he'd have turned them all into cinders. Some might have pushed on, but once Maeve got involved...."

He shook his head. "It would've been a bloodbath."

Joobel pictured the scene. She knew well what her Jack was capable of when angry. Seeing his cousin bleeding on the ground, a mob of armed men demanding he hand her over. Soldiers invading his sister's kingdom and threatening his people. A shudder rippled through her slender form.

"You saved him from himself."

Gray shrugged. "The act would have haunted him, even if it would have been necessary. Both he and his sister battle the darkness within as much as the forces aligned against them."

Joobel only nodded at this. She knew that both the prince she loved and her adopted sister relied on her to take the edge off their harsh nature. The stories of their mother, Queen Ornella, the Ashen Lady, gave contrast to how much more her children had worked to apply a balance of justice and compassion. Joobel's own utmost fear was losing them to that darker path.

"Thank you, for allowing him a less violent choice."

Gray's face went dark. "I worry that now he'll have to be the one to advocate peace. That sword gives me chills."

Joobel walked in silence. She also felt the hunger of the blade, though its magic never responded to her. Her attempt to ease Gray's doubts and fears had only brought out her own. Her nature didn't let her dwell long, though.

The distant shape of a red dragon flying high through the air grabbed her attention. It flew out of sight, turning around the mountain of caged flame.

"Woo hoo! Did you see it? How wonderous!"

Gray smiled at her excitement. He stopped and began to secure his gear. Joobel began to do the same. They'd walked into the Mountain Wyld, but the journey was long, and they needed to take to the sky.

Issabol had said that one of the reasons she needed to come along was that she could join Gray in the air without having to rely on him to carry her. The gnome was glad to leave the ground behind, not used to walking this far. She also felt they'd be safer in the sky.

Joobel soon learned that danger could find you anywhere.

***

Jack didn't mind the cold. One of the best things about the gift of heart-fire embedded in his hand was that he never felt chilled. Living in Autumn, where the cold was always just waiting for the sun to set, made it a truly useful gift.

As they trudged across the seemingly endless tundra of the hearty grasses in the southern part of Winter, Jack was quickly moving toward a foul mood. He was wearing 'appropriate' clothing; Joobel had made his current wardrobe of grey leather trimmed in light brown fur. His messy reddish hair was covered by a thick hat. Despite his arguments, sturdy warm boots covered his feet.

Jack had always unconsciously worn as little as he could get away with. He rarely ever put on shoes unless it was some royal silliness, and short trousers with a sleeveless tunic were his go-to fashion. Now he had to 'blend in.' Claire's plan would, of course, have to impede his comfort.

He missed the feel of Omisha's power flowing through him. The prince could access other sources to some degree, such as the stones in his hands. He couldn't channel power from them as he could through the jewel embedded in his chest, but he was able to store energy in the stones. Gray called them 'batteries,' but Jack was convinced he made most of his words up on the spot.

The river that ran between the border of Winter and Autumn had been simple enough to cross. The waters always ran slowly and Jack had used his new power over water to freeze a bridge they could safely walk over. After they'd crossed, he threw small orbs of explosive fire at each end. The center chunk of ice floated away to wherever the river led. That had been the only challenge so far, the only thing to hold back the boredom.

Raine was walking alongside him. She seemed comfortable now, her skepticism at entering Winter apparently unfounded. The young queen feared the great spirit would know it was her that had returned. Claire had changed her face along with Jack's, but the taste of her spirit might alert the realm of water that she was here.

Purification wasn't unique like Jack's change spirit of Transition, but there were only a handful with the skill, and her homecoming might not go unnoticed. If the realm spirit knew she was back, it gave no indication.

Fluvial had pledged to serve as her spirit and she no longer drew on the realm below their feet. Jack hoped that the lack of connection would keep Raine hidden, but there was a good deal they didn't know about how the great spirits perceived their territory.

They currently had the goal of reaching Afshaneh, a border town on the west side of the Winter kingdom. It was a decent-sized settlement, maybe half the size of South Harbor.

There would be inns and places to get a hot meal. Perhaps even some information. The town was one stop on the way to their goal of finding a dragon egg.

Sleet had slipped in and out of madness. His link to Winter was so strong. He could maintain clarity of thought for a short time after being cleansed of the corruption. The drake had used a moment of lucidity to reveal that he'd sired a nest.

Three eggs lay in a cave in the eastern mountains of the kingdom. Unfortunately, all Winter dragons were directly linked to the corrupt great spirit, so the mother and any other dragons would be just as mad as Sleet was.

The quest was a heist. They needed to steal the eggs. Jack could feed power to Raine and she'd hatch one. The Bitter Challenge required a loyal dragon of Winter, a frost drake to confirm that Raine had the approval of the great water spirit of Winter. In this case, it would be a different great water spirit, but few would know that part of the plan.

The roads would make travel more comfortable but would also create a much longer route. The tundra was boring, but it was flat, and keeping a good pace was easy enough. Maeve ran large circles around them, digging holes to sniff at the mice burrowed below.

Jack knew that talking would help keep Raine focused. Though he was good with the silence, he found it was best not to let the young woman brood over the details of her problems.

"Does it feel good to be back?"

Raine didn't hesitate, as if she'd known the question was coming.

"I feel like a stranger here. The power I hold comes from afar, not from the land I love. Winter is a wonderful and terrible place. I'm the rightful queen, yet...." She pushed her hair behind one ear. "I feel as if I'm intruding."

Jack spent a good deal of time in the Mountain Wyld, but even there, power flowed into him. The closest the prince had come to feeling cut off was in Heluvot, but it was so different from his home that he couldn't relate.

"Winter needs you, even if it doesn't know it. You're the best hope for your people."

Raine watched her feet trudge ever forward. "What if I fail?"

"Well... that would make for a bad day."

She chuckled, turning to him. "You're not going to tell me that fate will see us victorious, or some such nonsense?"

Jack gave her half a smile. "Fate tells me that my sister, who I once saw make a hard-left turn into a stone wall, is going to save a world and destroy another. I've seen her take a bite of soup and miss. While I'll not tempt fate, I also won't put it past her to have this go all rotten just to laugh at the show."

Raine giggled, the sound musical and sweet. Claire had changed her face but done nothing to her voice or personality. This was still the same girl he'd always known, even if time had added layers.

Jack wished for Joobel's optimism just then; she wouldn't doubt their success. He grew wistful, an emotion that was still new to him. He was worried for her.

While he'd not tried to talk her out of joining Gray on his quest, it was only the tall man's presence that made him comfortable. Jack rarely took a sparring match seriously, unless it was against Gray. If he didn't give a fight his full attention, Gray would, and had, beat him. Granted, Jack limited himself to only fire.

The prince rubbed at the spot in his left palm that held Fluvial's heart-dew. He smiled and thought the next fight would be more enjoyable. His thoughts were interrupted by the sound of Raine's question.

"Jack... why are you here?"

He lifted an eyebrow. "This is where I need to be."

"You could be in a lot of places. You aren't safe here. Why are you helping me?"

Jack stopped walking. Claire did this sometimes. The whole 'woe is me I'm not worthy of your help' conversation. Jack didn't understand why people did this sort of thing. He had trouble with some emotions. It had been that way since before he could remember.

One thing he took very seriously was loyalty. His family and friends could count on him. It was his code of honor.

Raine's view of family was probably seasoned with no small amount of suspicion. Her sister had tried to hurt her, and her own people had sent an army to capture her. It was no surprise she was looking at his help as a transaction. He tried to explain in a way she could understand.

"Raine, we're family. I haven't been to Winter to see you in some time. I don't know what family means in this never-ending pile of cold grass, but to me that means we will do what is needed to keep you safe and help you serve your people. That blade has two edges; if we need your help someday, I expect the favor returned."

He began to walk again; Raine stood chewing her lower lip. As he moved away, Jack added, "Besides, it's not my fault you chose to make a bargain with Claire. Even I'm not that daft."

They made respectable time that first day. Twice they encountered large packs of wargs on the tundra. Both times the animals got downwind, sniffed the air, and then let them be.

Jack wasn't sure which of them smelled like something scary to a pack of forty wargs. If forced to wager, he'd have put his coin on the happy brown hound bouncing around them as they walked. Maeve was excited to be part of the fun.

As night began to fall, Jack went to work on something Gray had suggested. Camping in the open was dangerous; any fire or light would be visible for great distances. If ambushed while you slept, threats could come from multiple directions. While he couldn't think of anything short of a dragon he wouldn't fight, and Maeve might be immortal, Raine was essential and seemed rather squishy.

Purification was an incredible skill. It had kept her sane while most every other water user in Winter had gone mad. However, in a fight, she'd have to rely on *that* sword. Jack didn't trust the weapon and didn't want to give her an excuse to use it.

With his new power over water, he began to draw moisture from the air and ground. He shaped a structure with a round base and a domed top. The prince looked up and heated a portion at the top to make a simple chimney.

Jack made a small covering for the doorway that faced down the hill and added some holes at the base for fresh air. He froze the whole of it solid.

At over a foot thick, the walls were quite sturdy. His power was over water, but he quickly learned to draw out the heat from it with fire and could effectively make ice. He was getting good at ice.

Raine went inside and spread out a bedroll. She took one side and Jack took the end closest to the opening. Maeve would sleep next to Jack, if not on top of him. Raine got out a cooking pot and he went to get firewood. As he walked out, he thought for a moment and then sealed the door. It would be just his luck a warg or something would corner her while he was out.

Jack could have skipped the firewood and heated the inside with his own flame for the night, but this far from his preferred source of power, he wanted to avoid wasting energy.

He looked at Maeve, gave her a hand signal, and said, "Fetch." The hound shot off like an arrow, chunks of tundra landing around him from the lumps she tore up. Jack also looked for anything he could burn. After nearly half an hour he gave up and went back to camp. There was Maeve. His hound had brought neither a stick nor a log, but a rather sad-looking tree.

Large pieces of dirt fell from the roots she'd ripped out of the ground. Jack shook his head and made a particular note to never send Maeve to fetch a person. He might not like what she brought back.

The prince lit a blade of fire and carved up several useful sized logs. Leaving some just outside, he melted the frozen door from the entrance. He gathered water from the air to fill the stew pot and set the portable stand that would hold it over the flames. They ate while they reminisced about their childhoods.

Raine was only a couple moons older than him, while Myrin had been a few older than Claire. As younger siblings, they'd often worked together to prank, tease, and generally annoy their older siblings.

She almost lost some of her stew when Jack told the story of how he had heated all of Myrin's dresses enough to shrink. The older princess thought she'd gained weight and threw quite a tantrum. The tension eased as they fell back into the memories, regaining a bit of the closeness lost to time.

Soon Jack pulled enough of the heat from the fire that it would burn slowly for the night. Maeve was still large, so Jack had her keep watch in front of the door. This was for security, but also to keep her from crushing him.

Jack was the first to fall asleep. The protective structure and the huge hound convinced him that Raine would be safe enough. The prince didn't hear her crying. He didn't wake as she tossed and turned. The prince did sigh slightly when she moved the head of her bedroll to his and took his warm calloused hand in hers.

Then she also slept.

# CHAPTER 8

It was unwise for a queen to rely too much on her dragon. In many ways, Harvest was her greatest weapon and her only real deterrent. Using him as such might show how little else she had in the way of military might. The death drake was motivated to protect his home and carried her the distance in short order.

This was Claire's first time using the mask that Gray had designed. Both Issabol and Joobel had helped construct the leather, fur, and crystal glass that made up what he called a 'flight helmet.'

Claire had thought it a silly idea. Yet for the first time she flew high and swift without having to squint her eyes or spit out bugs. She vowed to never fly without it again.

She'd made the journey so quickly that she had time to prepare for the encounter. Claire often heard Torg instruct Jack to always keep an enemy guessing. Make them think you were either weaker or stronger than you really were. She decided she should do the same.

Harvest could effortlessly kill all the Winter soldiers that entered her land. This would create new problems, though. It would show one of her greatest strengths before a possible enemy. Her dragon was strong, but Harvest was alone. Bloom would fight if she had to, but she was no warrior. Even both of them together would be hard-pressed if Winter committed a flight of frost drakes or ballista.

Claire never wished to rule through strength, preferring her people to follow her because of trust and respect. Not only were the soldiers marching toward Autumn, but they were also moving toward the bridge at South Harbor. Her people would see how she dealt with this.

If she slaughtered these soldiers with Harvest's claws and his horrible miasma, they would respect her, but they might never trust her. To be feared or to be loved. She might have to settle for a little of both.

Autumn's Queen had secrets. She held not only the spirit of Death, the power she was born with, but also Transmutation and her mother's spirit of Entropy. She had powerful allies in the water just on the other side of the city.

If things still went wrong, she also had a dragon who would rip Winter apart before he let anyone touch her. It was the drake who gave her confidence, but it was her own shrewd mind that would dictate the events to come.

Claire stood about fifty paces from the bridge with Harvest just a couple dozen paces behind her. She closed her eyes and spoke in the tongue of dragons.

"Mightiest of big fish, are you there, my friend?"

The response came from a reasonable distance off, but she had no trouble hearing the words.

"My queen, you've come to visit sooner than I had hoped. Are you up for that game of Ganteque?"

Claire smiled in spite of the situation. "I'm afraid there is the issue of an invading Winter army at the moment. I was wondering if you would mind lending some support."

Depth's rumble rattled her teeth.

"Of course. Would you like me to eat them? The armor goes down a bit rough, but soldiers tend to be a lean meat."

"I'll not say your offer isn't tempting, but I was hoping to pull this off with a minimal loss of life. Not to mention frightening the people of my own city."

"What do you have in mind?" came his disappointed grumble.

One finger began tapping her lower lip. "Well, how are you at mist?"

"Mist?"

"Fog, water in the air, makes it hard to see."

"Does the mist need to kill everyone?"

"I actually have plenty of miasma. Harvest is here with me."

Depth chuckled. "Hello, my little friend."

Harvest joined the conversation. "Greetings, elder."

"So, this queen doesn't want you to eat anyone either."

The death drake added his own rumble. "I haven't asked. I've only eaten one person and the taste was terrible. I was sick for days."

"Hmm, well then, I guess we do it her way. So, my queen, tell me about this mist."

Claire rolled her eyes. "I want to scare the spirits from these guys. I need to terrify them, to make them so afraid that Winter's madness doesn't drive them forward. It's hours until full dark and I expect them soon. A good fog will let them imagine what I don't choose to show them."

She spent some time going over her plan. Depth wasn't able to make the kind of mist she wanted, but he assured her that Fluvial would be happy to ensure the setting for her ploy. Autumn's Queen made her preparations.

As the Winter army approached the bridge, they came upon an unnatural fog. They could only see about twenty paces in any direction. The mist swirled and twisted, rolled and whipped, giving everything an eerie sense of movement. The leader moved ahead, almost seeming to sniff the air.

Claire knew that rumors of Autumn's Queen of Death had made their way through the other kingdoms. She hated the stories they told of the Banshee. The Necromancer of Blood Keep. A witch who required babies to sacrifice and specters to torment. Her own people mostly knew better, but both versions of her had made their way into other kingdoms. People tended to remember the bad stories more than the good.

The voice of Autumn's Queen pounded the minds of the soldiers, the words echoing both from the waters of the Loch and from somewhere in the mist.

"Who would dare bear arms against the kingdom of Autumn?"

The question was so loud in the minds of the men that many fell to their knees. Some of those mounted on the horse-like kelpies were nearly thrown as the frightened mounts bucked in surprise. The leader stepped forward.

"I'm Commander Coburn Kenn, leader of the fifth legion and steward of Queen Myrin of Winter. I pursued a murderer to your border, but she escaped with the help of some rough-looking men some days ago. It's said she's now hiding behind the skirts of the Banshee. We will see her returned to face justice."

Claire tapped her finger to her lips. She should be offended, but he was playing right into her hand. She smiled and spoke once more, the words a thunder strike in the minds of the soldiers.

"It is true that the Winter Maiden found her way into Autumn. She requested and was granted Hospitality, by the prince no less. Was she not heir to the throne? With Queen Eria's death, Raine Anahita is now your rightful ruler. Is that not Winter's way?"

Commander Coburn seemed a bit skeptical that the street urchin who had given him fits was really Autumn's Demon Prince. He yelled his response into the rolling mist.

"Winter's Maiden used her magic to kill her own mother. She didn't fight and kill with honor, she murdered with deception and guile."

Claire wrinkled her face, her own words echoing back. "What power does this accused murderer possess?"

The general seemed to grow impatient. He clearly didn't like where this was going.

"Everyone in Winter knows the powers of the royal family. The murdering witch used Purification magic to kill her mother."

"Purification? Explain how someone would use one of the least effective combat spirits to kill a dangerous water aspect with the power of a queen? That would be some trick."

Some of the soldiers began to murmur at this. Good. Claire assumed most water users would be prone to violence due to the corruption, but many of Winter's people were of air and earth. There were likely a few renewal users as well. She had fanned the flames of doubt. Her cousin Myrin was known more for her temper than her integrity.

Commander Coburn could already see he was losing control. The longer this went on, the more support he would lose among his own troops. Though he'd lived through one failure, he wouldn't survive another. He sneered into the fog.

"I'm not here to debate Winter business with a stranger in the mist. We'll march to the capital if need be, looting and burning every city on the way until we get the traitor in custody."

He began to lead his troops forward. Claire soothed Harvest through their bond. Her dragon might not like the taste of people, but that one needed eating.

She waited until the first of them were about to step off the bridge before she moved forward. Claire had lit her eyes to the unearthly shade of pale white that focused her spirit sight. All around her through the mist, ghosts stepped into view.

In Heluvot, she'd worked hard to find three souls who would come to her call. On the banks of Loch Mozeg, just east of the town of South Harbor, she'd given that same call. Hundreds had answered the queen in her homeland.

When she told the ghosts that Autumn was in danger, not a single one refused to help. When Claire explained their role in this, they began to get excited.

Most ghosts moved on in Fairie, but some felt they had more to do. Unfinished business, a loved one to watch over, or just a desire to see where events would lead. The specters were harmless. They weren't even visible without drawing power from someone who wielded a spirit of Death.

Claire had that spirit. As the Queen of Autumn standing with her feet on the soil of her realm, she had plenty of power to spare. They were a bluff, of course; they could only frighten, never harm.

The ghosts lurched and bobbed. Some flew through the air, and others crawled on the ground. It took everything she had to keep from laughing.

The scene was comical to a girl who had played checkers with a long-dead butler in the Blood Keep. She'd had tutors that only she could see and she'd heard gossip from maids that had passed on long before she was born.

These were her people as much as the living, and the display of utter ridiculousness was nearly more than she could take. To her, it was all so silly. To those seeing ghosts for the first time, it was horrifying.

Now she was in full view of Winter's army. The mist glowed with the light of countless ghosts moving and wailing. Claire spoke once again, this time not in conversation but in command.

"You... *dare*?! You plan to step into MY kingdom and threaten MY people! You intend to loot from MY cities and burn the homes of MY children!" A loud roar came from behind her, and another came from the waters of the Loch.

Her words exploded not just from her mouth or echoed from the dragons. A cry of her words left the open mouth of every ghost moving in front of the bridge. "You... will... *not*... harm MY children!"

The general had to shout to be heard, some power of his own bringing his words to his soldiers.

"You cannot kill us all; we are five thousand strong! CHARGE!"

Claire had hoped it wouldn't come to this, but she'd do what needed to be done. She was standing at a slight angle to the bridge; she would only hit those on Autumn soil.

The Banshee Wail only needed her own voice laced with her own power. She wanted to avoid having to use it twice. It drained her, but she'd recharge quickly. The sound echoed from all the ghosts and both dragons. Six men and two kelpies had crossed onto her soil. The scream ripped all the specters from their bodies.

Even though Claire had hoped that she wouldn't need to kill anyone, she'd planned for this. Pushing a mind back into a body was difficult. It took all her will and concentration, but she could do it. The ghosts of Autumn didn't fight her power; they welcomed it.

Eight of her specters moved forward, making a show of jumping up in the air and landing in the still forms on the ground. Six possessed soldiers leapt quickly to their feet. The kelpies were a bit slower; after a moment they also stood. The zombies turned back to the Winter army, eyes all glowing a faint white.

Her words came again in that otherworldly voice.

"Who said anything about killing you? Any soldier who crosses into Autumn this night will never die. They will serve me for eternity!"

The murmurs from Winter's army began to grow louder and more fearful. Commander Coburn could see he was losing this battle, but Claire didn't expect to see him lift a crossbow.

The bolt struck her right in the chest, the wet '*thunk*' followed by the keening of hundreds of ghosts and two furious dragons.

The voice of the Banshee through dragon-speak was calm and collected.

"Well, I didn't see that coming. I think I can make this work for us."

Claire reached down and pulled the bolt out of her own chest, the power of Transmutation knitting the flesh back together. In seconds the only evidence of her apparent death was a hole in her favorite riding leathers and the blood soaking the front of her shirt. She spoke twice now, once to the soldiers, and again only to her dragon.

"You will regret that. Come now and serve me!"

"Now, Harvest."

The death drake leaped into the air, flapping twice to cover the short distance. The mists rolled out as his ebony form slammed down on the ground between Claire and the bridge.

Harvest's typically yellow eyes were now glowing a bright white. The color was off, made of a layer of luminescent mist, but was still pretty convincing. He let out a roar flavored with the unearthly keening of the dead, the sound thundering through both ears and minds. The noise was deafening.

"ZOMBIE DRAGON!" screamed one soldier toward the back of the bridge.

The whole army broke. Every man crawled over the one behind him to get away from the Banshee of Autumn, the necromancer who could effortlessly raise the dead. In their eyes she was the evil queen who zombified her own dragon. Screams of fear and terror grew faint as the army retreated. Commander Coburn stood alone, his jaw agape.

Claire calmly strode to the base of the bridge. He couldn't hear her give the order for the mist to clear or the ghosts to cease being visible. He didn't know that the only reason the huge death drake wasn't chewing him right now was a direct order from this strange young woman. Or that most of South Harbor was watching from the city walls.

The man knew only that his life was forfeit. The Banshee would kill him now or Queen Myrin would do so later. He might not live through this night, but he had to know.

"What are you?"

"I'm the Banshee; you said as much."

He winced at her use of his word. "I'm humbled; I thought we couldn't fail."

Her feet carried her to the border, right next to him. "You never had a chance. You could have marched a hundred thousand troops over this bridge. They would have had no chance."

Her zombies moved to stand behind her, glowing eyes all focused on the man.

"Do you know why?" the Banshee growled.

He seemed to be fighting his fear but managed to shake his head no.

"Because I AM the Queen of Death. I AM the Banshee of Autumn. I AM the Necromancer of Blood Keep!"

She'd moved so close that her final words were screamed in his face in addition to rumbling through dragon-speak. A fine mist of bloody spit landed on the terrified man, but he made no move to wipe it off.

"No one THREATENS... MY... CHILDREN!"

In the distance, the people of the city began to cheer. The zombie troops and kelpies walked to the other side of the bridge. One by one, they fell to the ground. One soldier stayed behind, standing right next to his necromancer.

Commander Coburn was silently watching her work, the broad face of Harvest hovering just over him. Claire handed the man the crossbow bolt, still wet with her own blood. It had punctured a lung and hurt no small amount. Even now, the blood she coughed up stained her teeth and added much to her terrible presence.

"See that they're returned to their families. You know... that was an impressive shot. One I wager only someone with an aspect of air could make."

Commander Coburn nodded slowly.

"Commander, I think it's time we made a bargain."

The huge jaws next to the man's head widened into a toothy smile. It resembled his queen's more than a little. The leader gulped audibly.

It wasn't a request.

***

The mist cleared from the shore and the bridge at Claire's request. The thick layer over each of Harvest's eyes flowed away on the wind. The fog stayed on the water enough to obscure the form of an enormous head topping a long neck. Magic had enhanced the sounds and images so that the sea dragon and the tall, slender woman sitting atop him were able to watch. Both were smiling.

A couple of times, Fluvial had even clapped and squealed. Depth had broadcast the sound of Claire's voice and Fluvial had worked the mist on the queen's mark. The whole show had been rather spectacular.

The sea dragon let out a low rumble. "I could have eaten most of them, though."

Fluvial merely smiled. "Yes, but this way, the rumors will protect her kingdom. Claire embraced the image she hated. She did it for her people. They will love her for it."

As if to confirm her words, the cheers of the people of South Harbor rang into the night.

"The rumors in Autumn will ring a different tone," Depth noted.

The spirit nodded, eyes sparking with power. "They saw her fight for them. They saw the dead not as slaves but as her willing soldiers."

The massive dragon yawned; vast jaws popped as his triangle teeth snapped together. Depth slowly lowered into the water. "I don't know if this world will be saved from the March, but I'm glad we get to be here for the fight."

Fluvial nodded as she shimmered into clear water.

"Oh yes, I wouldn't miss it."

\*\*\*

Raine had slept quite well once she'd gotten out of her own head. Between the banked fire and the walking heater that was her cousin, the shelter had been quite warm, despite the walls of ice. She had to remember the design. Winter was a place to know how to deal with the cold.

The young queen stood and stretched, at least as best she could with the low domed ceiling. Jack was already up and moving around outside the shelter, his pack ready. Only her bedroll and some food were still lying out. Raine packed up and walked out, eating one of the deceptively filling cakes. She chuckled at the display of Jack launching small logs across the grasses of the tundra.

He appeared to be throwing them with a small amount of stored energy that would pop in midair. This launched them much further than someone could typically throw. She had seen air users do such things, but this was a creative use of fire.

The hound never seemed to tire of the game. As each one was launched, the hound would take off in a blur. Within moments she returned with the log. Most weren't worth throwing twice, as her powerful jaws turned much of the wood into pulp.

Maeve, the name Jack always called her, was insanely fast. Despite the speed and power behind the wooden projectiles, not one had hit the ground. She'd have the piece back at his feet before he could send up another.

Jack was different around this creature. His typical aloofness was shed for a more childlike and open manner. He kept praising her when she brought back the makeshift toy. Every few tosses, he'd stroke the coarse fur of the hound's head and neck.

Finally, it seemed the game was over. He hugged the creature and tossed her a small orb of pure spirit energy. The short tail wagged so hard that the whole back half of the animal shook with it. The force of the happy gesture almost pushed the young man to the ground.

Raine smiled despite all she was up against. Her cousin looked up and his face reddened, but he continued to hug the hound.

"Maeve needs the attention or she can get... clingy."

Raine only nodded. She'd never had any pets. Sroto had been her friend when she was young, later becoming her attendant and guard. Trust was a rare commodity in Winter and the yeti had earned hers many times over. Raine had loved her friend and shared much.

Yeti are large and powerful, with both males and females being strong of both body and spirit. Sroto had carried her for two days at a speed that stayed ahead of a mounted army. Ultimately, she died saving Raine, her last act one of friendship.

She found herself almost jealous of the hugs and praise Jack was giving the hound. Her loneliness, even among her family, was constant. Raine knew that would need to change when she claimed her throne. No one could tame Winter alone.

The young queen shook off the bothersome emotions and began to climb the side of the hill they had camped next to. Jack was next to her before she crested the low peak, and they both looked out across the grasses. In the distance, they could see the snow.

Most of Winter was covered in snow. It seldom melted and some parts were quite deep. Soon they would be making their way through the thick carpet of the soft frozen water. Jack made a disgusted face. He looked over and grumbled.

"We're less than a quarter of the way to Afshaneh. We will hit the snow by midday."

Raine winced. "Yes, it will slow us down quite a bit. It'll take a week to reach the town."

Her cousin shook his head. She could tell that the thought of days of trudging across the landscape bothered him more than any fight.

"Visibility is pretty low once you reach the snow, don't you think?"

She shrugged. "Well, yes, it will reach our waists in some places. It gusts up as well. Even so, it's much faster than taking the roads and...."

Raine trailed off. Jack had made a hand sign at the little hound and Maeve was doing something weird. Her front legs were pulling the hard soil and rock into herself; she was twice her standard size in only a moment, then four times, then eight.

In seconds, the hound was massive, maybe the mass of a frost drake. Her legs were long and muscled and she'd even taken on a whitish color. The color was almost the same as the snow in the distance. Maeve's shape hadn't changed much, though she was a bit broader. On her back was a makeshift saddle with a shaft of rock curving around front for a handle.

Jack grinned. "We've been working on this. She can get the color pretty close, though without reminders she reverts back to her normal brown. The saddle is a big improvement over our early attempts. Gray has been trying to get her to make, and I'm quoting here, 'plenty of trunk space.' Sometimes I think the man is crazy."

Raine looked at the strange mount, then looked at the distant snow. Her mouth hadn't yet closed and she worked it a bit like a fish trapped on the shore.

"What... I mean.... How big can she get?"

Jack shrugged. "Not sure. You met Depth, right? I once had her go many times his size. The problem is that she doesn't move any slower as she grows. We were playing and she knocked down a mountain. It's not safe for anyone if she gets too large. Also, she still tries to sit on me and it's all I can do to not get crushed."

Raine nodded slowly. The revelation was a lot to take in. She was learning many new things about her family to the South. Jack's hound was his friend and the young prince had probably never thought of what it would be like to use her as a weapon.

Perhaps that was why the hound had attached to him in the first place. If Maeve were unleashed on a kingdom, she would be almost unstoppable. What else had they kept from her?

No! These people were her family and had treated her with kindness and respect when her own sister was trying to have her killed. She wouldn't think them the plotting vipers she'd always dealt with in her homeland.

Raine walked over and put a hand on Maeve's side. She spoke loud enough for Jack to hear, but her words were to the hound.

"You, my dear girl, are absolutely marvelous. Thank you for offering to carry us through this harsh land."

It was hard to tell if Maeve understood the words, but she wagged at the tone. Jack took her pack and vaulted up. He leaned over and put out a hand to help Raine do the same. Maeve started at a trot and then moved to a quick, smooth run. They reached the nearest snowdrifts in only a few minutes and didn't slow when they hit them.

"This is a good deal smoother than she used to run. Claire and I almost died the first time we tried this."

"This is incredible!" Raine said.

She wasn't exaggerating. Only a dragon could travel faster than they were currently going. She wondered if he'd ever raced her against one. Miles flew by in minutes; the snow didn't seem to tire the tall, lean form in the least.

They stopped only once to rest and eat a brief lunch. Raine stretched, muscles stiff from the ride. She knew she'd be sore in places she'd rather not discuss, but on the whole, this was turning out to be rather fun.

She found a private spot to relieve herself before they continued on, and once finished, walked back to see Jack playing with a smaller hound. Raine stepped behind a drift and took a moment to flow through her sword forms with her blade. She wasn't trained as extensively with a long sword.

Raine was relatively small and preferred speed and skill over strength. Somehow the weapon felt like a feather in her hand. She favored a two-blade style using a short sword in her right hand while wielding a long dagger in her left.

With the lighter feel of Caledfwlch, she thought about using a knife, but instead chose to use the sturdy scabbard defensively like a shorter blade. It was only slightly weightier than she was used to and offered some protection.

This was only the third time she'd done these forms with her new weapon. Raine was nearly through her routine when she got the feeling of being watched. She didn't pause but focused her peripheral vision on the young prince standing several paces away.

Jack must have grown worried and come to check on her. He waited patiently for her final pose and she relaxed tense muscles before turning toward him.

"Care to spar?" he asked with half a smile.

She knew her cousin loved to fight. Not to kill or dominate, but the chance of a challenge excited him. Raine had only gotten the opportunity to watch one duel between Jack and his much larger challenger Gray.

Neither of them used weapons, at least not crafted weapons. They preferred to wield conjured items and weapons of various make. The reason no one had been able to give either man a good fight wasn't the skill either would use with any one style or weapon, but the constant shift between short and long-range attacks.

Raine felt honored to be asked, though she feared being made to look bad. Practice against a stronger opponent would help prepare her for the fight to come.

"I'll try to be gentle, cousin," she said with her own smile.

Jack winked as he extended his left hand. Water flowed from the snow to create a long sword. Frost crept down the blade as he consumed the heat within, freezing it solid. The cutting edge that would usually be razor sharp was round and dull.

The young prince took a stance low to the ground, the handle of the blade slack in his grip. She wasn't deceived by the clumsy look of the form; he could instantly react in a hundred different ways. Raine also took her pose, the sword held high with the point aimed at her opponent, the scabbard lower in a defensive stance. For a quiet moment, she held perfectly still as Jack swayed in his low crouch.

Then he shot at her, the blade coming at her face in a wide arc. She blocked with the scabbard and responded with the sword cutting down in a testing strike. His blade impacted her sheath; he rolled into her defense.

She froze. He held the tip of a slender spike of ice next to her throat. It was rounded and posed no danger, but was so cold it felt like it was burning the skin of her neck.

Raine grunted to concede the point and they parted to reset the match. Jack's opening stance changed; he now leaned forward with the tip of the ice sword on the ground. She regained her composure and had only started to exhale when he flicked snow toward her face.

She blinked and moved to restore the sight of him. The flat of the ice blade was already at her temple. She hadn't even had a chance to move. The young woman conceded once more, growing angry at the ease with which he'd bested her.

Once more, she took her pose; again, the prince was in a new one. Gone was the long blade, but instead from each fist was a forearm length spike of ice. He held both arms up, blocking most of the view of his face. Raine decided to push her attack. She whipped out using the long length of the blade to her advantage.

Jack ducked into a crouch. The tip of one spike shot out and hit the hilt of her sword so hard that it made her hand go numb. He spun under her guard and both barbs were touching either side of her neck.

Raine screamed and tightened the grip of the sword in her hand, plunging it down toward him. He rolled to her side and the stab entered the dirt. She didn't pull it out but sliced up and through the frozen ground. The tip missed the back of his head by so little that several reddish-brown hairs fell to the ground where he'd just been.

Jack regained his footing and faced her just as the blade was coming down at him. He jumped back as the tip sliced through the front of his thick coat. The prince landed and stood still as her overhead cleave came down at his face. She wanted to kill him, to open him up and let his blood flow. Only a second before he would die, he made a hand signal.

Raine felt the air leave her lungs as Maeve slammed into her chest. Long white teeth were at her throat. Her vision was tinged with red as she whipped the sword around to slice both back legs from the hound. A second chop removed the back half of the creature entirely.

She was lining up to remove the obstacle, when suddenly her arm couldn't move. Next her elbow, and finally her wrist and hand were unable to budge.

Her eyes narrowed as she looked over to see what dared to take away her revenge. That blasted prince was standing next to her, adding mass to the ice that now immobilized her right arm. Another piece was forming on her left, and it prevented her from using the free hand to wield the sword.

She screamed and tried to bite him. The fiend heated the ice around her frozen right hand and removed the sword from her grip. The wretched man took two steps and grabbed the scabbard she'd discarded. A low growling hiss escaped her lips as the brute sheathed the weapon and set it down.

Maeve crawled over to her missing pieces and reattached them in seconds. Her lean body reformed and trotted to stand by Jack. Both stood still, watching over Raine. She didn't notice their movements, her only emotion seething rage.

She was furious at him! How dare he make her look bad? How dare he stop her, how dare he....

Raine blinked several times, slowly at first. Her eyes began to flutter. Where was she? Why couldn't she move? She'd been practicing her forms, and Jack had asked to spar....

He was better than her, faster and so much more skilled. She remembered the anger, saw through her own eyes as she tried to kill him.

This young man, her own family, who'd left his home and was risking his life to aid her! She'd wanted to kill him, to feel the blade sink into his flesh. She'd wanted to taste his blood.

No longer. The sword's song was silent now. Her thoughts were her own. Raine looked up at the person she'd wanted dead. Her words trembled as the realization of what she'd almost done came down on her.

"I'm... so... *so* very sorry."

Jack shrugged. "I know. This was a long time coming."

He started pouring heat into the ice restraints. The resulting water didn't soak her clothes but flowed away as warm mist. He held a hand down to her. She almost didn't take it. She didn't feel worthy of his help.

Jack rolled his eyes. "We need to talk and I'd like to sleep in a bed tonight. Take my hand."

Raine gave in and he helped her up. When he saw her shiver, he pushed heat into her body. Her cousin moved over and sat beside the scabbard holding the blade. She sat across from him but made no move to touch the sword or its prison.

Jack paused, taking a moment to look at the frozen ground before returning his gaze to her.

"I've asked for guidance for this day from several. It was my Joobel whose advice I chose to take. Most of us feel the power of the blade even if we cannot wield it. Today you felt it try to take control. I didn't fight fair and made sure you got angry."

Her mouth dropped open. "You did that on *purpose*?"

"To be honest...." He shrugged. "I never fight fair. I might hold back sometimes, but combat is dirty. Only survivors get to tell the story. I wanted you to have to fight for control."

"I almost killed you!"

Jack shook his head. "I was holding back. You only thought you got close. The only real challenge was getting the sword away without hurting you. Maeve was a happy volunteer."

Raine remembered the hound and looked to see how badly she was hurt. Apparently not at all. The construct might be the scariest thing she'd ever seen. Right now, Maeve was digging a hole in the snow and shoving her head down to smell what was underneath. The woman regained her focus.

"I wanted to kill you; I was so angry. I—"

"You got your first taste of what you need to learn to control," he interrupted.

Raine wiped away a freezing tear. "In the end, it won't matter; I'll have to kill my sister. As I killed my mother."

Jack paused, frowning before he grunted and began a story. He told of how his mother died to save Claire. Twice. Circumstances demanded a sacrifice, and the Queen of Autumn did what was needed. As he finished, he looked her in the eye.

"Did you *want* to kill your mother?"

Raine gasped. "Of course not! She died because of me, though. If I hadn't tried to clean away the—"

He lifted a hand. "You acted out of love. You'd have saved her, but the corruption killed her rather than allow her a clear mind. It's your nature to help people. That's why Claire decided to assist you. That's why I walk this path with you. It's that same nature that makes you vulnerable. We need to prepare."

She pushed her hair behind one ear. "Prepare for what?"

Jack's mouth quirked into half a smile. "We need to save your sister. There's still hope for Myrin and I fear what killing her would do to you."

Raine rocked back. The Bitter Challenge was clear! The challenger must defeat the current ruler and free her spirit in front of the Black Citadel. The challenger must arrive with a loyal dragon of Winter, a powerful weapon of the realm, and the acknowledgment of a champion of the spirit of water.

She *must* slay Myrin. Even if they could find a way around killing her, the woman would never give up her claim. She was the eldest daughter to the previous queen. There would be many who would support that claim despite all else. It would cause a civil war.

"We can't; there isn't a way around the Bitter Challenge."

Jack waved a hand. "I have no intention of working around the Challenge, but I do need you to be able to hold back killing her. You need to control the blood lust."

Blood lust, a fitting term. The song wasn't a soothing voice of calm, but a call to war. It was a chorus of death and devastation. A dirge of destruction. She must learn to dance to the blood-song and somehow retain control.

"How can I possibly do that? You didn't feel what it was like."

Jack pulled the aspect of water into a glowing blue ball. "I tasted the power; it won't be easy. I think with practice, you'll be able to do so."

*Practice*? She couldn't go through that again! The man was mad if he thought she could start pushing through that regularly.

"Jack, I can't—"

"Are you a *queen*?" he growled.

"I'm the rightful heir to—"

"No! No one cares about the rightful heir. Or what law dictates or who's backing you. In our land, mad Queen Wenette was the rightful ruler of the land. She was overthrown by her own people. They didn't trust her; they didn't love her. They knew that they were currency to her. You know why my sister is a queen?"

"She was the Maiden of—"

Jack slammed a fist to the frozen ground. "Because she was worthy. Claire loves her people; she fights for them! She makes sacrifices and works ceaselessly to make the lives of her people better. Now I ask you again, are *you* a queen?"

"I am," she said without hesitation.

"Then make the sacrifice. Do the right thing when something else is far easier. Put the well-being of your kingdom before your own comfort. Earn the title, because right now we're the only two people in this spirit-forsaken snow heap who think you deserve it."

A long silence was counted by awkward seconds. The bitter chill of the wind was burning against the ice of her tears. The young Winter Queen took a deep breath.

"Hand me the sword."

She did her forms again, then sparred once more with the Demon Prince. Again, Jack trounced her, and the blood-song stirred her anger. Once she'd been disarmed, they decided to leave it there for a while.

Despite the long break, they finished out the day making good time. She'd thought it would take a week to reach Afshaneh, but they'd be eating dinner there this very evening.

Raine had worked up quite an appetite.

***

The skies above the Mountain Wyld were clear. This close to the Summer border, Gray found that he needed little of the gear made for the cooler skies of Autumn.

His flight was much smoother now. It reminded him quite a bit of the surfing he'd tried on a trip to California. Sure, if he fell he'd plummet to the ground like a stone, but the feel was very close to the same.

He hardened the air under him into a long wide plank of a conjured surfboard. Then he pushed air up to provide lift while pushing himself from behind with no small amount of force. Before he'd been clumsy, and the action had quickly drained him. The trick he'd learned wasn't to try to trap the air under him but to direct it behind him.

Now the effort provided both upward and forward momentum. He reached up to adjust his flight helmet before glancing at Joobel, who had an identical, if not cuter, version of the mask.

While he'd gotten to where he could fly with modest effort, the gnome had been born to it. She soared and darted seemingly without effort. Gray had learned that while Joobel would be a bit hungrier at their stops, her wings seemed to run more on magic than calories. It was hard to be in a bad mood when your companion was whooping and zipping all around.

They were making great time. In only a couple of hours, they'd put the smoking volcano of the Wyld at their left. Even now, the towering mountain that held the realm of Dawn appeared faintly in the distance.

This would be Gray's first visit to the home of the realm of air. Though he was starting to wonder if the air itself carried his brand of spirit magic in it. While Jack had always been notably weaker off of Autumn's soil, Gray really felt fine in the Wyld, Autumn, or even his brief unpleasant stay in Summer.

The southern kingdom was still on his list of things to deal with. His path into this world hadn't been a kind one. He'd been attending college in his home world when an agent of the Summer Queen knocked him out and dragged him into this world. Once he had eaten the food of Fairie, he'd bonded to a spirit of air. The transition was painful, but he'd gained amazing powers.

Sadly, if he went home, the lack of energy there would starve his spirit. Its end would precede his own. It was more of a symbiote than a parasite, but the bond prevented him from seeing his family again. Now more compelling reasons pushed him to find a way to visit his old home. He needed to find a way to save his new one.

There was no warning of the bolas that hit Joobel. The sound reached his ears as the snare hit his friend. Long leather cords wrapped around her form just before the dull impact of a heavy clay ball on each end. He heard a brief yelp as the gnome plummeted toward the ground.

Another struck his conjured platform followed by yet another. Gray could have held out against the barrage if he weren't worried about Joobel's hard landing. He had to drop the shimmering platform of his conjuring to see her and pull the air under her to pad her landing. The next two bolas reached him, and he felt the leather strips tighten around him, ending in the hard snap of the balls weighting the ends.

Gray couldn't see, but felt the wind rushing past as he hastened toward the ground. He'd often worried about this sort of thing and had a plan for a moment such as this. He pulled a shield of hard air into a bubble around all sides. Then he filled it with a weave of less dense air.

He'd gotten the idea from an egg drop experiment in school as a child. The hard outer shell crumbled as he struck the ground, while the less dense pillowy air spread the impact to his whole body. Other than getting the air knocked out of him, which he corrected instantly, Gray was fine.

The big man sprung quickly into action. Keeping up the hard outer shield, he smoked up the surface to make it even more cloudy. A thin blade of hardened air sliced the cords tangling him. He opened a line around the sphere to see the area around him.

Black and brown rock scattered the ground all around. He spotted an approaching figure but paid it no mind and scanned the area until he saw Joobel. She seemed unharmed but was still tangled up. Two more large figures were already carrying her away.

"Jack is going to kill me," he growled.

The approaching figure wasn't alone. They were walking single file, the other two obscured behind the first. They were tall and lean, with skin the color of evergreen needles.

Each had three fingers on each hand and wore loincloths. Tribal paints adorned their arms, chests, and faces, including their extended noses with dark tusks in the lower jaws.

Long pointed ears told him they might be a distant relation to elves. Coarse dark hair hung down the back of lean necks. They were taller than him, appeared fast, and seemed to have ill intentions, seeing as they had all but ripped him out of the sky. The first one was swelling up, muscles bulging as steam rose from its skin. The hulking figure had a short spear that he never got a chance to use.

Killing these creatures might be a mistake; he hadn't seen who'd snared him. For all he knew they saw him falling and were coming to help.

He eyed them as he ran for the distant shape of Joobel being carried off. A wooden spear came up, lining up a throw. Not a great sign. A ball of air the size of a softball shot out from his shield and hit the creature in the chest. Hard.

A loud 'oof' told Gray the creature was down for a bit. The air was packed into an orb that was essentially the consistency of jelly wrapped in a thin shell. It wouldn't kill, but it could put an enemy down for a few minutes. It also would make them think twice before bothering you again.

The second figure was staring down at his fallen comrade when he, too, was slammed with the jelled air. The third and final combatant dodged the ones meant for him, darting left then right. The creature also began to grow, muscle swelling out of his form.

After four misses, Gray acted as if a fifth was coming and then pointed toward the sky. The warrior glanced up just in time to see a wide thick shield swat him to the ground like a bug on a counter. He almost smiled. It would've been comical if not for his friend being carried off. He'd lost sight of her.

Gray was in the air again in seconds. The platform was thicker and wider than was strictly needed, but he wouldn't be taken down a second time. He moved in the general direction he'd seen Joobel carried. From an elevated position it was hard to see any tracks or signs of recent passage. Part of him wanted to land and look closer, but he'd be vulnerable.

He came to regret that choice. It took over half an hour for him to spot the encampment. Long bones were lashed together with strips of leather and string. Large tanned hides stretched over the macabre structures.

Scraps of wood and bone connected with more string encircled the camp, making a rickety fence. A stone ring in the center of the primitive civilization held a heap of cinders and ash. A spit over the pit contained the carcass of a large animal, now picked clean. Gray was glad that it didn't look to be humanoid.

In his haste and worry, the large man had worked himself into a frenzy. He flew low and landed just inside the fence. The place looked deserted.

Then he heard voices and laughter. The image of a tortured Joobel came into his mind. His friend. He was normally a thoughtful man, slow to act or speak. For the first time in a good while, Gray lost his temper.

For most people, this would involve throwing something, yelling, or perhaps trying to punch someone. Gray was no longer like most people. The spirit of air bound to his soul was powerful and he intended to put it to use.

Rage rippled across his face as he whipped the force through his spirit. At first, it was hard to notice anything happening. Then the breeze began. A gust of warm air traveled through the village. The hides covering the huts and tents began to flap. Then some started to whip and snap, cracking with the force of the ever-increasing speed of the wind.

Seconds later, it began to tear the fence apart. Chunks of wood and bone slammed into the side of the nearest dwelling. The structure didn't collapse with the impact; it was swept high into the air. Hides and ash were launched into the sky.

Another tent gave way, and several of the creatures took cover as best they could. Gray could now see the ones who attacked him running to the encampment. All three were having trouble walking through the tornado spinning around him. Gray began to shout his anger and defiance.

To his shock, Joobel ran out of one of the larger tents. She turned to look at him, but then made the mistake of flitting her wings in excitement. In an instant, she was gone, just a shrinking figure flying far into the distance. The hurricane-force gust of air caught her wings and dragged her through the atmosphere.

Gray was so shocked that he almost forgot to stop his attack. He dispersed the barrage and more of the creatures ran out. These were smaller than the others. Right after them followed two more that were obviously female, shorter than the ones he'd fought, and holding the softer curves of women.

It only took a few seconds for Joobel to fly back down to him. He'd made the mistake of letting his guard down, and some of the creatures were closing in on him. Just when he noticed and readied himself, Joobel screamed from above.

"Don't fight! He's my friend!"

The ones who had arrived just after him seemed not to care, but both females began waving and holding them back. Gray wasn't enjoying this at all. He didn't know who to attack, why Joobel was acting odd, or why he'd not worn more comfortable shoes. Things were going so well before it all went south.

The gnome landed next to him and turned around, speaking to the strange tall green beings.

"This is Gray... the friend I told you about."

The expectation when dealing with strange-looking beings who have tusks and wear loincloths is a guttural voice that is hard to understand. What he heard was the opposite.

"Well, young one, I expected him to come with our hunters. Not blow our town away!"

Joobel responded on his behalf, holding up a hand for him to listen and let her negotiate.

"In his defense, you did shoot us from the sky. He probably thought you were torturing me or something silly."

Gray's face flushed. Why would anyone assume differently? Now he was relieved no one had been killed. Joobel turned to him and in her cheerful way, introduced him to her new friends.

"Gray, I'd like you to meet the honorable Stone Spear Tribe of the trolls."

# CHAPTER 9

C laire had made it home late into the night, choosing to ride back with Harvest instead of using the portal in South Harbor. She was able to get a few hours of sleep and was now eating a light breakfast of fruit and one of Norim's pumpkin fritters.

She was wearing one of the unusual combinations of skirt and hose that Joobel had made for her. The thick golden-brown cloth was warm and trimmed with a darker black fabric. Claire looked up to see her advisor and former nursemaid sit at the table across from her. Norim smiled politely at her as the naiad picked up an apple and spoke softly.

"So, I hear we're not being invaded."

Claire smiled back. The short meeting with Coburn Kenn worked out well as far as she was concerned. The young queen tapped a quill to her lips as she looked at the schedule for the day.

"I should think it will be a while before we have to worry about troops from Winter again."

Norim looked concerned despite the news. She did so with her own face. The first thing Claire had done upon her arrival was return Norim's appearance back to her former lovely form. As a naiad, she had a deep natural beauty. In a couple of decades, she'd look much younger than the queen she had cared for as a babe.

"Do you intend to give details?"

Claire gave a short but descriptive version of the events of the previous night. Norim nodded slowly as the queen finished her tale.

"You've made a wager then."

Claire shrugged. "I prefer to call it a calculated risk. Winter has its challenges and I'll do all I can to help, but there is no way I'll allow Autumn to suffer the rampage of a foreign military force."

Norim sighed. "I don't know what I would've done differently, but this could all go very wrong."

"That was always the case."

A knock at the door informed Claire her escort to the throne room had arrived. The guards were surprised to learn that she still intended to hold court, prioritizing the meetings pushed back from the previous day.

Claire had forgone the tradition of sitting on the large stone throne that she found quite uncomfortable. Instead, she had a large table in a room to one side. She would sit at one end with her maps, books of law, and blank parchment to make notes. The idea anyone could sit as a pillar of wisdom without advice, resources, and a way to keep score was just plain silly in her mind.

The queen entered the large throne room to greet those present. There was a good-sized crowd and as the door opened and she stepped in, a cheer began. All of the voices of those present sang out in respect and admiration.

*'All hail the queen of the living and the dead.'*

*'Let's hear it for the defender of Autumn!'*

*'Our Banshee has driven away our enemies and saved our homes!'*

*'Your dragon is super scary!'*

Claire quirked an eyebrow at that last one. While accurate, it seemed out of place. She couldn't get the room quiet enough to get words out. She finally smiled and waved to the crowd before moving into the meeting room.

Her first appointment was with an earth spirit named Gorsh. The head of the Shaper's Guild was tall and just short of being elderly. His attire told the story of a man who had to dig deep in his closet for his dress clothes. The brown suit was several styles behind the current fashions of court.

Claire's own clothes were only in style because Joobel had made them the trend. Over the last year she saw many of the gnome's designs, or imitations, being worn by the more fashionable people in Autumn.

The man bowed deeply. Claire waited for him to rise back up before she sat down. Despite his low station, she valued him greatly.

Earth spirit users who could bend and shape rock weren't common outside of Summer. The irony that the southern kingdom preferred to shape living trees instead of stone and brick grated on her. She'd secretly had rumors spread that such people were welcome and well-compensated in Autumn. Some had already reached the capital, but her kingdom needed many more.

The man removed his worn hat before speaking.

"I'm here to update you on our progress, my queen. Before I do, I want to pass on the gratitude of the Shapers. Many of us have family in South Harbor and your efforts kept them safe."

Claire was trying to decide if she preferred the hateful scowls of her youth to the admiration of the present. She decided to just accept it and move on.

"A queen must protect her people. If I'd acted otherwise, I wouldn't be worthy of my throne."

"I, of course, agree. We're grateful just the same. Some of us remember a time when it would've been otherwise."

Claire knew this was a reference not to her mother but to mad Queen Wenette who came before. She'd used the people as pawns in a game no one else understood. Claire was increasingly worried that while Wenette's methods were terrible, the threat the woman feared was quite real. She shook off the thought and brought her attention to her duties.

"I appreciate the gratitude of your guild as much as I value the work you're doing for our kingdom."

The old man nodded, seeing she wanted to move on to business.

"The portal hub is nearly complete. It's fully enclosed and well ventilated. We incorporated the south-facing windows, darker walls, and roof. They have kept it quite comfortable. The one who designed it is a treasure."

Claire couldn't stop the smile his words brought to her lips. "Excellent news. Yes, he's a credit to our people. What of the school?"

Gorsh looked away, his brow furrowed. Claire knew that many of the older generation didn't agree with her edict to pull the children of the kingdom into the capital to be educated. He sighed and spoke.

"May I speak to my queen freely?"

She waved a hand. "I order it."

He swallowed hard. "Many of the workers are confused as to the purpose of such a place, and I wonder if you might have a harder time controlling an educated population."

"You speak with the assumption that *controlling* people is what I'm trying to do. Do you know what Autumn has in the way of trade?"

"Well, we have more crops than any other kingdom."

"But little else. We have nothing to mine other than red bricks. We make almost nothing, though the gnomes are helping there. Our greatest resource is our children, and leaving them ignorant and unchallenged is no better than leaving our harvest to rot in the field."

Gorsh pulled off his hat and began to rub the brim. The man still seemed to doubt, but continued his report.

"The school is coming along well, though we're months away from completion. We could go faster if we were to do away with the dorms."

Originally Claire only wanted the dorms. An orphanage would help with the multitude of children who no longer begged on the streets. Years of hard times had seen many parents dead, leaving young ones to fend for themselves. Many children were currently living in the Keep, with many more filling tents and camps outside the walls.

Gray had convinced her to add the school as a way to get the most out of the younger generation. It would give them a purpose and a source of pride.

"We have thousands in need of homes, young ones who are no less my children."

Gorsh nodded, still rubbing the brim of his hat. "The scope of the project is beyond anything we've done before; the craftsmen are spread thin."

"What resources would help you with your *urgent* task?"

"More earth spirits would, of course, be the most help. Our supply lines to the rock mines can bring us stone faster than we can use it."

Claire thought to herself. She wished Autumn had a hundred more Transition spirit users like Jack. They could fuel the craftsmen and increase the work of each many times over. She tapped her quill to her lips and pondered.

"How much time and energy are spent moving the rock into place?"

"Hmmm. That's the bulk of our work. Once we have built past our physical reach, the rock is merged into the base. Our power pushes it into position before it's shaped to add mass at the top of the wall."

Claire grinned. "What if the rock was already at the top? Could you merge it directly into the build?"

He thought about it for a moment, then nodded in confirmation. Claire looked down to her notes as she continued.

"We have no shortage of pixies and sprites that could use work. If we have those weak in spirit crush the rock into small pieces with hammers, and then the small, winged folk carry them to where they are needed, it should help conserve the energy of the craftsmen, true?"

The man paused, working the brim of his worn hat as his chin moved in a slow nod.

"I think that might work well. How should I proceed with putting the crews together?"

Claire waved a hand. "A representative of the messengers guild has informed me earlier this week that they have more applicants than they could hope to employ. We have numerous sprites and pixies out of work until the next berry harvest. Norim will have the meeting set up between you both."

She made more notes and then signed an order to hand to him.

"I'm approving the hire of two hundred laborers to prep the stone and as many carriers as you can find. I'd like another update this time next week. Again, let me say how much I appreciate your work. I look forward to speaking to you then."

The old man stood and bowed deeply.

"It is an honor to serve, my queen."

Gorsh followed the guard out, and moments later her next appointment followed the same guard back inside. The soldier moved at a slow walk, but the tiny man almost ran to keep pace. Claire usually stood to greet her appointments, but now she sat on the floor to welcome an honored guest whose support had helped much in her early rule.

"Ghamep, leader of the Autumn Gnomes, First among the Fallen Leaves Sept, you are welcome."

The gnome bowed deeply. "Meh queen is gracious and has honored meh greatly by showing er respect in the old ways."

"The honor is mine. Now that respect has been shown, won't you join me at the table?"

"I will, and I appreciate the accommodations," he said, nodding to the ramp and high seated chair that had been placed for him nearer to the queen so that voices would be easier to hear.

Claire had a full day but knew the importance of maintaining good relations with the gnomes. Less than two years ago, they'd been thought wiped out by the brutal pale goblins that had appeared in their homes in the caves of Blood Mountain.

Jack had learned that they were one and the same and had freed them from the curse that plagued them. The man who sat next to her was Joobel's grandfather. He was *much* shorter than his granddaughter.

Claire smiled as he settled in. "I trust the delay in our meeting wasn't too much an inconvenience?"

He waved a hand. "Well, one never likes to wait, but I hear ye were spendin yer time well and so I don't be mindin."

"We all serve our masters. In my case, I have a whole kingdom of them," Claire chuckled.

The little man laughed along, his voice much deeper than his size would suggest. He slapped a knee.

"Ain't it all kinds of true and just so. The more ye have serving ye, the more yeh have to serve."

Claire nodded in agreement. Her rule began alongside the gnomes' return. At first, many resented the promises she'd made them as the Autumn Maiden, but now no one seemed to mind. The gnomes were craftsmen of the highest order. They made everything from textiles to weapons, jewelry, and farm equipment.

They had helped her with rebuilding the infrastructure of the kingdom. The sept had become quite wealthy and added plenty to the coffers of both Autumn and her merchants.

No one wanted to insult the gnomes. Especially because Joobel had never hidden the fact that she was a gnome, and to humiliate her would upset Jack.

Only once had someone insulted her, calling her wings 'freakish.' Claire had the soldier relocated to the Summer border. It was safer that way.

"So, tell me of the expansion of your caverns."

The gnome gave her a wide grin. "Ah, they be a far cry from ye last visit. We've added several wings to our home and guest rooms to fit the taller folk. We were able to sell off all the excavated rock, too. Seems Autumn has been building."

His head for business was impressive. She'd just been discussing that with her prior appointment.

"Have you decided to allow our children to attend the school when it's built? It would go a long way to building future relationships with other groups in the kingdom."

Ghamep sighed. "That it would, that it would."

He paused a long moment, his face darkening.

"Arn ye sure our wee ones will be safe? I'm large for meh kind and I've teh dodge big feet when I walkabout. Our kiddies are so small and big children are so careless. I fear for der safety."

Claire had thought of this as well. Gnomes weren't even the smallest of the children. Some pixies and sprites were more diminutive, but they could fly and would be in little danger of a careless shoe. Luckily Gray had worked on the design of the classrooms and the smaller folk would never have to walk on the same floors as the larger races.

She grinned. "Perhaps we can make a bargain?"

"Ahh no, I won't be trying meh luck at dat."

Claire held up a hand. "Hear me out, my friend. When the school is finished, I'd like you to take a tour, to see where your children will be and the steps we've taken to ensure their safety. Joobel has already seen the designs and was quite happy with what we're planning. Then you can decide. I assure you this is for the best."

This seemed to appease him. Claire didn't blame him for being protective, but if a group as influential as the gnomes held back the attendance of their children, it would create no end of headaches.

Ghamep slowly nodded. "Aye, well, I keen not say no to deciding later. Ye say my granddaughter was involved; that will help persuade meh kin. How is my youngest and tallest family member?"

"She keeps me and the rest of the capital on their toes. I'd be lost without her. Jack dotes on her; she has him quite smitten."

Ghamep puffed up with pride. To the people of Autumn, Jack was loved and admired. A warrior of renown and the victim of many songs.

They'd also given him the name Jack of the Lantern, or more commonly Jack O'Lantern. Her brother hated the name, but the gnomes considered the young prince a hero of legend. Having him date a family member was a matter of pride for the Sept leader.

"So... have they set a date to walk through the pumpkin patch?"

Claire lifted an eyebrow. She wasn't sure of the phrase. Though she was well-read, much of the gnome histories and traditions had been lost for a time. Joobel had mentioned it, but her meaning was unclear.

"My apologies, I'm afraid I'm not familiar with the term."

The little man stroked his beard for a moment.

"Some call it bonding, others an espousal. Ye know, a weddin."

The queen's eyes grew wide. She was familiar with the last one. Her gasp made the little man jump.

"Jack's not yet sixteen autumns! It's much too early for such things. Joobel is also a bit young, don't you think?"

Ghamep shrugged. "Well, meh granddaughter is nearly thirty autumns. Surely, that is young but—"

"Joobel is thirty!"

Claire had no idea; she'd never thought to ask. Before the growth spurt, she hadn't given it much thought. Since then, Joobel looked younger than Claire did. Now that she thought about it, Joobel looked precisely the same as when they met two years ago, other than the size thing. She found herself upset that her adopted sister hadn't said so before. Her brother was only fifteen!

Ghamep held up a hand. "She's not quite there yet. Do remember that our kind matures slower than bigger folks. Not accounting for the time of the dark dream, I'm nearly three hundred. No gnome would even think of walking through the pumpkins before twenty-five autumns."

The dark dream was what the gnomes called the time they were cursed. That was several decades. If this were true, then Joobel would still look young when Jack was an old man, despite her age now. Also, Joobel was Named. It gave her size and allowed her to experience time even more slowly. That wasn't even considering her bond with Bloom and how that would affect her.

Claire put her fingers to her temples. "You've given me much to consider. Despite the shock of the differences between us, I love Joobel. I've already addressed the laws that would've prevented them from being together. When they are ready, they'll have my blessing."

This seemed to satisfy the gnome elder and they finished discussing the trade of gnome goods and the portals that would connect Blood Mountain to the markets.

Soon they finished the meeting and as always, the little man jumped up and hugged her tightly around the neck. The guards made no move to interfere. They were familiar with how affectionate gnomes were. This one had the queen's trust.

Claire stood up to greet yet another appointment. She wasn't yet caught up with her reschedules from the previous day. Ruling was easy.

Ruling *well* was a great deal of hard work.

\*\*\*

Jack entered the inn first, keeping Raine behind him and Maeve walking a few steps further back. The hound wore her mangy warg disguise. She could take several forms, but this one had taken months to teach her and it was a decent fit for Winter. As they approached the grizzled man at the bar, Jack spoke in a calm, even tone.

"Who would we speak to about a room for the night?"

The man didn't look up from his work of wiping down mugs with a questionable looking rag. His voice was low and gruff, like gravel in a bass drum.

"Yeh kin talk teh me. Rooms three bits, meal for both of yeh is another two. The mutt can't stay in here."

Jack handed the man five pale copper coins, "We'll grab a table. Send the food and key when you're ready."

"Whadabout the mutt?" the man grumbled.

"Feel free to throw her out," Jack said with half a smile.

The man glanced over at the mangy looking beast. Maeve bared teeth silently and went to lie under the table. Some people knew when to fight and when to back down. This man didn't bring up their furry companion a third time.

They hadn't quite gotten the meal when a man sat in the corner and began to strum a worn-looking lute. He warmed up his voice a few times and then started his ballad.

*From darkness of unholy dream,*
*The curse laid by the evil being,*
*Came the hope of lantern's light.*
*He pushed back the endless night.*
*All Haaail... Jack O'Lantern!*
*As our curse strong did hold sway,*
*He came to bring us a new day.*
*With cleansing fire and holy might,*
*He pushed back the endless night.*
*All Haaail... Jack O'Lantern!*

The look on Raine's face as Jack's began to redden could have lit a candle. She beamed as her blue-grey eyes took in his clear disdain for the song. The whole time he just shook his head slowly. Then she started to giggle and was unable to stop.

Other patrons were beginning to stare at them. When the bard finished his tune, Jack walked over to him. The man looked up and spoke with a smile.

"Oh, did you like the song? I learned it from a friend who heard it in the south. Hero ballads are always popular, you know, and that one has such a good melody...."

Jack silenced the man as he held up two more pale copper coins.

"Two talons if you agree not to play that song again tonight."

The man seemed torn between being offended and being two coins richer. Money won out quickly, and he began a different tune about the beauty of the Spring Princess titled '*The Alder King's Daughter*.'

Jack returned and started tearing up dry bread and tossing it into his thick stew. Raine ate in silence but couldn't hide her grin from Jack's reaction to the tune. Finally, she couldn't stand it anymore.

"Is that song seriously about you?" she whispered.

The prince scanned around to make sure their words were for them alone. After he was confident no one was listening, he turned and shrugged.

"So I'm told."

Raine rolled her eyes. "You know most people would brag about having a ballad written about them."

"Those people might have earned the honor."

She lifted an eyebrow. "I caught most of it. What deed earned you a song?"

"You know the pale goblins that used to live in Blood Mountain?"

Raine nodded. "Well, yes, but our intelligence was that they were wiped out and the gnomes had returned."

Jack swallowed his stew. "Those were the gnomes; they were cursed. I broke it."

Raine's eyes went wide. "You broke the curse? It must have been the better part of seventy years old.... You'd have to possess the power of a queen!"

Jack trusted Raine, but she was from another kingdom. She knew he could make fire and ice, and that he could manipulate energy. But the extent of his power was a well-kept secret for a reason.

There was no reason to burden her. Raine had seen him move energy the night she got the sword, but she might not realize what else he could do. He thought out his words and clarified for her.

"The realm spirit wanted the curse broken; I was the tool she used to do it. The gnomes were freed and they felt like I was the one behind it."

Raine looked to the bard for a moment. "Why not just tell them they're mistaken?"

Jack barked a short laugh. "If you figure out how to convince a gnome they're wrong, I'll pay you well for the information."

Raine laughed before she seemed to realize something. Her eyes grew shrewd.

"So, you saved an entire race of beings who can make some of the best goods in Fairie. Tell me you were paid handsomely."

"They gave me the best gift anyone has ever received."

"Oh, do tell. I'm dying to know." Raine's eyes looked hungry.

"I got Joobel."

Raine shook her head. "I don't follow...."

Jack's eyes went away for a moment. "She was one of the cursed. She's saved my life at least twice and she helps me understand people better. Also... I think I love her."

This wasn't what the Winter Queen had expected. Her face seemed to indicate something was bothering her, but Jack was terrible at reading people. He tilted his head, a habit he'd picked up from Maeve.

"Joobel isn't here, and as I said, I'm not good at understanding people. Is something bothering you?"

Raine bit her lower lip. "I offered to make Gray my consort."

Now it was Jack's turn to laugh. Like his cousin, he was trying to hold back, but her look of disbelief only made it worse. Slowly he regained his composure.

"You know he's in love with my sister, right? He's followed her around like a lamb for two years. I started taking him on missions to help him keep some of his pride."

She sighed, pushing her hair behind one ear. Her eyes narrowed for only an instant before she gave in and shrugged.

"I didn't see that Claire feels the same. Gray is strong and kind. He'll make a good father and would help me hold the powers of Winter in check."

Jack finished his bite, still grinning. "Claire carries the world on her shoulders. She does love him but has much to worry about. She'll come around in time. As for your proposal, what did the oaf say?"

"Basically, what you just did. The total gentleman turned me down while making me want him even more."

Jack rolled his eyes. "He isn't even good looking."

"You lack eyes, cousin."

"If you say so."

Raine grinned. "I do. Every woman with a pulse agrees. Maybe if he had silver hair and wings?"

Jack pictured her description, then slowly nodded. "That would be an improvement, sort of."

Raine stuck her tongue out at him and continued eating. They were just getting ready to head up to the room when a group of large men approached them. They'd started drinking early and hadn't finished. The men loomed over the pair. The closest, and possibly smelliest, spoke first.

"We was jus now talkin and think maybe this lady over er should come sit with us."

Jack looked up, wincing at the onslaught of smells.

"I'm afraid my sister is tired and we must depart early."

As Jack glanced at Raine, he saw her shake her head. He never got to have any fun. Another larger man leaned onto the table and leered at the young woman. He flexed large, muscled arms at the prince.

"Well, seein this ain't yer lady, she might want *real* men."

"I supposed that's fair. Let me ask her." He turned to Raine. "Sister, would you like to join these men at another table?"

Raine shook her head. "Why, no, brother. As you said, we must depart early. I do need my rest."

Jack turned back and grinned. "Well, I did try. She's just all worn out. Travel in the cold and all. If you'll excuse us."

The big man grabbed Raine's face with a greasy hand. He turned her face to him and snarled, "You'll join us, and then go upstairs and...."

The big man froze. No one saw the sign Jack had made under the table. The signal to grab and hold an enemy. Maeve would usually catch the throat, pin the enemy, and await Jack's orders.

The hound didn't like killing, but she'd learned that the hold was his way of avoiding it. This man's throat was on the other side of a solid oak table. It wouldn't have stopped her, but she got scolded when she crushed furniture. The hound grabbed the next best thing to get someone's attention.

The man let go of Raine's face. He slowly leaned back from the table and looked down at the mangy warg, who had long sharp teeth clamped firmly on his crotch. He tried to pull away, but she wouldn't move. He *really* didn't want to leave anything behind. Jack pushed his chair back and turned to Raine.

"Well, sister, I think it's time we turned in."

Raine stood as well, eyes wide. "Why... yes. I think you're right." She let out a long yawn.

Jack held out his arm and she took it. The two of them calmly walked to the stairs. The man's face was red as a ripe beet. His companions were afraid to make any move that might make the animal bite down.

After long moments, a distant whistle could be heard upstairs. The warg released the man and calmly followed her master to their room. The man started crying.

A smelly friend patted him on the shoulder.

***

As was her way, the gnome flitted her wings when she got excited. They were currently doing so constantly as Joobel told the story of how she'd been captured by the trolls.

They'd learned that the tribe had thought she and Gray were agents of Summer scouting for slaves. She flourished the tale with quick moving hands and made sounds to illustrate fear and tension.

The gnome liked telling stories and now her audience contained nearly two dozen little trolls. They were much like the adults except they had lighter skin with spots of the darker green, seemed to be more round of feature, and lacked the tusks that appeared to indicate age among the adult males.

Now she was dancing around and whipping her wings to illustrate the winds that had recently assailed the village. She finished her tale right where Gray had come in. There was a rise of happy clapping from the children and several adults nodded in approval.

Joobel took a bow, elegant and poised, before flitting her wings to hop into the air and land gracefully next to Gray, hugging his arm.

"Oh, aren't they just adorable? Someday I'll have many children and they'll be so cute. I can just see little toddler versions of my Jack; they will just be...." Her words devolved into a high-pitched growl.

Gray had been surprised to learn that these people thought he and Joobel were the enemy. He'd said as much and had asked about the slavers' raids.

The chieftain of these people called himself Rakash. Now that the squeaky bard had finished her story, the troll leader stood and took the center of the speaking circle.

Joobel could see that the ring was a form of local government. As guests, both she and Gray had been given a spot on the rim. They were now sitting on a raised mound of earth that stretched around a depression. The head of the circle would stand in the center and do the majority of the speaking. Those around that person could ask questions. Those outside the circle were to remain silent, though everyone could observe the proceedings.

The chieftain set aside the platform that had been used so Joobel would be visible. Most of the trolls were taller than Gray and she barely came up to his chest.

Joobel noted that Rakash was taller than most of the others, his dark tusks curling up almost even with his dark green nose. Like the other males of the tribe, he wore only a loincloth and had painted runes and glyphs on his head, chest, and arms. She couldn't understand the meanings they portrayed, but he had more markings than anyone else.

The females among the tribe wore long smocks that had no sleeves and came down to just above the knees. There were roughly the same number of males and females in the circle. Knowing Claire would want details, the gnome committed everything to memory.

Rakash began to speak; despite his tusks and primitive appearance, his words were clear and easy to understand.

"We have done our visitors a disservice. It is my decision how to punish the hunters who would have done harm to innocent guests. I decided they will know their actions were wrong but will pay no price other than the honor lost."

A murmur went through the circle, faint whispers through the crowd. Rakash raised his three-fingered hand, and slowly the trolls came to order.

"The larger of our guests was once a slave of Summer himself. He has granted that protecting our home from those who would take our people shouldn't be seen as a crime."

Gray nodded to the chieftain, clearly happy that his request was approved.

"He applied punishment to our hunters and they will walk tender for many days. I wouldn't wish to receive his wrath and we offer a gift as our apology."

The smile that crossed his lips pulled the corners of his mouth up and away from his tusks. Rakash waved his hand to a troll standing off to one side who was holding a large piece of leather containing something long and thin.

The troll strode to kneel by the circle and handed the package to the chieftain. The taller troll took it and unfolded the wrapping. A long yellow feather was revealed. Rakash held it high as he continued to speak to the whole room.

"Tradition teaches us that when a troll truly wrongs another, he must make amends by gifting his most valuable possession.

We, as a tribe, wronged these strangers. I, as chieftain, must pay that debt with the tribe's most valuable possession."

His hands lifted high and waved to the sides.

"Throughout the Wylds, there are dragons of the sky, sandworms of the desert, and men of the Wyld Hunt. All of these beings of power tremble before the master of the sky, the storm bringer, the great Thunderbird!"

Rakash lowered the feather, his deep voice holding a tone of reverence.

"In times of change, he will flap his wings and the winds will blow. He will shed his tears and rains will fall. When he cries out, the thunder shakes the world. When he rakes his great claws, the earth is torn asunder. Change has come and he shows his presence. I, Rakash of the Stone Spears, gift you this small piece of heaven."

The chieftain presented the feather to Gray. Joobel could see that by appearance the item looked merely like a substantial yellow feather. When it was placed in his hand, Gray jerked away from the power emanating within. She held out one slim finger and stroked through the stiff barbs, moving to the soft downy fluff at the base. Her finger tingled as the flow of energy ran up her hand through her arm.

Gray looked up at the troll. Joobel could hear Claire's influence on his words as he spoke.

"You honor us greatly, Chieftain, but you've given us an apology. We hold no ill will. The gift is extraordinary but not required. Would you accept it if I returned it to you?"

Rakash shook his head. "A gift returned is an offering rejected. You would dishonor both our tribe and its chieftain if you did not keep and honor this treasure."

Joobel tilted her head as she thought, a habit she might have picked up from Maeve.

"Pardon me, chieftain, but in Autumn, it's our tradition that alliances be formed with a gift. We'd never dishonor your tribe by rejecting such a wonderful possession. Perhaps you would allow us to try to secure our friendship by offering something to you as well."

Rakash rubbed one tusk before shaking his head.

"Honored guests, we are a people. Our tribe is many and you are but two. An alliance is made by leaders. While we appreciate the thought, we couldn't reach treaty with you."

Joobel gestured to the center of the circle. "Perhaps, honored leader, you'd let me once more address the tribe?"

Rakash nodded, moved the platform back into place, and moved to the side. She knew he couldn't refuse right after he'd given them such a gift.

With a few flits of her wings, the gnome once more stood with all eyes on her. Many of the children seemed to think another story was coming and bobbed up and down in excitement.

Joobel turned slowly on small, graceful feet, looking at what must be several hundred trolls. Then she turned to face the chieftain once more. With a perfect curtsy she addressed the tribe.

"A more detailed introduction is in order, it seems. As you know, my name is Joobel. What you don't know is that I'm the chief advisor to the Queen of Autumn. It is within my authority to offer aid or sanctuary to those who have allied themselves with our kingdom. You see, Rakash, I *am* a leader of a people, a kingdom... as it were. You say you're being hounded by slavers. Have they taken your people?"

Rakash seemed to have his doubts, but he nodded. "They have taken many. They often try to steal the children as they are easier to condition to a life of servitude. We are a *free* people."

Joobel noticed his three-fingered hand clenched into a fist so tight that the dark green skin paled. Gray, too, was visibly angry at the words. She held the chieftain's gaze.

"Are you aware of the laws protecting the freedoms of the people of Autumn?"

"You will excuse our lack of news here in the Wyld. We know not of your laws."

Joobel turned to the crowd with a dazzling smile. "Slavery is outlawed in the kingdom of Autumn. No one may own or transport a sentient being within the borders of the kingdom. The queen is quite stern on this matter and has the full support of the great realm spirit in seeing the law enforced. *All* people in Autumn are *free*."

The chieftain now looked even more doubtful; Rakash shook his head as he replied.

"Such words are pretty and painted, but our people have been betrayed by empty promises."

"My companion was once a slave in Summer; he now has his home in Autumn. Perhaps he could persuade you?"

Joobel looked to Gray, who was still stewing in the news of captured children. He snapped out of his angry fugue and looked up.

"When I freed myself from Summer, I looked at the places I could settle. The words of my friend are true; Autumn is protected and free. There is change taking place and all peoples are welcome if they are willing to contribute to our future."

Rakash paused a long moment before he nodded and looked back to Joobel.

"Our people are hunted. We are hungry and must fight for every scrap of food this land has to offer. We are thought ugly by many of the races of this world. That which is ugly is evil to most."

Joobel gestured to her own small form. "And those who are small are stupid? Do you know that I'm a gnome? Only two short years ago, I could have stretched out on your forearm and not touched wrist or elbow. The Queen of Autumn *sat on the floor* to speak to my kind."

Her eyes went around the room, meeting the gaze of all watching. The gnome continued.

"The respect of the old ways was given by a queen. My Sept is now wealthy and respected. We have a voice in the rule of our kingdom. Your people are proud and strong. I assure you that neither would need to be sacrificed to seek a home among us."

It was clear that the chieftain wanted to believe her words. The trolls were battered down by generations of raids, famine, and the leers of travelers from all over Fairie. Now someone stood with a piece of sweet bread in an open hand, seemingly an obvious trap.

"You offer much... vastly more than the value of our gift. Nothing is free; what is your price?"

Joobel began to hover a few inches above the platform, the excitement of her wings too much for a little thing like gravity to stop her ascent. She smiled widely, and her bright blue eyes bore into the troll.

"We want your knowledge, your tradition and culture. Your children would learn alongside all the other races of the kingdom. You would share your magics and medicines and would gain access to ours."

Again she looked out to the watching crowd.

"You would hunt the forests and share the meat; you would craft weapons and help us fight those who would take our children. We don't want you to serve our tribe; we want you to join it. My offer is a home and the protection of the western kingdom. My price is you playing your role within it."

Joobel had said her piece and now slowly landed back on the platform. She could fill the silence, but right now, the quiet served her purpose. She'd been speaking not to the chief but to the tribe. Mothers held their treasured children; hunters gripped weapons. All awaited the words of the chieftain of the Stone Spears.

Gray spoke now, his words few but his meaning clear.

"It would be an honor to count the Stone Spears among the people of Autumn. A great war is coming, and great warriors will be needed. I only see great warriors among you."

Rakash looked upon his beloved tribe, strong but hunted, proud but hungry. His answer was painted on all of their faces. He sighed and looked back at the gnome.

"When would we leave?"

# CHAPTER 10

Issabol was in one of her moods. Several soldiers had arrived from the Keep to help relocate her workshops to the new hall within the same world as the war room. Inside, she'd be able to work on her creations while allowing time within Fairie to move at a snail's pace.

She had much to do, and time was, for once, not on her side. Claire's insane plans had asked much of her skill and it had become clear that the complex tasks would need her to do more work than she could attend to in such a brief period.

Now soldiers carefully moved the tables and benches into her new workspace. When finished, she'd change out the portals to rearrange the rooms in her home.

The Shaper's Guild had been pulled into this world of speeding time to build the larger structure. Despite being instructed that time would stretch there, they were all unsettled by the experience. They finished a long day of shaping stone and moving earth, only to come home and find they'd been gone only a half hour or so.

Now soldiers had to carefully time the movement of items into the new workshop. One could move in, spend a few minutes arranging, then run into the man who was walking in right behind him.

Issabol snapped and shouted at the burly men, her child's voice in contrast with the authority of her words. They all tolerated the strange girl because they were instructed to respect her as if she were the queen herself.

The new workshop was almost three times as large to accommodate the additional people utilizing the space. Claire was coming along well in honing her Transmutation. She even incorporated Entropy to make day-long processes take seconds.

One corner was also set up for Joobel. Sewing supplies and materials sat next to her large staging table and the desk where she drafted designs. At first, Issabol found the company of the gnome to be a bit much. No one could dislike the woman, but she was tiresome in large doses. Her upbeat, happy manner could grate on those who couldn't keep up.

After they had worked together a few times, Issabol saw the gnome's skill and began to respect her more. The recent work on the flight helmets had actually been enjoyable.

She'd grown accustomed to being alone for the most part, but knew Joobel wouldn't age quickly. That friendship could last for centuries thanks to her Naming. Most people were hardly worth getting to know, as they would be gone as soon as Issabol got comfortable around them. Maybe Joobel could be different.

It only took a couple of hours to move the contents of her workspace to their new home, but she hadn't made a change this significant in well over a thousand years. Things felt odd. It took her the rest of the day to move the venting portals and doorways into the usual spots within her altered home. There were now over a dozen locations built into the halls and rooms of her house. It was getting harder to fit everything together.

The latest change was small, but she couldn't believe she hadn't thought of it sooner. Inside the cookstove in the kitchen was a portal into the heart of the mountain of caged flame. She'd set it so that only heat and light could pass through. Her stove was always ready to use; she only needed to adjust the reflective heat shield to control how much warmth it produced. Gray had given her the idea.

"Claire, I wish you'd hurry up and marry that man. If he passes down that mind of his, our family will be smarter several times over," she muttered as she worked.

She'd usually bathe and sleep in her comfortable room down the hall, but time was too short. The soldiers had set up a four-poster bed with drapes so that even sleep could occur in a world where time was faster. Despite her age and skill, Issabol had a child's body and needed no small amount of rest. That was time they couldn't afford to lose.

The ancient child left the note next to the Keep portal that explained where to find her if Claire had an emergency. Issabol would eat and bathe in her normal home, but sleep and work in a place of speeding time.

She was all alone now. Areena was on one of her adventures and might not be back for weeks, months for her here in the world of fast time. Claire would come to visit for tea each day, but weeks would pass for Issabol between those visits.

Growing accustomed to company had been hard at first. Now she found herself wishing for a verbal duel with her many greats nephew, or a barrage of questions from the curious, dark-skinned Gray. Even an over-enthusiastic story from Joobel would help keep loneliness at bay. She sank into the bath and let the warm waters engulf her, easing the tension from her tiny frame.

The ancient child pondered about how a portal into the flame mountain would do an excellent job of heating the water.

***

Raine was just starting to move the next morning when Jack came back into the room. The swishing of a warg's wagging tail came from next to her bed as the door opened and he slipped in. His gear was packed and he handed her a bowl of hot oats with honey.

She'd slept in a set of clean clothes, so all she needed was to eat and relieve herself to be prepared for travel. She'd thought about trying for a bath at the inn. But the thought of the oafs moving about made her decide against it.

Jack had asked that she let him or Maeve deal with danger until she was able to tame the blood-song. He seemed to think that controlling it would be more difficult once the sword had been used to kill, and she agreed the risk was too high.

The porridge was quite good considering the more rustic feel of the inn. She knew he'd gotten it for her because they would be eating rations for a good while after this breakfast. He was thoughtful in his way; being considerate didn't come naturally to him. That made it seem more significant.

She finished the food and walked down the hall to the bathroom. It wasn't as complicated as the ones Gray was setting up in Autumn, but one of the benefits of Winter was that frozen things tended not to smell.

On her way back, two of the men from the night before were walking toward her in the hall. She almost cried out, but when they saw her, they turned around and moved away. She bid them good morning in a voice that carried her smile.

Raine hated the way they'd made her feel small and helpless. When she was queen, she'd see that the women of her kingdom never felt that way again.

She knocked on the door before entering, more from habit than from worry that Jack would be changing. He had been ready to go long before she was up. He was standing right at the door with both packs and a wiggly warg.

As they left the inn, Jack stopped and patted the arm of a man sweeping the floor. He nodded toward the warg and cleared his throat.

"She ate the dresser in our room."

Jack handed him a few extra coins. The man looked cautiously to the mangy animal walking through his dirt pile and leaned on his broom.

"Well... I thank yeh for putting it right. Safe travels now."

Soon they were heading south on the road out of Afshaneh. After about an hour, they turned left toward the frozen lake that bordered the town. The road would soon lead east toward the next town, but they weren't in Winter for towns; they needed to go further north and to the west. They were heading for the ice caverns.

Once they'd moved far enough away so as not to draw attention, Jack signaled Maeve. Soon they were traveling quickly across the ice of the large lake. Winter was a land of water, but much of it was encased in thick sheets of ice. If not for the slight depression in the land and the perfectly level layer of snow, it would be difficult to know they were running atop a body of frozen water.

With no hills to slow for and no dangers to avoid, they practically flew across the distance. Jack seemed happy that with the air so cold, no bugs were getting stuck in his teeth. Raine didn't know why he didn't wear some sort of mask, but she was sure Jack knew what he was doing.

Her trip was pretty nice, as far as barreling over a frozen land on the back of a shape-shifting Hel-hound made of stone, earth, and wiggles goes. By the time the sun had reached its peak in the southern sky, they had reached the far edge of the frozen waters. Now she was glad to stop and stretch.

In moments she was going through her sword forms. Once she finished, she dueled Jack. She was amazed at how irritating it could be to fight someone who seemed to slap away her best attacks as if she were a toddler. Her most advanced defensive maneuvers were bested as if she weren't even moving. Soon the blood-song overwhelmed her and Raine tried to kill her cousin.

Once she returned to herself, the prince helped her up and handed her the sheathed sword. Three times they went through this process. On the third, she fought a bit longer before losing control. A small victory, but they were both glad to see it.

After a lunch of Issabol's cakes, they were off. Hours of further travel pushed them closer to the caves. They stopped for the night and again slept in a dome of ice.

This time there was no wood to be had. The prince warmed both her and her blankets with a push of hot air. The cold was much worse that night.

In her sleep she tried to warm herself next to Maeve, but the wiggle hound didn't give off heat. Her stone body was as frigid as the ice Raine's bedroll sat on. Finally, Jack gave in and lay his mat next to hers. The heat rolling off him had her comfortable in moments.

"Jack?"

"Yeah?" he muttered sleepily.

"I never got to say I was sorry about your mom. I wanted to come, but it wasn't allowed. I think my mom still resented Aunt Ornella. It wasn't fair to you and Claire. I'm sorry you lost her and sorry I wasn't there for you."

There was silence for a long moment as she waited for him to respond. Nothing came.

"Jack?"

"Still here," he said with a yawn.

"Do you forgive me?" The girl felt a wave of fear that he might have some resentment for her. A warm hand reached out and took hers. The young man's skin felt almost feverish.

"I'm not mad, Raine. I never was, at least not at you. I'm sorry about your mother as well. I suppose we're both orphans in a way."

Long moments of silence passed before more worry forced her to speak.

"Do you think we'll win the Challenge?"

"Go to sleep. Let my sister fret about such things."

The young queen squeezed his hand, not willing to let him have it back. The warmth plus the exertions of the day soon pulled her into slumber.

They started the next day uneventfully. The cakes were growing tiresome, though it was better than an empty stomach. After breakfast they pressed onward.

Shortly after their lunch break, complete with sword forms and duels, they saw the mountains Sleet had described in the distance. Raine had seen the emotion in the frost drake's eyes as he told them how to steal his hatchlings.

After she'd cleansed the maddening corruption from him, the frost drake could see the danger posed to his young. Dragons are precious to any realm, and while Winter had around a dozen, the loss of three eggs would be devastating news for the whole kingdom.

She knew that cleansing the older dragons would return them to the previous sanity they enjoyed before the corrupting influence of the tainted realm spirit. But there was no way to know what would happen if dragons were hatched by that horrible energy.

Their pace resulted in a tough decision to either push forward to look for the eggs, or to wait till morning and have a full day to search. In the end, they set up for the night and decided to get an early start.

Raine was much too excited to sleep. The process of the hatching Claire and Joobel had described was both thrilling and terrifying. Part of her was afraid of the attempt. After all, Joobel had nearly died helping Bloom from her shell. Her kingdom, on the other hand, needed her to take the risk.

The next day they pushed out before the sun had even begun to light the sky. Raine saw Jack pull out the secret weapon he'd brought. The prince unwrapped a folded piece of oilskin and pulled out a piece of white cloth. It was a tunic she'd rubbed on the head of the frost drake Sleet. The fabric carried the scent of the eggs' sire.

Jack gave a command to Maeve and the hound stiffened. When commands were given, treats were at stake. Several deep sniffs of the cloth and she was ready. Jack wrapped it back up and ran to follow the hound.

Raine had been impressed by Maeve several times even before this trip. The hound had helped Jack hold off the Winter soldiers that had tried to take her back after she made it into Autumn and had saved her from an assassin her first night in the Blood Keep.

The construct, though it was hard not to think of her as alive, was able to do some impressive things. Raine shouldn't have been surprised when she saw the hound follow the scent straight up the side of the mountain.

Her paws slipped several times before Maeve growled. The construct's feet seemed to shift and suddenly she had the claws needed to climb up the wall of frozen stone. Jack tied a rope to his waist and knotted the other end around hers before following the hound.

It quickly became clear that Jack would keep up through pure athleticism, but Raine's hands weren't strong enough for the narrow handholds he was gripping with strong fingers.

Her frustration changed to annoyance when she saw the first perfectly formed hand and footholds of shaped ice appear before her. Jack never stopped moving but she could just see his little smirk. She loved her cousin but longed for the day that someone would show him up.

The climb still tired her out, but she was holding up pretty well. Every once in a while, the loose pebbles Maeve knocked free would fall into her eyes and hair, but the handholds started moving off to the right and it was no longer an issue.

After about an hour, her arms were so sore and tired that she wondered if she might fall. Then she made the mistake of looking down at the drop below.

Jack slowed and touched her forehead with a finger. The energy of the warm spirit power gave her the strength to move on for another half hour. He repeated this twice more as she needed help.

Now she pulled herself over a cliff edge. Jack was stroking Maeve's brown fur and giving her little balls of pure white energy. Apparently, the hound was a 'good girl' and had done a 'good job' and she was his 'best friend in the whole world.' *Yes, she was!*

Raine found herself both disgusted at the display and saddened she wasn't a best friend in the whole world.

The thought was tossed from her mind as she looked up at the round opening in the cliff face. It was a huge hole dug right into the ice and stone, excavated by mighty claws. It was a frost drake cave. She moved to run inside but Jack held up a hand.

"Not yet."

Sleet had told them that three eggs rested within the cave. The nest would be guarded by his mate. River wouldn't be quite as large as Sleet, but they didn't have Harvest here to subdue the mother dragon. Even Jack might find a direct blast of frost fire a bit much to handle.

With a command, Maeve began to grow. She soaked up so much rock that the ledge began to narrow. Raine had to start moving into the cave to keep from falling.

Now the hound was massive. Maybe not quite as large as a dragon, but big enough to give one a good fight. Maeve sniffed the air, then circled and tried to sit on Jack. Fast as the prince was, he barely avoided the huge wiggling backside. Finally, Jack signaled her to stay, and they entered the cave.

Raine had never been to one of the dragon caverns. Her mother had told her about this one once; Sleet had taken Eria long ago. Her mother's description was nothing like what she witnessed now.

The cave had been scratched and torn all about. Where once stood a nest of shaped ice, now lay shards of broken rock and frozen ooze. Raine looked down and began to weep. At her feet were the shattered remains of a dragon egg.

The shell was a bright blue like the crystalized waters of a beach on a clear day. On its surface were several black splotches. She mourned the sadness of such a magnificent creature's flame snuffed out before it ever drew breath.

Raine felt a hand on her shoulder and heard a voice in her ear.

"There will be time to weep for the dead later. We must work for the living."

Nodding, she wiped her cheeks. Three eggs, a small clutch. There would be two others, and time was short.

Dragons contained strong magic; they were unchanging pillars of the element that nourished them. Dragon eggs were different. Like babies, they were waiting to be fed. They needed to be nourished and cared for.

The corruption had sent away the father and driven the mother so mad she'd destroyed the most precious thing in her world. They had to find the other eggs and save them. Her kingdom depended on it.

Raine moved through the rubble. The sight of the broken egg made her glad that the vast form of Maeve waited outside. It would be unforgivable to step on a tiny dragon.

Then she saw it. In the corner had rolled another egg. It was almost completely covered in the black spots she saw on the other shell. She picked up the treasure, cradling it to her chest. Raine held back her magic. Claire had told her that once it tasted energy it might want to feed. This place wasn't safe.

Jack touched her shoulder again. He also held an egg. This one had fewer spots and seemed to have a bit more shine to the surface. He opened his pack and gently set the egg inside. She did the same, settling the precious orb in her own travel bag.

Jack removed the orb cluster from his satchel. Issabol had asked them not to use a portal in Winter until they'd completed their task. It would be a foreign form of power and might draw attention. Now it didn't matter. In moments they would be gone, safely back in Autumn.

He started to power the orb that would activate the array, but a screeching cry and crash from outside told them both that River had come home.

Another collision caused part of the cave to shudder. Large cracks appeared in the walls. Then the frost drake was rolling into the chamber, snapping and biting at the huge hound made of earth and stone.

A blast of frost fire hit Maeve in the side. The cold blue flames were tinged with the corruption that plagued Winter. As the hound was doused, the construct shed the layers of frozen tainted stone. Even as she fought, Maeve pulled fresh rock and dirt through her back legs pushing against the frozen rock.

Bigger and bigger the construct grew. River threw her head from side to side as she fought. Raine knew that if she could just touch the dragon, she could begin to clean the corruption from its mind and body.

Then the furious drake saw her, still packing away the egg. River's eyes narrowed as she spotted the round treasure. Her egg.

A blast of frost fire shot out toward Raine. Her arms came up to defend herself from the deadly wave of cold. Then Jack was there, facing her and holding on to her wrists. The crackling of fire meeting ice could be heard as the young man took the full force of the dragon's breath to his back.

His gaze locked with Raine as the deadly cold was held away from her. His heat almost scorched her face as he fought the power of the drake's breath. Then the wave of chill stopped.

Raine caught Jack as he fell forward. His back was black from the cold, the hair on his head dissolving away. His clothes started to fall off as the back half of his coat and trousers were worn away by the impossible cold.

She screamed. Maeve heard the noise and looked down. Jack had given her the command to hold the enemy, but her master was hurt. Her Boy.

Raine covered her ears as the hound howled. It was deep and sad. The baleful sound grew in anger and fury as the hound realized she'd lost her master. Her size grew even faster and her mouth filled with long sharp teeth.

The dragon turned her attention back to Raine and readied another blast of the chill breath. The attack would never come.

The eyes of the frost drake River went glassy as the furious hound ripped her neck from the base of the drake's enormous, winged body. The dragon continued to struggle, claws scratching at the stone hound. Slowly the movement faded and River went limp.

Maeve instantly started shedding rock and earth as she moved toward Jack. By the time she reached them, the hound was her smaller brown self. Maeve whimpered and whined, seeming to understand that touching Her Boy would only bring pain and more damage.

Raine looked around frantically. The young man had terrible frostbite over the back half of his body. He would go into shock in seconds if he hadn't already. She only needed one thing from him; she didn't know how to work the portal.

The Winter girl saw the cluster of orbs. She grabbed it and leaned down in front of Jack's face, her words a frantic scream.

"Jack, show me what to do. You don't have much time; I need to get you home. Jack, please. PLEASE!"

The young man slowly opened his eyes. For the first time Raine could remember, her cousin was shivering. She held the cluster in front of his face.

"How do I turn it on?"

He moved a finger and pressed the control, running his power into the device. It began to hum as he passed out.

Raine set the portal a few feet away and moved to watch the construct open, like a door standing in space. She was suddenly looking into the dim room of Issabol's portal hub.

She seized both bags and set them down inside as gently as she could while moving at speed, then she grabbed Jack's hands. The back of his arms had grown black with the frostbite, but she couldn't spare the time to be gentle.

Screeches were echoing in the distance. Other frost drakes had heard the fight and were coming. Maeve might well be able to kill them all, but Jack would be dead in minutes.

As she dragged him, the man whimpered in pain, his head lolling to one side. Maeve growled low at his discomfort but seemed to understand Raine was trying to help.

As she moved the body through the portal, the hound hopped through. Another long blue neck whipped through the opening to the cave. Just as the drake began to breathe its revenge, the portal contracted closed with a hiss.

\*\*\*

Despite the urgency of their quest, Gray and Joobel spent two days and nights working out details with the Stone Spear trolls. Gray was surprised that he also had made many assumptions upon meeting them that were clearly untrue.

They were a ritually hygienic people, and while water was scarce, oils and soaps were used that allowed them to stay quite clean. They were all taught how to read as children, a skill that many of the people in Autumn didn't have access to. At least not yet.

They had several odd traditions that he found different but couldn't really label as primitive. They had no one they called 'father.' All the little trolls had mothers, but every adult male was considered to have the role, if not the title, of father.

If a child went hungry, it was every man's shame. If a mother had no hut, then every man would help build one. Since the men were the ones who hunted and earned the tribe's resources, there was no such thing as a needy family or a rich one. Everyone was taken care of, or no one was. It was hard for him to imagine, but it admittedly had advantages.

Joobel had always been quite intelligent and before the gnomes were cursed, she'd been educated in the capital. By now she'd spent enough time with Claire to have picked up some of her better habits. She produced quill and parchment and started writing a formal alliance treaty that would grant the trolls a home inside the borders of Autumn.

They, in turn, would agree to pay taxes after the first year of residence, allow the young trolls to attend school with the other children of the kingdom, and conscript to service at arms should Autumn need to be defended. It was a standard agreement that would benefit both parties.

The trolls would get to choose from the available lands, have access to kingdom builders to construct necessary infrastructure, and have portals connecting them to the other parts of the kingdom.

Gray found it really strange that they accepted the idea of portals without question, but the idea of getting breathed on by a dragon brought concerned inquiries. Several trolls were terrified when Joobel insisted that every village got a stop by Bloom about every two weeks. The sick and injured were gathered up and the dragon would breathe on them.

What he came to learn was that Summer had a practice of doing the same thing, only their dragons didn't breathe a healing mist. Instead, wood dragons breathed a noxious fog that turned the victims into stone. This was Summer's way of dealing with the sick and weak.

It's what would have happened to him if he hadn't proven strong enough when he was first captured. Joobel quickly cleared up the confusion and then looked nauseated at the misunderstanding. The woman was a beacon of light in a world of darkness. He wished everyone had her compassion.

After the terms and details were discussed, the trolls were given two options. They could travel to Autumn on foot or await a portal to be made to move them. Gray understood why the trolls chose to await transport. He and Joobel had flown far from the lands of the Wyld Hunt for a reason.

Next, Joobel made copies of the treaty and asked about other races who were having similar difficulties with both survival and the raids from Summer. Many groups lived in the Wyld and most were hurting. As more and more left the area, the attentions of the slaver raids grew more focused on those who remained.

Gray was worried that Joobel's gift to Rakash would be diminished by offering it to all who were in need. Soon he understood that by having the chieftain act as an intermediary, he was honored much more. Gray had a lot to learn about politics. The whole process made him think fondly of Claire.

Finally, Joobel wrote a letter explaining the negotiation and her promises to the tribe. She was making sure they were taken care of even if something should happen to Gray and herself. He knew the risks involved with their quest, but the thought that something might happen to his friend made him feel sick.

It was midday before they had everything cleared up to a satisfactory degree. Gray gathered up their gear, wrapped the yellow feather in oilskin, and put it carefully in his bag. They bid farewell to the tribe and took once again to the skies.

They were able to cover the distance to the mountain peak before nightfall. They only stopped to rest once, and they flew a good deal higher to avoid further attacks.

The realm of Dawn was really only a mountain. It reached so high that its summit stretched up through the clouds. Claire had explained that many had gone on pilgrimages to the top. A narrow staircase spiraled around the base, beginning near where the mountain pass would lead to the kingdom of Spring.

Gray was sure it was an enlightening walk along perilous old stairs through the chill Winter winds blowing from the north.

Today he didn't feel like enlightenment. He was just going to fly straight to the top.

He looked over to see a smiling Joobel. She was so excited to have an adventure. Jack was always telling her the stories of places he had gone and battles he'd fought. Joobel didn't lack courage, but while Jack would struggle to win out over an enemy, she'd just charm them into being a friend. The trolls were only one more example.

Despite the frail appearance of her paper-thin wings, Joobel was climbing high into the air better than he could. He couldn't hear her whoops and squeals with the rushing air around them, but he saw her mouth making the motions and could see clear excitement on her face.

Gray felt glad he hadn't made this trip alone. As they moved through the thick fog of clouds at the peak of the mountain, they followed the staircase to the large balcony of shaped stone.

Pillars rose up from the structure to a rocky roof above. A worn red carpet covered the floor inside. In the center of the room stood something Gray once thought to be a myth. A griffin was staring at a hefty tome.

The creature had the head and front claws of a great eagle. The white of the feathers was as crisp and clean as fresh snow. This merged into the body and rear legs of what Gray guessed would be a large golden lion. One massive wing was neatly folded next to the powerful body. The other was dragging on the ground, the bones broken and poorly healed.

The griffin hadn't seemed to see them yet and Gray stood open-mouthed as the legendary beast was reading with the eye on its left side. After a few moments, a taloned claw moved up to turn the page.

Gray started to step forward. Claire had given him tips on diplomacy. He ticked off his priorities as he moved in. First, don't stare at or mention the wing. Second, address the being with a flattering title. Lastly, do *not* stare at or mention the wing. He readied his greeting when a loud buzz shot right past him.

"Oh dear, what have you done to your wing? Are you in pain? Oh, do say you will let me help you."

And...Joobel got to him first. Gray sighed as he moved to catch up with his friend. The griffin didn't seem to be surprised at having visitors. The rigid form of the beak gave the impression of a slight frown, but it would look that way regardless of mood.

The mythical beast turned to look at the woman that was fretting over the damaged wing. Cocking its avian head to one side and looking at her, it spoke. The voice was strained, and clicks came as the beak moved, snapping the hard material together every few words.

"My wing is my business. *Click.* What brings you to the realm of Dawn? *Click.*"

Joobel frowned, her face a mask of concern. "Oh, but you cannot fly with a wing damaged this badly. Does it hurt? Are you in pain? Oh dear, you certainly have to let me help you!"

Gray saw the creature's beady eyes narrow. It was clearly insulted, but it was so hard to be mad at Joobel. She honestly had forgotten everything they were trying to do upon seeing someone who needed help. He sighed and stepped forward.

"Honored representative of the realm of Dawn, we seek your counsel."

Joobel was kneeling down to look at the point where the bone had been crushed, her hand hovering just above the knotted break that had healed at an awkward angle. She paid no attention to Gray or the griffin.

"I need to feel it to know what to do. May I touch the wound?" Joobel asked.

Without actually waiting for permission, she set one small hand down on the break. Gray could tell she was using her magic to probe the wound and remove the pain and stiffness.

Joobel had nowhere near the restorative powers of her bonded dragon, but she could ease suffering and often diagnose what was wrong. In this case, Gray could see what was wrong from twenty paces away.

"Oh dear, there's a good deal of pain. The break couldn't be set because the hollow bones were shattered. I see. This couldn't be healed; it would need to be reshaped. Hmm. OK, it should feel better now, but there is only one person I know who could fix it. We'll need to arrange to take you to her. When can you leave?"

Gray was worried that the beast might take offense at her forward intrusion, but the creature had relaxed significantly after she began to draw away the pain. Its mood improved, and it somehow seemed to smile down at the gnome with a beak that didn't alter its shape.

"What have you done? *Click.* Though that is... now that is much better. *Click.* I thank you for the relief. *Click.*"

Joobel waved a hand, attention still on the break. "Why I took the pain away, of course. There's nothing that I can do to fix it, though. Even if we rebroke the bone, there are too many shards and pieces to arrange under the flesh. As I said, only one person could help you to fly again."

Gray watched as the creature's big head awkwardly turned to look at both its wing and Joobel. Its eyes were near enough to the sides of its head that it was mostly able to do both at the same time. The griffin spoke again.

"I thank you for the relief. *Click.* Many healers of Spring. *Click.* Have tried to fix my wing. *Click.* None were able. *Click.*

No renewal magics can repair what has been done. *Click*. The wound is too old. *Click*."

The gnome rolled her eyes. "Oh, you silly bird, I already told you we couldn't heal it. No renewal magic can fix it; I said as much. But there is still one person who can help you. Now stop being stubborn and tell me when we can take you to her!"

Gray had to step in now. Joobel got impatient when people fought her help. They'd come a long way, and offending this creature could put a stop to any advice it might offer.

"Honored host, we mean no offense. My companion only wishes to help, and it's hard for her to set aside her nature. We've come seeking your assistance. If we were able to help you regain your lost wing, perhaps that would earn us the grace of your wisdom."

There, he was sure Claire couldn't have done better. Joobel pouted at him, but then went back to doting on the wing. The griffin looked back to Gray.

"Sharing wisdom is my job here. *Click*. If you were able to help me fly again. *Click*. I would need to find another way to repay you. *Click*."

The gnome clucked, shaking her head. "Oh, you silly bird, we don't care about payment. I simply cannot stand to see someone in such a state. You should be ruling the sky, not dragging the ground."

Gray was once again afraid of the offense their host could take, but the griffin seemed to be considering her words. Finally, he looked at Joobel and Gray both, each with one large golden eye. At the same time.

"Do not call me a bird. *Click*. I'm the second of the three great brother chimeras of this realm. *Click*. You may call me Shirdos. *Click*."

The mighty creature softened his tone as he continued, his right talon clicking the floor.

"If you truly can return me to the sky. *Click.* I would accept your offer. *Click.* First, I must fulfill my duty. *Click.* Why have you come to our realm? *Click.*"

Joobel continued to prod the broken wing while Gray took a deep breath and tried to sum up his quest.

"It's my pleasure to meet you, Shirdos. My name is Gray and my companion is called Joobel. I'm an immigrant to Fairie. I've been bonded with a spirit of air. I have a crafter who can make me a jewel to allow me to travel to my homeland."

He motioned to the mountaintop. "To do so, I'd need a piece of the bedrock of the realm of Dawn. It is the element that sustains me, and my only way home."

Gray had decided to keep the reason for his urgency a secret as long as possible. The threat to this world was subtle and there was no way to know if agents of the Black March had appeared throughout the other lands.

The griffin cocked his head, switching the eye that stared at Gray.

"You may be able to make your jewel. *Click.* Only the sage could say for sure. *Click.*"

Gray bowed slightly.

"How would I find the sage? I'm afraid there are urgent matters in my home I must attend to."

Shirdos jerked his head twice more. "He is not a part of this land. *Click.* He sits above those who crawl in the dirt. *Click.* He resides on a Celestial Isle. *Click.* Only the inhabitants of Dawn can reach him. *Click.*"

Gray sighed. "Where could I find an inhabitant of Dawn? It seems I require a guide."

Shirdos blinked. "You did not climb heaven's stairs. *Click.* You walked the skies to arrive. *Click.* You are both citizens of Dawn. *Click.* As for your guide, I will take you to him. *Click.*"

Gray looked at the griffin's wing and understood. The creature had led him right into keeping his word about returning the griffin to the sky. He would've done it anyway, but he was impressed that the creature had maneuvered him so. He smiled and nodded.

"Shirdos, for you to guide us, we must attend to the wing. Would you allow us to make good on our offer before we depart?"

Again, the griffin seemed to smile with a beak.

"Just so.... *Click.*"

Gray reached into his pack for the orb cluster that would carry them back to Autumn.

# CHAPTER 11

I ssabol was sitting over her workbench, tinkering with the thread of magic that controlled the destination of the small portal. Portals had five essential controls that must all be adjusted properly for the doorway to work correctly.

Origin was simple and usually would activate at the location the portal was opened from. Destination would determine where the entrance would lead to. Size had two calculations of height and width, while Angle would decide the relationship to the vertical axis. Finally, Resistance would determine what could pass through and in what direction it could do it.

The origin orb would have the controls built into it and was usually located at the top of the array. This control was often simple; a normal-sized portal with full two-way access was relatively easy for her to build.

This particular project was proving difficult because the destination wasn't a place she had been, could see, or could even have described to her. She had to make assumptions, and doing this by trial and error would be dangerous.

Issabol was so caught up in her work that she almost didn't register the shriek. In her defense, it didn't sound like a scream. Such a shout lasts a few seconds and is both shrill and loud. What she heard in her workshop lasted for almost a full minute and was deep and muffled as if coming from far away. When she did notice, she couldn't quite recognize it for what it was.

From her perspective, time was moving as if in fast forward. The sound was stretched, and the pitch deepened as it moved from her portal hub down to her workshop. She thought her house was empty, so who could be calling out? Understanding sent an icy pulse down her spine. The portals she'd given to the young ones!

Issabol carefully set the orb down and walked briskly to the opening into her home. Right before she crossed the threshold, she moved to a run.

The hub was just down the hall. Doorways to many places were open, though most were one way. Only the door to the Blood Keep and the portable portals could open here without her activation.

She turned into the room just in time to see a large bright blue head getting ready to breathe frost fire through the doorway. It closed before the dragon could launch the attack.

Issabol could hear the crying of the young woman who was frantically using Purification on the mass of blue-black flesh on the floor before her. A little brown hound was guarding over the Winter girl as she worked. Maeve's tail drooped and she whined softly as she paced frantic circles.

The girl was Raine. The hound was obviously Maeve. Where was Jack? The scream that echoed in the hub was hers now. Her many greats nephew was a mass of blackened skin. Jack's healthy air of invincibility was clouded by the rasping breaths he was struggling to take. Small convulsions racked his lean form. He didn't have long to live.

"Raine, we need Bloom! Go get Claire to send for her!"

The young woman didn't move, her terrified gaze locked on Jack.

Issabol shook her arm. "Now, girl!"

Raine snapped out of it and ran for the portal leading to the Keep. Issabol was afraid to touch Jack's bruised skin, fearing it might damage him more or cause him pain.

Jack had gone out of his way to annoy her. He called her 'Aunty' every chance he got. They jousted verbally every time they were together. Now, seeing him broken on the floor, she realized just how much she loved him.

Issabol leaned over the prince and her tears left tiny spots of moisture on the black flesh of his arm. She'd buried so many people over the years that one more shouldn't matter.

This one did.

***

Raine came through the Keep portal at a full run. Things had been going so well, and the fact that they went wrong so quickly made the situation seem surreal. As if she'd wake up and Jack would be himself once more.

She hadn't spent very much time at the Keep, but she knew the corridor that would take her to the royal quarters. Jack's best hope was the dragon that had saved her only a few weeks before. Bloom could work miracles but was usually out visiting the various villages of Autumn.

Raine needed to talk to someone who could call out to the dragon, someone who could perform dragon-speak. Joobel was off to the east with Gray, but Claire should be here. Her cousin would be able to help.

Her mind was so focused she didn't hear the guard down the hall shouting at her to halt. Though the one that barred her path, pulling out a short sword and holding up a hand to make her stop, couldn't be missed.

Part of her wanted to pull her own sword and slice his blade in two, but she needed to speak to Claire with a clear head. The blood-song would have her fighting all of the royal guards. Instead, she spoke in hurried tones.

"I have to speak to the queen!" Raine tried to push past the man who shoved her against the wall. "I need to talk to Claire. It's an emergency!"

The guard shook his head. "You need to explain why a stranger is running around the royal floors with a sword on her hip."

Raine unconsciously put her hand on Caledfwlch's grip. The guards reacted as if she was going to attack and she quickly put up her hands. It was then she realized that she was wearing Winter clothing, was armed, and didn't wear her own face.

She was a stranger to these men. Only a handful of people knew her new look, and none of them were here except Claire. She had to reveal who she was.

"I'm Raine Anahita, cousin to your queen! The prince is in danger and I need to speak to Claire!"

The guards seemed surprised but didn't move. The one behind her grabbed her arms and pulled them behind her back. The other looked her right in the eyes.

"Well, now... you've given yourself away. We know that isn't true. Raine Anahita is dead."

She fought to get free, but despite her skill with the sword on her belt and the lessons Jack had taught her, she wasn't nearly as strong as the guards. Caledfwlch remained sheathed, and Raine was led toward the holding cells down below.

***

The attendant had worked in the Black Citadel of Winter for many years now. He'd first been called to service under Queen Eria Anahita at the start of her reign over twenty-five years ago. The weight of recent events hung heavy on his narrow shoulders.

His perfectly pressed uniform of dark blue silks hung over a frame that had been much more robust only months ago. He'd lost weight and seldom slept. Something was wrong with his kingdom.

Hurley Irving had risen to the role of chief advisor to Queen Eria almost eighteen years prior. While he'd never really loved the queen, he did hold a great deal of respect for her.

It was he that had convinced Eria to pass up the typical tradition of naming the firstborn spirit eligible daughter as the Winter maiden and heir. His efforts in securing a competent heir went further than most knew.

Myrin was extremely powerful and had inherited the rare offensive spirit of Frost Fire. To many, this was an omen of future greatness. Hurley had seen only her cruelty. He saw it while she was still a child.

It was known to many how the elder daughter would demean and bully her attendants and the other children in the Citadel. While she was always proper in court, she was another person when no one of authority was around to keep her in check. As a princess, the only person who could do so was Queen Eria.

Hurley had convinced the queen to wait until Raine was old enough to judge her character. He'd arranged to have both girls tested by having a water spirit user of Sight turn a bowl of liquid into a viewing pool. The two princesses were sent through the Citadel to meet people and deal with various problems.

The queen watched as Myrin acted haughty and spoiled. She frosted a maid who dared to scrub a floor she wanted to walk on, and she threatened a guard who failed to open a door for her quickly enough.

He was relieved to see Raine's test. She greeted the servants and lords alike warmly. She found that a butler had eaten some rotten fish and went out of her way to use her power to relieve him of the blood sickness.

The same guard Myrin had threatened met Raine with a smile as she asked about his oldest daughter and her lessons. In only one afternoon the nature of both daughters was revealed. Eria made her decision that very night.

That had been well over a year ago. He hadn't loved Queen Eria, but he knew he'd love Queen Raine. The girl cared for people. Her power was more common and not a sign of strength. But Hurley planned to work around that. Her natural grace and charm would overcome those who would protest.

Now it had all fallen apart. Some sort of sickness of the mind had afflicted over half the people of this kingdom. He'd only recently realized that all of those who seemed affected had spirits of water.

It was the Winter Maiden who'd confused him. Raine was still herself, the same kind girl walking the halls and looking after people. Even though she held a water aspect, she was also immune to poisons.

Hurley had come to this realization too late. His own aspect was of change; he controlled a spirit of Chance. He was the perfect advisor. He could see the odds of various outcomes of decisions. This had led him to push for Raine as the Maiden. Her odds of being an effective and respected ruler were 97%. Myrin's were only 8%.

The combination of his intelligence and his spirit abilities had allowed him to lead Eria through some severe problems. She had come to take his advice every time he would give it.

Until a few months ago.

Queen Eria had begun to grow unpredictable. Her decisions became more and more erratic and selfish. She began to punish minor crimes with terrible consequences while letting horrible criminals free because she found them entertaining.

Even her dragon had seemed to go mad. Who knew what Sleet was out doing? All the hard work and planning to bring Winter to greatness had fallen apart, and his only hope of a better future was miles away.

As he opened the door to allow Queen Myrin's next appointment, he looked into the face of Commander Coburn Kenn. The Commander carried a case and a look of uncertainty.

Hurley knew the man was as good as dead. Twice now, he'd been sent after the former maiden. His first failure had cost him his honor and nearly his head. Rumors of his embarrassing defeat, at the hands of one woman no less, had run through Winter like water through a stream.

The Citadel had gotten several reports and though Hurley was confident that they were embellished, all attempts to recruit another force to invade Autumn had fallen flat. His own efforts had helped see to that. He turned to his queen to announce the visitor.

"I present the Commander of the 5th Legion, Coburn Kenn."

Hurley watched as Queen Myrin sat upright on her throne. She slowly turned to look at the commander who'd failed her a second time. Drool was beginning to form at the corner of her mouth. She giggled like a child as she rose and moved to stand before her guest. Myrin spoke in bursts as if she only had the barest amount of air.

"I'm surprised you came back... since you failed me... a second time...."

Commander Kenn stood straight and tall. Hurley noted that he showed no signs of the madness that had affected so many. His opinion of the man went up, though slightly.

"My queen, I don't understand. I freely admit to failing you the first time. Today I'm here to give the official report of the second chance you gave me."

The queen sneered. "You think I've... not heard about... your defeat?"

The Commander lifted an eyebrow. "I've no doubt a great and wise queen hears everything, but the rumors of my defeat were part of our plan to do as you asked. We had our scouts locate the target, and the diversion at the Autumn border allowed us to act on that information."

Myrin narrowed her eyes. "I don't... understand...."

The soldier set the case on the floor at Myrin's feet. Unlatching the top, he opened the lid and tore out Hurley's heart. There on a red velvet cushion lay the severed head of Raine Anahita, the rightful Queen of Winter.

He'd adored that girl! Spent years preparing Winter for her rule. Now her kind face lay in a box, frozen from its time of travel through Winter.

Myrin squealed and clapped, hopping up and down, her stained royal blue robes swaying with her movements. She reached down and picked up the terrible remains of her sister. Then she walked right out of the throne room, talking to it as if Raine were standing before her.

"Who is mother's... favorite now... little sister? ...Oh, it is me!"

As the crazed young woman walked out of the room, she didn't see the tears sliding down her advisor's face. Hurley wanted to kill this man, the monster who murdered the rightful queen. Raine couldn't have killed her own mother! The girl caught and released spiders, for spirit's sake.

Before he could work up the courage to strike, the Commander leaned over to him and whispered.

"We've much to discuss. Is there a place we could have a... private conversation? I have information that I believe will change the outlook of Winter."

Hurley was suspicious, but if nothing else, he could stab the man in private. He only had a 19% chance of success. He'd accept those odds; the old man had nothing to lose at this point.

He led the way to his quarters down the hall.

\*\*\*

Joobel had been happy that Shirdos had agreed to let them work on the wing. She'd probed the injury and knew any healing would have just reinforced the bones that had come together all wrong.

She'd let Gray discuss their plans and was glad to hear that Shirdos would allow them to open a portal on the wall of his outlook at the realm of Dawn. With permission, Issabol would enable the return trip to be much faster.

Gray set up the portal. The griffin seemed impressed to see it power up and open a door into a large chamber. Other portals lined the walls of the room that was a bit dimmer than the light of the outlook.

Joobel tilted her head as she saw a girl with blonde curly hair and one lavender lock leaning over a lump of black... well, it was hard to say what it was. As she glanced around the room, she took in the satchels, the size of the black form, and finally the scraps of clothing under it. She was in the air and yelling before Gray had even looked into the opening.

"Jack! Oh, what happened? Jack, can you hear me?"

For the first time since he'd worked the portal, the young man tried to stir. The pain was overwhelming and many of his muscles didn't respond. Jack gasped out a noise that could have been her name, but it was so faint the gnome couldn't be sure.

She didn't need to have Issabol tell her the best hope for him; the cry for help through dragon-speak was out of her in an instant.

"Bloom, can you hear me?"

There was no response. The hub was in Issabol's home in the Twilight Vale. If Bloom were to the east or far enough south, she'd be out of range.

Joobel put her hand to Jack's forehead, taking the pain and calming him. She needed to get help, and the best way to get into Bloom's range was to go through the portals.

"Jack, I will be right back. If you die, I'll never forgive you!"

Issabol's hair flew out as Joobel's wings stirred the air around her. Gray and the griffin came through the portal and gasped in shock at the scene before them.

Joobel left them to work it out. She usually didn't use her wings indoors, except when she wanted to distract Claire or was in a hurry. She was in a hurry.

The gnome entered the hallway so fast she had to spin around and catch her momentum with her deceptively strong legs, and she pushed off to shoot through the portal to the Blood Keep.

The door to the portal room was open as if someone had already come through this path. She was just happy she wouldn't have to slow down. The hum of her mighty wings echoed off the stone walls, making it sound like an avalanche roaring through the halls of the Keep.

The noise didn't affect her dragon-speak, yet there was still no response. Bloom was still out of range. She almost stopped to weep but then she remembered the griffin. Claire could reshape flesh, could fix damage in another way. Jack's wounds weren't old, but why should that matter? She headed toward the throne room as fast as her wings could carry her.

She approached two guards escorting a young woman with reddish hair and Winter clothes. Raine?

Joobel flew right above them. "She's with me, let her go! Head back to the portal, I'll meet you there!"

They started to ask Joobel to explain; no guard could mistake her for anyone else. But before they knew what was happening, the gnome was gone. The rushing air of her shooting over them knocked one guard's helm off his head. Joobel heard it hit the stone floor but never slowed.

Twice more, she had to catch herself on tight turns and soon she launched into the throne room, leading a gale of wind and noise. A quick glance told her Claire was in her meeting room. She made a tight turn and landed right before the door, booted feet sliding as she pushed the guard aside. He made no protest. The look on her face told Jasper it was urgent.

Claire's face lit up when she saw her adopted sister and advisor. That expression melted into worry as she noticed the tears streaking her friend's face.

Joobel moved to pick up her queen. "You just have to trust me!"

They both shot out the door. She flew back the way she had come, slowing only on the turns she couldn't take with a passenger. She could've let Claire run, but the queen tended to ask questions and wasn't that fast.

Even now, Claire was trying to talk, but the echoed thrumming of her wing beats made hearing words impossible. That really wasn't necessary. Claire was the only other person who used dragon-speak. Joobel focused the words in her mind.

"Jack is badly hurt. I think he got hit with frost fire and the damage is really bad. Oh, Claire, I'm so scared. Bloom is out of range and he might not make it till she gets back. The only thing I could think of was for you to repair him with Transmutation."

Claire's face went pale. "He what? I'll certainly try. Where is he?"

"He's lying in Issabol's portal room. We must hurry!"

Joobel was nearly back to the portal that would carry her to Issabol's. She shot over Raine, who had finally gotten free of the guards, but didn't stop to talk.

As she neared the door to the portal room, she set Claire down. The queen had to get her legs up to speed to keep from falling. Then Claire was running under her own strength. Joobel didn't fight to get around her, wanting the queen to reach her brother as quickly as possible.

All three women entered the hub within a few seconds of each other. All three promptly attended the prince. Gray had gotten a sheet to drape over him, protecting his modesty to a degree.

Joobel knew Gray would be feeling helpless. The man got his chance to help when Claire asked if they could get him on a table. He reached out his hand and a soft platform of air lifted Jack to Claire's waist.

The Autumn Queen laid her hands on the blackened skin of his back. Raine began cleansing the corruption that had infested the dragon's breath. Joobel was fighting back tears as she knelt by his face, her hands on his cheeks. She took the pain away through her power, kissing his cheek and whispering her worries and fears into his ear.

All three women worked to repair and cleanse the damage of the terrible cold. What Bloom could do in moments took them over two hours. Tears dripped onto the prince and the floor.

Even Gray wept for his friend. Shirdos was confused and seemed lost as to what to do; he only stood in stoic silence.

After the first hour of work, Issabol went to get refreshments. Raine had finished her part of the process much more quickly and went to help. They came back with fruit juice and bread. Joobel was able to feed herself, but Raine put food into Claire's mouth as both her hands were focused on the delicate task.

Once the process was finished, Claire stepped back and wiped her cheeks. She looked at the people gathered, her gaze finally moving to Joobel.

"He'll live, though he will be much weaker for some time. The cold damaged much of his body. I had to use some of his healthy muscle to repair the damage. He's lost close to half his physical strength and will be both tired and hungry."

Joobel stood up and looked down. Jack's body looked as if he had been starving for weeks. His skin hung loose around thin limbs and his shoulders that had been broadening out were bulging with bones. The tan skin of his torso was wrapped around the protruding ribs. His stomach had always been slim with defined ridges, but now it seemed caved in.

Joobel was so relieved he'd survive that she began to laugh through the tears. She hugged him close. Raine broke the silent relief of the room.

"It was me. He was saving me. Jack was too fast and strong to be hit.... He almost died because I hesitated."

Claire put her arm around the woman. They'd all been afraid at the close call. She whispered to her cousin in understanding.

"Some people will sacrifice themselves for others. It is their nature. They are the best of us. He's ok and you'll have the chance to make him proud. For now, you have another task that cannot wait."

Claire looked meaningfully at the satchels. Joobel looked away from Jack for the first time and followed the gaze of the queen. Both bags were full. The flap on one of them was open, and the crystal blue of the dragon egg was visible. Now Shirdos spoke for the first time since his arrival.

"Are those what they. *Click.* Appear to be? *Click.*"

Joobel moved over to look, careful not to touch the precious orbs. She glanced up to Raine.

"You did it! I'm so proud of you!"

Joobel turned back to the Autumn Queen.

"Sister, I cannot thank you enough, but we've one more favor to ask of you this night. Gray will explain when he gets back from taking Jack to his room. My prince needs rest; I'll sit with him until you can stop by later on."

Turning to Raine, the gnome finished, "I know you can do it! Just share yourself and it will happen."

Gray finished wrapping Jack up in a sheet. He carried the prince out on a soft platform of air, Joobel following behind him. The prince had a small room up the hall he could rest in. Others wouldn't be resting.

It would be a long night.

# CHAPTER 12

C laire was still shaking from the adrenaline of her brother's brush with death. She was relieved Jack was ok, but the sight of him so thin and weak still made her feel guilty. Gray returned only moments after carrying Jack to his room. He glanced at the griffin and spoke.

"Claire, er... my Queen of Autumn, this is Shirdos. He's offered to help us with our task, but he cannot take us to where we need to go without his ability to fly."

Gray held his dark hand just over the break in the wing. Claire could clearly see the griffin had suffered a terrible injury that had healed without being set. He continued.

"Many healers from Spring have tried and failed to restore the limb. It doesn't need to be healed, but to be reshaped. Joobel seemed to think you could fix it."

Claire gave the griffin a nod and then leaned in to look at his wing. She put a hand on the wound and closed her eyes. Her head nodded slowly as she probed the joint with her spirit. As the queen stood, she stretched her back and looked to the griffin with a nod.

"I think I can help; do I have your permission to try?"

"You are generous. *Click*. To offer your help. *Click*. You have my permission. *Click*."

Claire nodded, tapping her lip with one finger. "I'll need to probe your good wing; I need to know how the bones and tendons are supposed to move."

She stepped over to the working golden wing. Her hands moved, probing along his feathers and joints. Claire bit her lip in concentration, speaking absently.

"Move it out slowly, as if you were flying."

The griffin did as she asked, using his full range of motion. Claire stood up straight, tapping her lip again.

"I'm ready. I am afraid the pain will be bad. I can move flesh around with mostly a tickle, but the bones and tendons will hurt. I can get Joobel if you think you'll need her."

Shirdos tilted his head. "I'm no stranger to pain. *Click.*"

The Queen of Autumn closed her eyes as she used her stolen power. The bones began to separate on the lines where they'd healed wrong. The harsh edges smoothed as loose shards seemed to melt into the larger pieces of bone. Tendons stretched and popped as bones were reassembled into a mirror image of the proper wing.

Claire's face went red as the griffin's tendons and ligaments reformed from the hard misshapen parts. Finally, she pushed her Transmutation spirit through his stiff, unused muscles, stretching and toning them enough that the griffin would be able to move them without pain.

"Ok, that's as much as I can do."

Shirdos spread the wing wide. Just the one side took up a good portion of the room. He flapped it twice, testing the joints. Claire nodded in satisfaction.

"Start easy on it; it will feel weak for a while. Within a few days, you should feel more confident."

The griffin tapped his talons on the ground in excitement. He reared onto his rear lion legs.

"It has been decades! *Click.* Since I have walked the sky. *Click.* I owe you a great debt. *Click.*"

Claire shook her head. "Actually, I did a favor for my friend. Gray asked this of me, and for *him* I repaired your wing. Your debt is to him. Help this man as best you can in his quest, and I'll be satisfied."

Shirdos gave her a curt nod. "It shall be as you say. *Click.*"

The queen turned to Raine and sighed.

"Well, I intended Jack to help you with this. Now we're the ones who need to ask a favor."

Claire picked up the packs and handed one to Raine. She turned to Issabol and requested the portal be readied, then left the hub just long enough to get her coat and hat. The moist air would be cold this late in the day. Raine looked confused but didn't argue.

Claire looked to Gray. "Please see to our guest."

He met her eyes, then silently nodded.

The two women walked out onto the misty shore of Loch Mozeg.

\*\*\*

Raine breathed in the cool, wet air. Portals really were a marvel. In the last few hours, she'd been to four different places that were all days apart by foot.

Claire set down the pack and looked out onto the waters of the loch. After a few seconds she turned back to her cousin.

"Depth heard me and is coming; our Lady Fluvial will be with him. I'll owe him several rounds of games after so many visits. I called Harvest before we left. He'll be here in a couple of hours to watch over us. This will take a good long while."

Raine nodded and then realized she hadn't eaten since her early morning breakfast. Appreciating what was still sitting in her pack, the young woman set it down. She moved the egg to the ground, careful not to touch it with her power yet.

Pulling out the wrapped travel cakes Issabol had made her, she took out two and handed one to Claire as she walked over to sit by her. They ate in silence and Raine found herself leaning on Claire's shoulder. They were just over three years apart. Myrin was just a bit older than Claire. Raine felt that she wanted to grow up to be more like her cousin. The Autumn guard's words echoed in her mind.

*We know that isn't true because Raine Anahita is dead.*

Raine realized that Claire might have something to do with that. She kept leaning on her cousin, her head resting on the woman's shoulder. She spoke in a dreamy tone.

"Say, Claire?"

Her cousin chewed slowly. "Hmmm?"

"You didn't happen to... oh, I don't know... kill me recently, did you?"

Claire was still chewing the cake; between the griffin and her brother, she was famished. She paused until she could answer with an empty mouth.

"Oh, you know. I think I did kill you. Yes, now that you mention it, I'm certain that I sent your head to Myrin. Is the news going around Winter already?"

Raine sighed. "Your guards told me that I was dead."

"Yep, that sounds about right."

"Claire?" she sighed.

"Yes, Raine?"

"If you find you need to kill me again, could you let me know? I felt awfully foolish."

Claire nodded, covering her mouth. "I suppose that's fair. Next time I'll make sure you're informed."

Both girls laughed despite themselves, more from the stress of the day and the task ahead than from the morbid joke of Raine's not quite demise. They sat in silence for only a few more minutes before the loch opened up to allow Depth to emerge from the water. Fluvial walked beside him as he waddled toward them.

Raine stepped forward, surprising Claire. The Autumn Queen was quite good at this, but this was Raine's bargain, and she needed to make it. As the great water spirit stepped forward, Raine went to meet her.

It was her intention to curtsy and give Fluvial the formal greeting her station deserved. As she drew close, Raine felt her spirit revive. The emotions of the long hard day rushed over her like a wave.

She opened her eyes to find herself hugging the spirit who'd agreed to bond with her and her land. Raine wept as her core was overwhelmed by pure warm power. The rightful Queen of Winter sniffed, wiping her eyes as she stepped back. It wasn't the diplomatic negotiation she'd pictured.

"My Lady, I need your help."

Raine told the story, starting with the climb into the cave. The condition of the nest and eggs. The fight between Maeve and the frost drake, River. Finally, the moment when Jack took the blast of frost fire that was meant for her.

Depth seemed quite upset at the news. Claire explained that while he was weak, the prince would survive. Raine walked over to pick up the packs and carefully set down the two frost drake eggs. She looked to Fluvial and stiffened her spine.

"When Claire and Joobel hatched the eggs of Bloom and Harvest, they had a source of power that could rival that of a dragon. Jack siphoned the realm spirit of Autumn's power into each woman to allow the dragons to emerge. He was to do the same for me, but he's weak and tired. The hatching will take several hours, and he's not able to do it. I came to—"

Fluvial moved to stand before Raine. Her hand moved to the young woman's cheek. Her other came up to halt her words.

"Of course, I'll help you! Let's get started. This is exciting!"

Raine couldn't help herself; she hugged her great spirit again and then found a comfortable spot on the ground. She picked up the first of the two eggs. To her surprise, Fluvial turned into a wave of clear water and wrapped around her shoulders, covering her like a cloak of warm mist.

Words whispered into her mind. "You have all the power you need."

The first egg was the least coated with the black sludge. Raine touched the little life inside the egg with her spirit. The corruption was thick. The tiny drake was soaked in greasy energy that had just started to seep into the creature's very core. She began to clean.

Raine visualized her power moving in, tentacles of pure water spirit wiping away layers of filth. She worked from top to bottom and then side to side. Once the egg was free of the tainted spirit magic, she began to push her own Purification toward the tiny dragon inside. It rejected her instantly.

It could tell she wasn't a dragon; she wasn't family. This dragon tasted her magic and found it lacking. Raine finished her work and then looked up. Claire nodded in understanding.

"Jack and I were both rejected by Bloom."

Raine handed the egg up to her cousin. That was the one she'd been most hopeful for; the corruption was weaker and it looked less battered. Claire handed her the second egg. Raine took a deep breath and again began to send her spirit into the soiled orb. The other egg had been coated in corruption; this one was drowning in it.

The greasy black taint had worked roots of contamination into the flesh of the tiny creature. The nose and mouth were sullied inside by muck and little lungs were full of ooze; she thought it would never take its first breath.

Raine knew beyond a doubt that this was her dragon. No tiny spirit could need her power more than this one. Cloaked in the power of a great spirit, she could purify even this wretched soul. As before, her magic formed tentacles of the pure water spirit, but as she began to wipe the filth away, it lashed out at her.

The taint was so strong and pervasive that it was fighting her. For a moment, Raine was back with her mother, trying with all her might to take the maddening filth from her spirit. She'd failed and the taint had torn the queen's core in half rather than let her have her real mother back.

Raine had been alone and afraid. No longer. Now she was wrapped in power and she stood alongside formidable allies. This little creature belonged to Winter. It was hers! This drake needed the protection of the true Queen of Winter.

Jack's words came back to her.

*Do the right thing when something else is far easier.*

She'd save this dragon. Raine pulled back the tentacles of pure water spirit as if giving up on her task. Then the prodding fingers of magic were replaced by a tidal wave of her purifying water spirit.

Raine had tried to fight the taint like she battled with a sword. She was weak but fast, small but skilled. Raw power was never her gift; she worked with subtlety. No longer.

She opened her core to the tiny life and shared the truth of her power. The essence of purity hit the corrupted dragon like a falling mountain. The tiny life felt this last hope of pure spirit and pulled it in, drinking the energy while cleansing its body and core.

The dragon hadn't just accepted her, it was consuming her. Claire's warning of not touching the egg with her magic had been wise, as the draw of energy would have drained her core instantly. The combined flow of power to both feed and cleanse was making the spirit paths in her arms burn. In long seconds the purification was complete. The feeding had just begun.

Unlike the two women who'd gone through this experience before, Raine wasn't getting power from Jack, but from a great water spirit of both age and strength. The energy was perfectly aligned with her as Raine was now the source that fed the creature.

Claire's magic had been so close to that of the death dragons that Harvest emerged much as any other dragon of his species would have. Joobel, on the other hand, had changed her dragon. Her nature was too different. During the hatching, little cores are still forming.

Bloom had emerged in the shape of a death dragon, but her color was different, and she was altered in both personality and power. Her aspect was the opposite of change. Her power the opposite of death.

Raine had learned as much as she could from the experience of her friends. But nothing could have prepared her for this. Power flowed through her and though she was of a similar element of water, she wasn't like her sister.

She couldn't make Frost Fire. The brutal nature of Winter had produced dangerous and cruel protectors. If Myrin had been feeding this dragon, she'd have made it nearly identical to the other frost drakes.

Myrin wasn't here. Raine was very different from her sister. Though she was the only close family Raine had left, and she still loved her, Raine could never be like Myrin. She wanted to lead her people to a better way.

Like Joobel, her magic shaped the soul of her dragon. Her personality and kindness altered the little life feeding on her core spirit. This dragon that had been so corrupted accepted her essence and held it tightly.

The passage of time became remote and fluid, her whole world tied to the creature consuming the ocean of energy. Finally, the flow of power began to slow. Words appeared in her mind.

"Glferdig."

The emotion coming with the word was one of gratitude. The cleansing had so affected the hopeless soul of the dragon that it was focused on the act. Cleansing. Filtering. Purification. It felt her power and saw it as the greatest weapon in the world.

"Fdertesv."

The emotion of love and friendship. Raine heard dragon-speak. She'd waited for this moment since Claire had explained the plan to attempt the Bitter Challenge. She could speak to the creature in her mind. Raine formed a word and pushed it to her new friend.

"Family."

She sent a picture, not of her face, but of the taste of her spirit. Along with this, she sent her love for the dragon and the people of Winter who needed them both.

The words went back and forth for what could have been seconds or months. Raine didn't know. The power from Fluvial's cloak kept her feeling strong and she cherished the time with her new bond-mate.

Then came the word 'herflig' with the emotion of stretching and needing to take that first breath. Raine felt the sensation of pushing, then resting. It repeated again and again. The draw on her spirit increased, spiking at each exertion.

The Winter Queen felt the shell under her hands begin to shift.

***

Depth watched as Claire worked to make her cousin comfortable. Once the bonding had begun, she gave the younger woman and the spirit sustaining her room to work. This was part of the Autumn Queen's plan.

He liked the woman; she was cunning, devious, and quite strong for a morsel. She hid that power like a dagger under her skirt.

He'd felt the bonding begin. This was a relief to him, as Raine's magic was so unlike that of the other dragons of the water realm. The young Winter Queen was almost too kind to bond to something so brutal.

Depth was well aware of how a hatchling could be altered; in his world, it was once almost common. Powerful rulers had used a similar process to create loyal dragons of specific powers.

The mighty sea dragon had enjoyed working with both Harvest and Bloom. They were both extraordinary in power and intelligence. He had helped them learn how to be dragons in addition to being bonded.

Dragons were often larger than other races and all were gifted with a magical breath that manifested their essence. That was just the start. Depth could crush a lesser mind with his voice. He could manifest his element from pure spirit energy.

His power was so great that he was one of only a handful of beings who'd survived the Black March when it destroyed Heluvot. In a way, he'd lowered himself to make friends in this world. He didn't want to be alone.

Now he watched the girl Raine begin her bonding to the second egg. The first had rejected her. Its nature wouldn't abide by her kind spirit. He knew that this egg's mother was dead. Its sire was still fighting through the madness of Winter's corruption. Depth craned his great neck down until his large yellow eye was only a few feet from the egg in Claire's hands. He spoke to his queen in the language of dragons.

"My queen, I'm glad to see Raine was able to bond with her dragon."

Claire nodded. "Yes, this is great news. It should last several hours, but I think it will be successful."

Depth looked to her burden. "Might I ask a question of you?"

"Big fish, you can ask me anything you like."

He rumbled laughter, then continued. "What is to become of this other little one?"

His eyes focused as the woman stroked the egg. She seemed disappointed.

Claire sighed. "I'd hoped each would accept her. I was planning to have her bond with them both. I think the other egg was so corrupted that it was more open to her spirit."

She frowned, still stroking the egg gently. "Raine is possibly the only water user in Winter who isn't mad from the taint. With Jack hurt, Fluvial is the only being powerful enough to power the hatching."

His massive head moved slowly from side to side. "I'm sorry, my queen, but you're wrong on both counts."

Claire looked at him, confused. She looked back at the egg, then to him again. As the realization sank in, her mouth slowly gaped open. The three scars on her cheek stretched as her mouth worked like a fish out of water. Finally, she got her words out.

"You! *You* can power the hatching?"

Depth nodded. "I have enough power to hatch a dozen eggs at once. I'm Named and very, very old. What boon would you ask if I were to accept the egg?"

Claire seemed to think for a moment. Depth liked the queen but was wary of her bargains. She had a way of coming out way ahead. Her offer surprised him.

"Mighty big fish, if you agree to train the new dragons of Winter, continue to teach those of Autumn, and hold this young drake to the same standard of behavior as you've held yourself, then I grant you the bond of this drake. I also agree to help it learn both flight and friendship."

Depth thought she might try for some future favor or a similar boon. He'd have done all this anyhow and the idea of having a disciple appealed to him a great deal. He nodded his promise.

"I agree to your terms."

Claire laid the egg on the ground before him. Her eyes grew big as he leaned down and somehow gently scooped it up with large triangle teeth. The egg sat safely inside of his mouth, nestled atop his huge tongue.

Depth backed up into the water to be more comfortable. The time it took to hatch wasn't a measure of the power of the one feeding energy; the egg could only absorb so much so fast. He also would take several hours to complete his task.

Just before he began, Harvest landed several paces up the beach, quietly for once.

Depth knew that the death dragon could also feel the hatching Raine was working. Harvest reached out to him.

"It's good to see you, elder. I see you too are guarding this miracle."

"No, little one, I'm here to help. I also will be hatching this night. Watch over us and soon our family will grow."

The death drake's eyes got a bit larger for a moment, then Harvest broke out in a toothy grin.

"Nothing will disturb you, Elder. May you bond well."

Depth focused on the egg. This wasn't like a human feeling around for a candle in the dark. He knew he could hatch this egg before he even got close to the beach. If the girl had been able to handle both eggs, he'd have said nothing. It wasn't his place to interfere.

Now this young one was doomed to either death or madness. He knew that his power would alter the spirit of the hatchling. It was a power that had been rare even in his world. He was of the vast sea, the deepest part of an ocean in a world mostly covered by water.

Pressure. The compression that only came from surviving miles underwater. Countless tons of crushing saltwater were his to call. It was his spirit. He could breathe devastating power as a thick fog of mist and those caught inside would be smashed to paste. It was almost too destructive.

Using it around his fragile new friends would certainly crush them. His power was, in many ways, a burden here. It was like trying to slice an apple when all you have is an ax. Few things would benefit from his immense power. This was one of them.

Depth ran the smallest trickle of energy into the egg, the spirit of pressure running through the top of his tongue. The egg seemed startled at the vastly different quality of spirit from what it had tasted just a short time before.

Raine had been a power of cleansing and purity. The soul had rejected the nature of this; it sought strength and power. The power to kill and protect. This was a soldier with a soul much like that of Harvest.

In the spirit of Pressure running through Depth, the dragon found more than it could have hoped for. It sensed something else, though. Depth had survived for so long on Heluvot because an ancient great spirit of water had sustained him. As powerful as Depth was, the hatchling also tasted Fluvial's power within the sea dragon.

Fluvial had once been a girl, born to a poor family in a small river village. She had, like so many before, received a spirit in her mother's womb. Spirits grow more powerful with each lifetime. The one she received was ready to ascend.

A child, in a now long-dead world, had been gifted a power many considered to be the most coveted spirit in the many incarnations of water. Flow. This was the spirit Fluvial had nurtured until it allowed her to become a fledgling great spirit.

Pressure was a power of destruction. The hatchling felt it and would have accepted without question had it been the only option. However, the power of Fluvial was also present within the sea dragon.

The magic of a great spirit like hers was ambient and diluted, usually changed by the vessel that received it. But Depth had so many years of direct flow of her power that much of it had remained unchanged.

The hatchling wanted the power to protect home and family. A power that could only destroy was good, but a power that could be used both offensively and defensively was better.

Depth was shocked to find the tiny drake latching onto Fluvial's power rather than his own. The ancient aspect of water called Flow. No person in Fairie had ever seen or heard of such a power, and yet the foreign sea dragon had carried it inside him.

He couldn't use it; he was shaped long ago by his brood mother. No amount of Fluvial's magic would change his abilities. He wasn't a hatchling. This was true for Depth but not for the egg resting on his tongue.

The egg pulled the strand of spirit that had only been stored in him. Depth wanted to fight at first, offended that his power wasn't accepted, but compassion for the young one won out. He began to push the stream of his own power aside and filter the egg its preferred food.

The experience of hatching wasn't the awe-inspiring bonding that a morsel would experience. He wasn't overwhelmed by the sense of wonder and emotion, but instead had to shield the tiny form from his own crushing will.

There remained the similarity of that first word and the emotion that came with it. 'Gerdespab' came into his mind, with the feeling of satisfaction and curiosity.

Depth formed a term in his mind and lightly pushed it back to his new youngling. 'Family,' with the emotion of unity and safety. For a powerful being that had spent so much time thinking he'd die alone, the bonding touched his heart.

He'd have centuries to build a relationship with this disciple. The bond that was only minutes old meant more to him than the power he'd coveted for so long.

Then there was a slight sense of effort and rest. Depth knew what was coming. The sea dragon's next thought was to himself, but the emotion leaked through the new bond.

'*I have a son.*'

# CHAPTER 13

G ray watched as the queen he loved walked out of the portal onto the shore of Loch Mozeg. He wanted to go with her. Hatching was a miracle unmatched by any other he'd experienced, including being able to fly or make things from air. Duty had urged him to remain at the hub.

He had petitioned Issabol for a place that would allow Shirdos to rest and heal the changed wing. She'd led them through a portal and to the large room that had formerly been her workshop.

Gray wasn't surprised to see the room empty; he'd been the one to suggest setting up a new one. He brought in a chair, then went to the kitchen for food for both him and his guest. There he grabbed some fruit, bread, and jam.

Traveling had worked up quite an appetite and he'd eaten nothing but travel cakes for days. The Stone Spears had offered him some kind of roasted meat, but he and Joobel had both declined.

He also grabbed several chunks of cured meat. It wasn't raw like Shirdos had requested, but he hoped the griffin wouldn't care too much. He placed it all on a small table and carried the whole thing into the room with his guest. The griffin was taking advantage of the larger room to stretch and flap his wings. He looked over as Gray entered.

"It would seem the wing repaired. *Click.* It is the stronger of the two. *Click.* Long years of not using the other, I think. *Click.* Your queen has worked a miracle. *Click.*"

Gray set the table down and pulled up the chair. He was already shoveling food into his mouth and had to talk around his food to speak.

"She's an amazing woman."

The griffin tilted his head. "Forgive me for asking. *Click.* In what manner do you serve? *Click.*"

Gray shrugged. "I'm afraid I don't understand."

"Are you a guard? *Click.* Perhaps a soldier? *Click.* A consort? *Click.*"

The last one almost caused Gray to lose a mouthful of bread and jam.

"No, I'm just a friend and resident of her kingdom."

The griffin paused, its head cocking left and then back right.

"Citizens do not speak. *Click.* Freely in a queen's presence. *Click.* They do not gather. *Click.* Her look of respect. *Click.*"

The man sighed. "We were friends before she was queen. I'm sure that's why we remain so informal."

"Perhaps. *Click.*"

Gray was growing uncomfortable with the direction this was taking. He spread more jam on a crust of bread and put it in his mouth as he laid the meat out to feed his guest. The griffin seemed to stalk the meat with his eyes.

Suddenly, his head moved forward, like a snake striking, his thick beak snatching the closest piece. He swallowed it whole. Before the griffin could continue this line of questioning, Gray asked the question he'd so patiently waited to ask.

"Will the sage be able to help me?"

Shirdos clicked his talons on the stone floor. "The sage of Dawn would be. *Click.* Able to more than anyone else. *Click.*

Though wisdom will not be shared. *Click.* With any who have not passed the trials. *Click.*"

Gray lifted an eyebrow. "Trials?"

"The three great Chimeras. *Click.* Of the realm of Dawn. *Click.* All must be defeated. *Click.* Before he grants an audience. *Click.*"

Gray thought this over. A chimera was a mythic beast that was a combination of other animals. A feeling of dread washed over him as he remembered Shirdos' introduction.

"You're the second chimera!"

Shirdos nodded. "I am part of the trial. *Click.* It seems I am nearly back to full strength. *Click.*"

Gray groaned. "So, I went out of my way to bring an opponent to fighting fit?"

"I did not make the request to be restored. *Click.* As I remember it, your companion was quite insistent. *Click.*"

That was true enough. He wouldn't have been able to stop Joobel short of knocking her unconscious. The woman had too much heart. He sighed and continued.

"Well, can you at least tell me who all I have to fight?"

The griffin snatched another piece of meat, swallowing before nodding.

"The challenger has the right. *Click.* To have a champion fight two of the three trials. *Click.* The ability to delegate. *Click.* These tasks is part of the test. *Click.* Only one can prove worthy. *Click.* To consult the sage. *Click.*"

"I guess that takes away the issue of being tired out after the first fight. Who would we be fighting?"

"The first chimera is the manticore. *Click.* Lampago also has the body of a lion. *Click.* We all do. I am not sure if the creator really liked lions. *Click.* Or just had a lot of them lying around.

*Click*. We also all have eagles' wings. *Click*. Though I got more eagle than the others. *Click*."

Shirdos cocked his head back and forth, then continued. "Lampago also has the head of a man. *Click*. Though lighter skin than yours. *Click*. Finally, he has a long tail that is covered in long venomous spikes. *Click*. If one of them breaks the skin. *Click*. You will die in seconds. *Click*."

Gray held up fingers. "So big claws, really smart, and poisonous. It sounds like he'd be fun at a party."

The griffin cocked his head and stared in silence. Gray just waved off the confusion. The creature snatched another piece of meat and gulped it down.

"I am the second chimera. *Click*. As you can see. *Click*. I am eagle, lion, and rabbit. *Click*."

Gray wrinkled his brow. "Wait, where's the rabbit?"

"It is... on the inside. *Click*. I have the liver of a rabbit. *Click*."

"That seems a bit random."

"I know; I still don't know why. *Click*. Anyway, I am the fastest and best at flying. *Click*. Both my beak and talons. *Click*. Are very quick and deadly. *Click*."

"Ok, so beak, talons, and really fast," Gray said with a nod.

"Finally, Hawlabu is a sphinx. *Click*. He is by far the most dangerous. *Click*. He has a man's head. *Click*. Lion's body and again the eagle's wings. He is quite vain. *Click*. And will pretend to give you riddles. *Click*."

"Pretend?"

"The riddles will be real. *Click*. But in the end, he will attack you no matter what you do. *Click*."

Gray leaned back, eyes narrowed. "So why the riddles?"

"It makes people let down their guard. *Click*. Or maybe he just likes to toy with his food. *Click*."

"Sounds like a real jerk."

"Lampago and I serve the sage out of duty. *Click*. We fight our best but have never killed. *Click*. Only a few have defeated either of us. *Click*." He looked down at his wing for a moment, avian eyes remembering the pain. "Hawlabu enjoys killing his opponents. *Click*. After toying with them. *Click*. Like a cat with a mouse. *Click*."

Gray nodded slowly. "So, whoever faces the sphinx needs to be wary."

The griffin clicked his talons. "Also, very, very strong. *Click*."

"So has anyone ever completed the trials? Beaten all three of the chimeras?"

"I sincerely hope you are the first. *Click*."

Gray began planning his strategy. At first, he thought of asking two of the dragons to take on two of the challenges. The thought of Harvest getting asked a riddle and then just eating the sphinx had more than a little appeal.

That would show that he had powerful friends, but no real thought on his part. The manticore poison could be an issue. He only knew one person with natural immunity to poison and Raine had enough to deal with.

He must choose carefully.

\*\*\*

Claire had snuggled up with Harvest only a few paces from Raine. Depth too, was performing his own exchange of power. The sky was clear beyond the mists of the Loch. She cherished the time she got to spend with the dragon she herself had hatched.

With Depth and Fluvial both involved, she wasn't really worried. It was an excellent excuse to spend time with her bond-mate. The death dragon curled around her and she leaned against his long neck. She noticed he'd gotten a bit bigger in the past couple of months.

Though it felt like she'd carried the burden of rule for many years, it had only been two. He was less than three years old but seemed to grow in intelligence and understanding far faster than the other races.

Harvest had trained with Depth but had never met another death dragon. Well, maybe if you counted Bloom, but she was more different from Harvest than the frost drakes. He was the last of his kind.

Moments when they could just sit and enjoy each other's company had become rare as the kingdom had grown and expanded. She was able to speak to him most of the time, the range of dragon-speak extending many miles for her now. They both had a role to play, and she was content.

They'd been waiting for several hours. The bonding had begun before sunset. Now it was only a few short hours until morning. Her eyes had grown heavy, and she almost slid into sleep before Harvest warned her of the miracle about to take place.

Claire had been drawing her spirit for this moment. Raine had to leave no doubt in her Bitter Challenge. She would need to arrive with not a tiny hatchling, but a dragon that no one could deny. This little drake needed an edge. She was going to give it one.

The Autumn Queen walked toward where Raine was in silent communion with the crystal blue orb, though she realized it was no longer the same shade. The blue had faded. The egg now had the color of a fresh winter snow.

The shell had lightened and soon began to crack. Tiny black lines spider-webbed across the surface. They grew wider each time the dragon pressed its tiny head against the inside of the thick shell. Bit by bit, the little dragon pushed the shell apart.

Finally, a large piece of the thick pale blue material slid to the side. A tiny head popped out. The dragon was even paler than the shell. The tiny face was as white and pure as new linen.

Raine awoke from her trance, the bond complete, and little eyes met hers. The only blue left in this dragon was the bright crystal blue of its eyes. Lively and intelligent, the little dragon jumped out of the shell and met Raine's gaze.

The woman smiled as she met her new bond-mate. The dragon let out a squealing roar and crawled into her arms. Then it gently rested the top of a white head against Raine's chin.

Frost drakes were shaped much like death dragons, long serpentine necks holding up their snake-like heads. They had short horns over the eyes and tiny ridges on either side of the tips of their broad noses.

Both types of dragon had front limbs that served as both legs and wings. The back legs of the white drake were lean and built for speed and the mighty jumps that would carry it into flight. A long whip-like tail ended in a single sharp barb.

Raine gently hugged her new friend. Looking up at Claire, she formed a broad grin.

"Isn't it perfect?"

Claire laughed and put a hand on her own dragon.

"I prefer my dragons to be black and intensely scary. This one is just adorable."

Raine beamed with pride. "So adorable!"

"Are you ready?"

Raine sighed as she looked at the dragon in her arms. "Do I have to put it down?"

Claire shook her head. She carefully sat next to Raine, then firmly set both hands on the soil. The realm spirit of Autumn tingled with excitement through her fingers.

The Autumn Queen had grown much stronger since the last time she'd used her power of Naming. Over two years ago, she'd last given her gift to Joobel. The effort almost made her pass out, but it was the only time Jack hadn't been there to feed her power. Now she would share the gift again.

Naming wasn't part of her spirit; it was a rare skill that was a part of her. Her core would help power the ability, but the aspect of both the person giving and receiving the name was inconsequential.

Now three spirits were helping her channel the ability. Raine held the back of the dragon to her chest. The little drake looked at the woman who was leaning close to it. Then the tiny dragon breathed right in Claire's face.

She'd forgotten to explain to Raine how to mentally safeguard her friends from the dragon's attacks. Little dragons didn't know who was friend or foe; only their bond-mates were safe from assault.

Raine jerked up in fright, but Claire only coughed twice from the mist in her face.

"Ug... it went right in my mouth."

Raine gasped, eyes wide. "Are you ok?"

Harvest was panicked; even a small frost drake could blind a person with the power of frost fire. Claire waved to everyone that she was fine. Was she fine? She felt fine. She'd have to figure out what the moisture even was.

"You're unharmed."

Fluvial stood beside Claire. She put a hand on her shoulder and then sat on the rocks next to Raine. The great spirit arranged her dress of flowing water, then turned back to the women.

"When different spirits are used on a hatchling, the dragon inside is changed. Long ago, the original rulers of the various lands would breed dragons with the greatest offensive power and then replicate that power through the generations."

The great spirit's gaze moved to Harvest. "In some cases, such as Death or Frost Fire, the dragons are mostly unchanged. I don't know what would happen if Claire were to hatch another; it could take any of her three spirits, or some combination."

Claire had wiped all of the moisture from the dragon's attack from her face. She spit on the ground. Not very ladylike, but no one blamed her. The queen turned to Fluvial.

"That explains Harvest. How did Bloom come about?"

Fluvial shrugged with a grin. "Oh, I have no idea how that happened. I didn't think such a thing was even possible. I've never heard of a dragon feeding off a different type of spirit magic, much less a polar opposite. From a gnome no less. You all have the most wonderful oddities."

Raine perked up, still shocked her dragon had assaulted Claire. Now she heard that her perfect little friend might not have an offensive spell. She turned to Fluvial.

"So does my dragon not have an attack?" Raine was pouting, biting her lower lip in concern.

"My dear queen, your dragon has what might prove to be the best attack of any dragon in the kingdom. *She* is truly your creation. Have you forgotten your own spirit, daughter?"

Claire tapped her lower lip. "Purification. She just purified me, right?"

Fluvial laughed, the sound light and joyful.

"Well, yes, I suppose she did. If you were, oh say, corrupted with a terrible ooze from another world, you might have reacted quite differently. This dragon may just be the bane of their existence."

Claire was already plotting. They could use this dragon much the same way Bloom worked. They could hit whole groups and let the corrupted be cleansed. She couldn't hide her smile.

They could work all that out soon. For now, she needed to Name this little dragon. Before Claire was going to move her face that close again, she had a few instructions.

After Raine learned to define her friends to her dragon, Claire once again moved close. This time she looked into crystal blue orbs with eyes the color of falling maple leaves. The power flowed through her.

Her voice took on a deep echoing tone as she spoke to everyone and no one. "I NAME you Mist." Her energy stores dropped, but not to empty. She'd grown stronger. Claire drew on Autumn, already replacing the energy she'd spent.

"I love it! Hello, Mist." Raine snuggled her new friend.

Claire looked at the hatchling, now a Named dragon of water. Perhaps she was the very weapon they needed to fight the Black March. She smiled at Raine.

"Your bond-mate is a lovely little lady."

Her power was refilling quickly. She had one more round to go. She looked up as Depth slowly moved onto the shore and gently used his tongue to lay the other egg on the cold stones.

The shell was also changed.

***

Joobel sat next to her prince. He didn't know it yet, but she was going to walk through the pumpkins with this man. She had names picked out for their first four children. If he ruined everything by dying, she was going to be furious.

She'd helped Gray set him on the bed and turned as the larger man dressed him. Claire's rules were quite clear and Joobel could only break them if the woman was being silly.

The gnome had a special bond with Claire, Named by her power and forced to obey her commands. She'd sought out the Naming for only one reason. It worked in the fact that she'd gotten much larger.

Joobel was born with the weakest of spirit magics. Before her Naming, she could bless people, but her ability was weak. She'd never been able to take away pain before, at least not enough to notice. Now she had yet to have an issue removing any level of agony.

There were other new gifts, not all understood. She had rarely used her power of blessing. Before, it had seemed so weak that it only helped when someone was already ok. Now it was so powerful that it felt intimate, like a passionate kiss.

There was only one person she wanted to give a kiss to, and she'd agreed to wait until his eighteenth birthday. Claire had made it clear that boys full of hormones produced brash decisions. One kiss from her and Jack wouldn't think clearly for a decade.

Claire hadn't restricted the blessing, though. To him it would be no different than getting healed by Bloom or having Claire alter his features. It meant more to her, though.

Joobel knew that as strong as she was now, the blessing would bond her to him. It would link them forever. She knew it as much as she knew that moving her wings would lift her into the air.

She'd thought him dead. She had saved his life before but never had she thought him already dead. It had crushed her. Now he was so weak he was looking at months or even years to recover. They were so close to the battle and he'd be stuck in bed.

Jack would be months rebuilding the strength he'd worked so hard for. He was the one that had to train Raine. The Winter Queen still needed the control that Jack could teach her.

So many depended on him. None of them loved him as she did. To Claire, he was a brother. To Raine, a cousin. To Gray, a friend. To Maeve, a master...?

Ok, well, she didn't want to know how Maeve would react. But to Joobel, he was her world. From the moment she'd imprinted on him in that filthy room under Blood Mountain, she could love no one else.

He might not even notice the blessing; it would be subtle from his perspective. To her, it would be a bond no less evident than the one she had with Bloom. If she did this and he rejected her, she didn't know how she could cope with that. No matter what he chose, she loved him.

Joobel laid her hand against Jack's brow. He stirred lightly. His skin felt warm; she'd think him feverish if it had been anyone else. The power flowed through her. She blessed him with the power that linked her spirit to his. The gnome felt her own core drain as he sighed and began to rest more easily.

It was done.

\*\*\*

Depth set the egg on the rocky shore of Loch Mozeg. It had drained all the unchanged magic of Fluvial and then some of his own. His stores of energy were mostly unchanged, having so much to begin with. Even now, he felt the bond.

He'd never sired a brood, mostly due to his arrogance. No one was as grand as he and so who could measure up to be his mate?

Foolishness. He already cared more for the hatchling he was yet to meet than he did for the whole of his power.

The shell was different. His eyes were better for seeing in darkness than picking out colors, but even he could see the change. It wasn't so much the color of the egg as the fact that it was moving.

The surface seemed to swirl like the surface of a river. It reminded him of something. His huge yellow eyes looked to Fluvial sitting on a rock next to the young queens. Her dress moved with that same color and motion. Depth's eyes widened.

He'd felt that the draw of power was different than he expected, but this wasn't what he'd thought would come of it. He had questions for the great water spirit, but they would have to wait.

The bond brought him a sense of effort and rest; the arrival had already started. The top of the strange orb was just starting to reveal tiny cracks that pushed and spread. Then one crack widened. A stream of clear water flowed from the opening and down the side of the egg.

The fluid moved a pace from the shell, then shaped into a wobbly, iridescent dragon. Once formed, it gained color, and the scales of its skin seemed to writhe with various shades of blue. It looked around and then saw Depth.

The tiny drake shifted effortlessly into the stream of water again and flowed into the loch, moved up his side, weaved around his long neck, and reformed atop his massive head.

The tiny head pressed down on his. 'Femole' came into everyone's mind, along with the emotion Depth had given to 'family.' His reply came despite his shock and awe at the form of his adopted child.

"Very true, little one. Family."

Fluvial stood straight up and with absolutely no regard for her station or dignity, jumped up and down while clapping like a child of eight winters.

"I've no idea what's going on.... This is just the very best day!"

Depth looked down and Claire walked up to the water's edge with her fists on her hips.

"You're going to explain what you did, and spirits help me, if I get breathed on one more time, I'll have Issabol move you to Summer!"

Depth couldn't help but laugh. The rumble through dragon-speak was no surprise for Claire, but Raine almost fell over. Her new senses were still raw.

The sea dragon blamed everything on Fluvial, who was much amused by his story. Neither expected her residual magic to have an effect, and the resulting dragon was both incredible and a bit frightening.

The iridescent hatchling got curious and cascaded off the sea dragon's head, landing with a splash on the ground. The water coalesced into solid form and hopped about, wanting to play.

Raine lost hold of Mist, and the white drake ran over to her happy sibling. As she approached, the other dragon aimed its tiny head in the air.

Dragon breath is a manifestation of the magic that brought the creature from its shell. All dragons had a power they could breathe, with both Bloom and now Mist having a unique ability that was less offensive in nature but quite useful. This dragon didn't aim its breath at anyone, but instead just breathed a small blast of fine mist into the air. Then it was gone.

Everyone looked around for the missing hatchling. Except for Fluvial. She too disappeared into a thick fog of mist. Water swirled in the air for a few seconds, and then the great spirit was back in her spot next to Raine.

As suddenly as he'd disappeared, another cloud solidified behind Mist. The new dragon pounced playfully on its white sibling.

Fluvial smiled widely. "He's magnificent!"

Claire didn't know how the great spirit knew it was a male, but she couldn't argue with the statement. His breath wasn't a projection of his magic, but of himself. He could shift into the different stages of water. It seemed to be a natural skill, like a spider knowing how to spin a web.

The Queen of Autumn had gathered the power for the Naming, but she was wary of scaring the energetic little dragon. After a couple of minutes of letting them play, she appealed to Depth.

"Can you reel your little friend in? I'd like to Name him, and I don't think I can catch him."

Depth smiled with large triangle teeth. His large head leaned forward, and the hatchling turned to him. After a moment, he splashed into a stream that moved over rocks and debris, once again taking solid form right at Claire's feet. He squeaked up in greeting. Claire was a little jealous that Harvest hadn't been so well behaved.

The emotion must have seeped into the bond, for a moment later, Harvest grumbled into her mind.

"You must forgive me, my mother was inexperienced."

Claire rolled her eyes; Harvest was spending too much time with Jack. The thought of her brother made her feel a bit guilty. He was supposed to be here for this.

Sitting down cross-legged, as she still wasn't quite sure the second Naming wouldn't knock her out, Claire looked around at the people gathered to see the miracle. She leaned over and picked up the dragon, who once again squeaked at meeting her.

Before she could look into his eyes, he nodded his head down and put the top of his head on her chin. The dragon sign of friendship. It was as if he knew they were to be bonded through the Name.

The queen smiled as she waited for him to look up. Then small eyes of shifting blue met her own. Her voice took on the deep echoing tone as she once again spoke to everyone and no one.

"I NAME you Puddle."

Then the energy she'd gathered left her. All of it. Claire slumped forward, darkness closing in around her vision. As she faded, she heard Depth's disgusted rumble.

"You Named my disciple Puddle!"

# CHAPTER 14

It was dark inside the sea dragon's mouth. It was also damp and smelled of whatever Depth had for breakfast. Raine was now deep under the water of Loch Mozeg. Her moment had arrived and soon she'd issue the Bitter Challenge. So much preparation had come down to this day. She was no longer the young girl who was carried from her home.

Raine was no stranger to politics. If Myrin could have her killed on sight, her sister would do just that. This fight had to be about optics. The people had to see her, a true Queen of Winter, issue a challenge under one of the oldest laws of her kingdom. She had to create a dispute no one could refuse.

Less than two months ago in the world of Fairie, Myrin had sent an entire legion after her. Only the resolve and strength of Sroto and the intervention of Jack and Gray had seen her make it to Autumn. Only the healing of Bloom and the protection of Maeve and others had seen her survive that night.

The next attack had a much larger force pushing right up against the border of another kingdom, an act that would certainly start a war. Yet the actions of a clever and terrifying woman had seen that fail as well.

If something wasn't done, the entire world would soon be fighting a war that could only have one winner. The Black March might seem like an unthinking poison, but she could see now that what was attacking her people was akin to a diabolical plague.

None of her time had been wasted. She had the components of the challenge and they were all so much more than she could've hoped for.

The forged weapon of water was so powerful that it frightened her. Caledfwlch sat on her hip, sheathed in the scabbard Issabol had made her. She was riding in the mouth of her champion, a being of water so powerful that he could crush the whole of the Black Citadel. Finally, she'd acquired Mist.

Raine had found Claire and Joobel's descriptions of the bond with their dragons hard to understand at first. Yet in short order she couldn't imagine life without her bond-mate, the drake Mist, white as fallen snow. She'd thought about riding her drake to the front of the Black Citadel, but having her fly so close might give away the element of surprise.

Though her dragon was undoubtedly of water and Winter, Mist would be hard-pressed if multiple frost drakes attacked her before Raine could issue the Challenge. Besides, this way would make for good theatrics. This whole thing was more about the show than the actual event. This being the case, she couldn't bring any of her allies who weren't of water and Winter.

The voice of Depth rumbled into her mind. "We are here; it is time."

She replied to her allies with her own dragon-speak. "I want to thank you all so much. Your faith in me is everything. Let's save this realm!"

Depth didn't wait for further instruction. There was a jerking halt as his massive head hit something. Then again. She was lurching forward, her hand braced on the back of a large triangle tooth.

The third impact gave way to a forward stagger. Raine knew that Depth had just broken through a sheet of ice several feet thick. They had traveled underwater right to the edge of Loch Mozeg's northern shore.

The Black Citadel was built on the northern tip of the giant lake. Despite the ice, water could be harvested for the needs of the capital. The proximity of the lake to the home of the queen made Depth the perfect transport.

As the ice cracked, Depth sank back down. Up from the narrow breach flowed a stream of clear water. The trail of liquid moved across the ice the short distance to the shore. Then the water shifted in motion and transformed into snow piling onto the clearing between the drifts next to the lake. More words filtered into her mind.

"It's clear; the only guards are further up near the Citadel. No sign of any drakes."

Puddle was much less rumbling than his adopted father, who seemed to say everything through a huge bass drum. Now Depth lifted through the frozen water far enough for his open mouth to allow Raine to step out onto the shore. She nimbly hopped onto the thick surface of unbroken ice and scanned for Mist through her bond.

The white drake was flying high and staying in the clouds. The snowy sheen of her scales would be something no lookouts would expect to see. Raine heard huge chunks of ice creak in protest as Depth smoothly settled back below the surface.

One deep breath, then another. The tips of her pale fingers lightly touched the handle of the sword, its blood-song crooning a dirge of battle and death. Her other hand pushed long white hair behind one ear. There was a tremor of fear and anticipation. After so much preparation, it was now time.

"Alright big fish, I'm ready to start the show."

There was no indication her next words would sound different, but she had faith in the sea dragon's ability to relay her speech through the entire citadel. The true Queen of Winter issued the Bitter Challenge.

"Under the Unseelie Pact, I of royal blood have brought before the Black Citadel the components to compel the Bitter Challenge."

Another deep breath, and she continued.

"I stand wielding an unknown weapon forged of the aspect of water. I have at my side a loyal dragon of Winter. At my back is the most powerful champion of water this world has ever seen. My Challenge is legitimate under our oldest law and cannot be denied. You must meet me in combat, Myrin Anahita. Your crown can only be regained through freeing my spirit!"

The sound of Depth's relay of her words was silent in the air but thundered through the mind of every sentient creature for miles. Guards a hundred paces away looked out and saw only a young woman.

She was wearing a blue coat, trimmed in white and cut to allow movement. Her thick blue leggings attached to a matching skirt. She wore no hat despite the chill wind, and her long white hair flowed to the side, carried in the biting breeze. Despite the Challenge, they saw no champion and no dragon. Both guards came to investigate.

Raine didn't move as they approached. Depth rumbled a message just for them.

"Do not approach the challenger. The *queen* must answer this summons."

One guard seemed to be ok with that, while the other had drool running from his mouth. He rushed toward Raine, his club raised. The madness was strong in him. When the guard was ten paces away, Raine sent the command to her bond-mate.

"Now, Mist!"

A jet of glowing fog came down from the sky and covered the guard. The thick stream of rolling white consumed the man. He stumbled forward, convulsing. The other guard ran back the way he'd come. Raine walked over and held out a hand as she smiled.

"No longer will my kingdom suffer this poison. I've come to take back what is mine. Tell Myrin Winter's true queen has come home."

The guard was sputtering. He began to retch a thick black sludge onto the frozen ground. Then he looked up into the face of Raine Anahita. The slain Maiden of Winter, back from the dead.

The man screamed and ran after his fellow guard. Raine only waited another minute before issuing another taunt to her mad sister.

"Would the queen wait in the walls of her fortress and deny the Bitter Challenge? I stand to defend my kingdom as any *true* queen would. It would be the heart of cowardice if I had to drag you trembling from under your bed!"

Raine heard the laughing rumble from the hiding sea dragon. Depth was really enjoying all this.

***

Hurley was running to keep up with the queen. She wore priceless armor over a stained royal gown. Her white hair looked matted and greasy and she'd dropped her crown again.

Wild bloodshot eyes darted all around as if looking for danger in every shadow. The line of drool down the corner of her mouth reached all the way to the damp collar of her gown.

"My queen, you need to wait for the council to go with you. I doubt this challenger can meet all three requirements, but you must have witnesses."

Myrin leaned down to pick up her crown, only to lose her breast plate. "Who is this horrible wench... that calls me a coward... in my own capital...? I'll bite her nose off!"

Hurley helped her stand. "Of course, my queen. You'll no doubt settle this. If we just wait, you won't even need to fight. Surely no one has a dragon; they're loyal only to you. No champion of water would stand with another while you are on the throne. If she has failed to meet the council's judgment, then you can simply have the army flog this usurper."

Myrin sneered. "I'll have her fed to a pack of wargs."

"Of course, my queen. Please let us wait only a moment. The legion has already been mobilized."

She turned, brow wrinkled. "So quickly?"

"They are ever vigilant, my queen."

Hurley watched as the queen went to her throne. She sat down and spoke to the head sitting frozen on a table next to her.

"Did you hear what they said... about me, sister? The nerve! You'd never talk to me... that way, would you? No, you would tell me... I'm smart and pretty. No one is queen but me!"

The lean man shuddered at the sight. He'd known this moment was coming. Coburn had explained the corruption of the great Winter spirit. He'd described the death witch taking a fallen soldier's head and shaping it into this uncanny thing. Yet the false head was a perfect match, and it had once left even Hurley convinced that Raine was deceased.

Now hope filled his heart. He had to make sure he did his part. The council and the military must all be present for this night.

He felt sorry for Myrin. She was never fit to rule, but he'd known her since she was born. He had argued against her as queen but never wanted to see her hurt. Seeing the madness so thick in her was heartbreaking.

A knock sounded at the door; Coburn leaned in and nodded to him.

It was time.

\*\*\*

The main doors to the citadel began to open. They were so large and tall that they were clearly visible from the shoreline. Raine had only shifted around enough to keep the blood in her legs pumping. Slowly the military moved out of the outer wall of the capital.

Hundreds of soldiers marched through every minute, lining up in rows. They parted as an honor guard moved past. Between these soldiers of more ornate armor were several litters.

Banners signified what great families were represented by each member of the council. Finally, there appeared the largest of these, signified with the royal crest and that of the Anahita family. Myrin's crest, and her own.

Raine always found the idea of having people carry you around rather foolish. She might have the royal litter turned into a boat, or perhaps a house for owls. The pace of the things was slow and she was getting both impatient and cold. Depth's mouth had been gross and smelled like fish, but at least it had been warm.

Finally, the pretentious carriages were each set down about thirty paces away. A council member crawled out of each litter. The council of seven would decide if her Challenge was valid. The honor guard walked forward with the seven ancient people.

Four men and three women each represented a powerful family of Winter, and every one of them was older than mountain snow. A hunched-over man raised a hand, and the murmuring slowed. He spoke in a high croaking voice.

"The Bitter Challenge has been issued. You have claimed to have the blood of a great Winter family. What surname gives you this right?"

Raine stepped forward three paces. Putting her hands together in fists and making a slight bow, she answered him, words carried by the sea dragon.

"I descend from the Anahita family. My name," she announced, pushing her blowing white hair from her face, "is Raine."

The murmurs rose again. Cries of disbelief and anger came from all sides. Shouts of 'murderer' and 'liar' could be heard from every angle. None were louder than the feral scream that came from the royal litter. Myrin flew out through the curtains. She ran straight for her sister, sword gleaming in the faint Winter daylight.

The council chair raised a hand and the honor guard stepped in front of the woman. She screamed and hissed at the soldiers, but the old man kept speaking.

"Until the Challenge is judged, you are *not* the queen. If it is valid, you'll have your chance to fight. If it is not, then you may have the woman punished."

He seemed to run out of the moisture needed to speak and worked his mouth for a moment before continuing.

"The Bitter Challenge requires a weapon forged of the realm of water. Do you bear such a weapon?"

Raine slowly drew Caledfwlch, the blood-song filling her ears. She held the sword out from her, point toward the ground. Twenty paces from the council, Raine slowly lowered the blade into one of the large cold stones lining the shore of the Loch. She stepped back as Depth relayed her words.

"Feel free to examine the weapon."

The old man waved a guardsman to bring him the blade. The large man moved over and grabbed the hilt, turning to walk back. His arm jerked and he almost fell over.

The guard looked around as if he was the butt of a joke, then pulled with all his strength. He couldn't move the sword. Another went to help him, but both together could not budge it. Raine let them fail for a while before stepping in.

"Perhaps a demonstration would allow you to judge?"

The old man was getting cold and impatient. He gestured for her to go on. Raine strode over and grabbed her weapon. It slid easily from the ground.

Deft hands swiftly spun the blade and struck against the side of a large rock. It looked as if nothing had happened. She set one booted foot against the top of the stone and pushed, sliding the perfectly cut piece off and onto the ground.

The crowd grew hushed. Like most crowds, they seemed more interested in entertainment than anything else. Raine smiled; they had no idea. The show hadn't even started yet.

The old man looked to the others. They gestured and argued for only a moment before turning back to her.

"We accept the weapon as genuine. The second requirement is a loyal dragon of Winter. Two of the frost drakes are missing, but all others are loyal to Myrin Anahita. Can you produce a dragon, young lady?"

Raine sheathed the sword, relieved to have the blood-song out of her ears. She made a show of looking around for a moment before looking at the old man's feet. She gave a broad smile and a showman's gesture as her words boomed through the minds of the crowd.

"I almost thought I misplaced my dragon. Turns out, you're all standing on him!"

Nothing happened. Raine tapped one foot, waiting. Then she crossed her arms and rolled her eyes. Finally, she spoke again, her tone halting and exaggerated as she had to repeat the missed cue.

"Turns OUT... you're all STANDING... on HIM!"

Whispered dragon-speak came into her mind.

"Oh sorry, I was looking at the banners."

Raine gritted her teeth. "Just do the thing already!"

The snow surrounding the council and honor guard began to vibrate, then a swirling mass of powdered ice rose from the ground in a cyclone of cold stinging air. The snow gathered and climbed high, where it coalesced into a huge blue dragon.

The drake's scales flowed with shades of sapphire and cobalt and the sheen of iridescent magic covered every inch of his form. He whipped his head around, looking at the gathered crowd with large eyes of flowing azure. The old man gasped and fell down.

Guards helped him back up, but he swatted the strong hands away. He looked both shocked and angry. Raine still stood with arms folded, not bothering to describe that which spoke for itself. The old man looked like he wanted to fail her out of spite. In the end, duty won him over.

"This looks nothing like any frost drake I've ever seen."

Raine smiled and made a sweeping gesture.

"The law states 'a loyal dragon of Winter.' Frost drakes are no doubt dragons of Winter, but they're clearly not the only ones."

She moved her voice to a tone that dripped of sarcasm.

"A dragon that can shift into snow is of Spring perhaps, or maybe Summer. Ours is a realm of water and no dragon embodies that more than this one."

Raine could tell the old man was no longer on her side, but the crowd was nodding. Many openly exclaimed that this was very much a dragon of Winter, the realm of water.

Once again, the old man conversed with the other old family heads. Several looked at the crowd, and all had to glance up at the dragon who was now blowing thick rings of mist into the air. Raine rolled her eyes.

"You're supposed to be intimidating. That's just showing off."

Puddle grinned. "You said yourself that we're putting on a show. These people love me."

She groaned. "Depth... your boy is impossible."

"I've never been prouder," came the rumbled reply.

The old man now moved forward and spoke with a clenched jaw.

"Though we have our doubts, we concede that this is indeed a dragon of the Winter realm. You must know that your dragon cannot serve two roles. You must also have a great champion of water. I see no other companions. Perhaps I'm standing on another one...?"

Raine caught the jab, but smiled a sweet grin at the old man as she flourished.

"Don't be silly... you're not standing on him." The woman finished her bow, blue-grey eyes looking back up with a twinkle. "I am!"

She bent her knees as the thundering crash came. The ice under her erupted in a cracking explosion. Depth had taken several hits to break the ice before. That wasn't a lack of power on his part, but an attempt to keep the woman held in his mouth from being tossed about. Now he crashed through the thick layer of ice as if it were wet parchment.

She landed on his massive head as Depth came up through the ice. He didn't stop with the head and neck. His powerful long tail flicked and his enormous body crashed out through the thick sheet of frozen water. Most of his girth was now on the icy shore.

He lowered his head down next to the council. Some guards moved to protect their charge; others fainted or froze. One threw down his sword and opted for an early retirement. The old man stood staring at the sea dragon. No one moved. No one except the young woman.

Raine hopped off the colossal head and landed next to the council. The guards no longer saw her as the biggest threat, and she moved freely. She leaned over and whispered in a conspiratorial tone, but the words were heard by everyone present.

"I hope he'll do. His older brother is more impressive, but we couldn't fit him into the loch."

Only Raine heard Depth's rumbling laugh.

***

Issabol stood over the portals. She had thought Claire mad when the young queen had come up with this plan.

On the table before her were two small squares. She had made many doorways to other worlds and had become so entwined with time and space that she might be effectively immortal. Mastering her craft had taken centuries and she'd felt there was nothing left for her to learn.

How wrong she'd been only confirmed her worry that long years had affected her thinking. She could do things no one else could, but she was trapped by her own lack of imagination.

Each of the squares was a masterpiece of her craft. The creation of the first had taken over a year, the second only a couple of months. If Gray hadn't convinced her to move the workshop into the world of faster time, she wouldn't have been able to have them done in time. All the planning and preparation would be for nothing if her task didn't prove successful.

On the wall stood another portal. Like most of the active portals that were down the hall in the hub, this one only allowed light to pass through. Only enough to see while in the shadows of a dim room; too much and it would appear to be a dark square for those near where it was located.

While the image was on the wall, the angle was straight down. It provided a view from above, the portal's existence further obstructed by the low hanging cloud hovering over the events taking place in front of the Black Citadel. Some of those watching with her had grown dizzy from the mixed messages of looking down and straight ahead at the same time. She had no such issues after thousands of years.

Her many greats niece, Claire, stood beside her. Beside the queen stood her advisor and adopted sister, Joobel. Gray stood behind them all, having no issues seeing over the shorter women. On the floor to their right was a simple portal, only three feet square. The swishing of a mangy warg tail could be heard, the hound ready to join the spectacle.

All were silent except for Joobel, who couldn't contain her emotions. The gnome laughed, clapped, and gasped as Raine put on the show they'd rehearsed for months.

The workshop was now attached to sleeping quarters and a large living space. Issabol had spent just over two years in the world of fast time with a few guests. Claire and Joobel still spent most of their days in Autumn. Gray was with them most of the time as well. Together they plotted a strategy to complete the trials he'd learned about from the griffin. Raine and Jack, along with two very unique dragons, had spent almost all of their time living with Issabol.

For the first few months, Raine had worked with the dragons on how to play the roles they would have, as well as on their skills with communication. Harvest and Bloom had each taken turns visiting through a more extensive portal that opened into the dragon sanctuary of Autumn.

They had helped each water drake learn how to fly and have more basic control. Depth had even come for a short period to teach the young dragons some of the old ways of power and skill.

The sea dragon had grown so attached to his protege that Issabol wondered if he might just call Puddle home. In the end, he allowed the young dragon his time to grow so that he might help in the battle to reclaim Winter.

Once the dragons had outgrown the help they needed from Raine, the Winter Queen had spent her days helping Jack recover from the frost fire and the efforts of relearning to walk and build his strength.

Issabol had been impressed by how hard Jack worked to regain his abilities and the attitude he had while doing so. Many would have cursed the world for the challenges of basically building a body from scratch. He did spend a short time each day in the central garden of the Blood Keep, drawing a store of power from the great realm spirit. That time was always spent with Joobel. The gnome seemed to always know when he was near.

All the time and work had come to this. The ancient girl knew the others were feeling useless at the moment, though it was Raine who'd pointed out that only Winter could involve themselves in the Bitter Challenge. Claire had agreed and made it an order.

It was essential to not be seen tampering with Winter politics. If the great families knew how much Autumn had done to put Raine on the throne, they might revolt out of principle. As it was, Raine had a long road to travel in getting Winter back in the hands of the sane.

Issabol made the final adjustments to the mechanisms that would either make all the difference or fail the world of Fairie. Her breathing began to grow faster, her stress level at a breaking point.

A hand rested on her shoulder. The aches and pains that had been plaguing her faded away. She took a slow breath as the calm voice came from behind her.

"We've done all we can. Now we must trust in our friends."

Issabol hoped the gnome was right.

***

The council was clearing away, along with the ornate honor guard that escorted them. The soldiers who'd been standing back began to move forward. Many eyed her with outright hatred and disdain.

Of those, most showed signs of madness. Those had spirits of water. The stronger the spirit drawing on the power of the realm, and the more often they drew it, the faster they were affected.

Raine thought of her mother, of how far gone the queen was months ago. All of the frost drakes were utterly insane now. River was evidence of that. Only Sleet was still somewhat protected from the madness, and that was with regular purification to keep the corruption at low levels.

Raine had known Myrin would be bad by now, but she wasn't ready for how far gone her sister was. Myrin was wearing armor that had been put on poorly. She almost seemed to stumble out from the guards that had been holding her back.

The moment the Bitter Challenge was issued, the woman was no longer queen until it was declared invalid or she slew the challenger. Nothing about her looked like a queen.

The parts of her robe visible under the armor were stained and wrinkled. Her ice-blue eyes were bloodshot and seemed to dart all over as if she could see monsters in every shadow. Long white hair, the color of Raine's own, was matted and greasy. A long line of drool ran down the corner of her mouth, freezing where it dripped onto her breastplate.

Raine almost wept for her. If there hadn't been so much at stake, she'd have run to her sister and tried to help.

Whatever had happened, she still held love for her sister. With both her mother and father gone, Myrin was all she had left. Raine had made new friends and allies, ones that supported her in more ways than her family ever had, but the burden of what must be done still weighed heavy on her conscience. She didn't want to kill her only sibling.

She took a deep breath as the woman stepped into the circle. Raine had grown during her efforts in the world of fast time. She was now slightly taller than Myrin, and would be about the same age now. This time she spoke only to her sister.

"Myrin... please don't make me do this. If you concede the match, I'll cleanse your spirit and give you a place in our kingdom. I don't want to fight you."

Raine might as well have been speaking to her coat. Myrin hissed at her, spittle flying out of her mouth. The woman was barely in control.

The old man raised a hand and started the fight.

"Begin!"

Cheers for both fighters rose from the crowd. Raine held up the scabbard in her left hand, sliding Caledfwlch out with her right. The blood-song filled her ears; her mind filled with battle and carnage.

It had taken Jack months to once again be her match. Then she'd begun her training. Every day for the past six months, at least as they'd experienced it, they had fought long and hard. In every moment Raine had swum against the current of the blood-song. Now she was in control, mostly.

Myrin rushed her at full speed. In her hand was the long sword her mother had once wielded. It, too, was a named blade. Frost-bite looked to be crafted out of pure ice. One cut from the blade would freeze all the blood in the victim's body. A tiny scratch was fatal.

The sword was only a hint shorter than her own. It had served her family for generations. A totem of the brutal rule her family had enjoyed, it was a deadly weapon wielded in a closed fist. It had taken many lives.

As the older sister charged, she swung down with the weapon of ice and death. Raine held her ground until the last second. Then she caught the blade with her own, spinning away as the flying end of the ice sword stuck into the frozen ground. The crowd grew silent.

The broken blade glistened as an omen of change. Myrin screamed and swung her shorter cutting edge at Raine's throat. The scabbard caught the attack and the sword Caledfwlch cut a thin line on Myrin's cheek.

Once Raine had feared this fight. Myrin had been a much better fighter as they were growing up. Her spirit power was one of the most potent offensive spells Winter knew. Raine had a spirit that was used to clean and help. In a fight, she had no spell, until now.

Against a person overflowing with corruption, Raine was a thing of nightmares. Myrin watched as Raine put a finger to the blood on her blade; the taint sizzled and steamed out of the crimson liquid.

The woman didn't understand that she was sick. From inside her insanity, Myrin thought everyone else had gone mad. The corruption inside recognized Raine, and Myrin lost control.

Raine had waited for this. There could be no question who the queen was. The body of Myrin shuddered as the tainted power in her veins took over. Her eyes went pure black. Those who could see what was happening began to murmur in fear.

The Black March had come to Winter. Raine smiled a vicious grin. She was the predator now.

"I'll be taking her back... just so you know. I'd suggest you run. Your kind won't survive this night."

The possessed woman screamed in a baleful howl of rage and hunger. As Myrin approached, she threw the shorter blade at Raine's head. The younger woman dodged, her reflexes taking over. The spin of the blade brought one edge against her cheek.

The magic of the blade attacked her. The scratch began to blacken and freeze. Then it stopped as the intrusive magic was purified from her blood.

Raine didn't have time to think about the close call as the blast of frost fire came directly at her. No one had ever survived a direct hit of the essence of cold, at least no one that this crowd knew about. Raine swept the sword in front of her and caught the spell on the flat of the blade.

Issabol had been the one to realize that the magic emanating from the thing had to do more than just make it cut through solid objects. The blade could cut through the weave of spirit that held a spell together.

To those in the crowd, it appeared as if Raine had just batted away the powerful attack. They saw this challenger shrug off two things everyone thought were always lethal. Unfortunately, the cut and the spell did one thing that Raine had been trying to avoid.

The blood-song blocked out all other sounds, its melody of destruction assaulting her control. Her arm moved as if it were no longer her own. Myrin ran at her, holding another blast of her tainted frost fire. Raine knocked the hand away with the scabbard.

Then Raine drove the ancient blade deep into the chest of the *former* Queen of Winter.

\*\*\*

Hurley stood next to the litter as the queen stepped into the circle. Part of him was worried about the fight, but he'd been assured the real battle would come later.

For weeks he had conspired, moving all the water spirit users into individual regiments in the military. The higher-ranking officers had been strategically removed or arranged to prevent them from issuing orders that would endanger the citizens.

Coburn Kenn had gotten a higher command after he'd delivered the fake head of Raine Anahita. They and others had made sure everything was carefully arranged for this night.

He exchanged nods with several who were in position. As Raine stepped into view, his heart sang with joy. Hope was here. She looked older and more confident, more than should have been possible in the two short months since she'd left. He watched as the fight roared on.

His heart dropped as the blade of Frostbite nicked the girl's cheek and he almost cheered when she fought on. He was dumbfounded that she seemingly soaked up the frost fire that was feared by all. Hurley began to weep as the sword entered the chest of Myrin. He'd never wanted to see her hurt.

Now he was glad they'd worked so hard to maintain control of the situation. He had succeeded in every single detail. At least he thought he had.

The false report of a Spring raid on the eastern border had a 93% chance of keeping all ten frost drakes away for the duration of the Bitter Challenge. Sometimes no matter the odds, the dice fall poorly.

Hurley hadn't considered that the corruption in the realm could call those drakes back sooner. As the sword slid effortlessly through the thick armor of Myrin, the screeching cry of several furious dragons rang across the dim sky. Hurley held up a red kerchief. It was done.

All he could hope for now was a moderate bloodbath.

***

Raine leaned over her sister. Myrin was pale and seemed to have trouble taking in a breath. The black of her eyes still stared at Raine and the thing inside Myrin tried to hiss. No sound came out.

The blood-song had thrust the sword at Myrin's heart, but Raine managed to steer it into a lung. She slid the sword out and stood to hold the weapon into the air.

The crowd roared, seemingly at her victory. Then she saw that the black of Myrin's eyes was spreading through the crowd, the soldiers, and even through some of the council members. Those who had corruption were being taken over. Swords began to draw and shouts rose up. Raine sent the command through her thoughts.

The mist gathered above began to descend toward the ground. Raine was out of sight now as she kneeled beside Myrin. No blood leaked from the wound; none coughed up from her short gasping breaths. Wedged in the gap between the woman's back and rear plate of her royal armor was a very unique scabbard. The injury wouldn't bleed as long as she was in contact with it.

Now Raine put a hand on each side of her sister's head. Once again, she used Purification, but not to poke and prod. She was bonded to a dragon of like power and kneeling amid the mist of the great Fluvial. Raine opened the floodgates of her spirit.

A wave of pure white energy hissed through the core of Myrin. The black of her eyes grew cloudy and they rolled up in her head. Her mouth let out a silent scream of pain and anger. Not Myrin's, but of the shadow that had claimed her.

Finally, when it was clear Raine couldn't be defeated, the corruption tried to crush the core of her sister. Raine was once again in a waiting room with her mother, the feel of her queen's life force being torn apart.

Raine screamed, "Not again!"

She pushed her power in between Myrin and the shadow, then spread all around it. Raine squeezed with her will and the last of the taint was burned away.

"Now, Depth!" came her dragon-speak.

The sea dragon let out a roar and his huge tail slammed down against the icy water of the Loch. Many in the crowd mistook it for an attack. In truth it was a signal.

A small portal of about three feet square opened and a small mangy warg trotted out. Raine slid the sword Caledfwlch into the scabbard that still rested with her sister. She also grabbed the shorter half of Frostbite's blade and set it on Myrin's chest as she moved her to the portal.

Gray's large hands grasped the arms of Myrin and pulled her through the door. Then as fast as it had opened, the portal shut once more. The mist began to clear.

The cries of ten frost drakes echoed in the distance.

# CHAPTER 15

R aine turned, her shorter sword catching a blade. The possessed honor guard shuddered as she pushed her power into the man's face. His eyes went milky and he screamed an inhuman cry of anguish.

She rolled to the side, dodging a spear thrust. All around, tainted soldiers were fighting any who weren't possessed. It seemed most were tasked with killing her, the one who could hurt the corruption inside. It was time to begin the real fight for Winter.

"Mist, we're ready. Remember everyone, try not to kill. These are victims, not enemies."

Raine had held back her own dragon. The original plan was to have the white drake serve the role of loyal dragon for the Bitter Challenge. In the end, Mist, who was no more built for combat than Bloom, was the most effective weapon against this enemy.

Out of the cloud that had formed over the battle, flew the huge cleansing dragon. She slammed down to the ground and launched a thick puff of purifying fog at the soldiers attacking Raine.

While her bond-mate needed time and concentration to take the corruption from a being, Mist could use the primary tactic of a Named dragon. Overwhelming force. The two men both cried out, the sheer strength of the magical fog dissolving the shadow from their spirits. There's no fighting against a tidal wave.

As Mist began to ready another blast of her power, a man slid down her neck and landed next to Raine. He wore only a pair of short trousers and a sleeveless tunic. His pale skin was covered in a light layer of frost, while his short hair was slicked back with a light blue sheen of ice.

A half-smile formed on the man's lean face as he walked to stand next to her. The mangy warg moved alongside him, tail wagging so hard it made his leg shake. He looked over the crowd and spoke with a calm voice that had deepened with the many months spent in the world of fast time.

"Well... you've quite the mess here."

Raine waved a hand. "On the contrary, this is all going according to plan."

Jack looked at the approaching frost drakes. If there was any residual fear from his near-death to frost fire, he showed no sign of it. His only reaction to the danger was a wide grin.

Raine knew it had been a while since he'd gotten to enjoy a good fight. Today he wasn't here as the Demon Prince of Autumn. No one could know the true identity of the man at her side. His face wasn't his own.

Jack had lost a battle, at least as far as he saw it. Instead of brooding or getting upset, he'd been determined. She knew he felt that better control of his power over water might have seen him unharmed. The man had mastered hot and cold as much as she had learned to control the cursed blade.

Although in Autumn this night had been planned two months ago, Jack had almost two years to prepare. He wouldn't use fire this night. For this battle he was a warrior of water and a champion of the Winter Queen. The drakes were going to make this enjoyable for him.

Jack lifted a frosted eyebrow. "Those weren't part of the plan if I recall."

Raine pouted, her blue-grey eyes narrowed; Hurley had told Claire they shouldn't be an issue. The woman sighed as she pulled on her power and held up the broken half of Frostbite.

"Are you saying you want to retreat?"

Jack smiled even wider. For only a moment, his eyes flashed in the yellow hue of his fire.

"Oh, I wouldn't miss this."

Then he was gone, his body older and stronger than he had been before the incident in the ice cave. The Queen of Winter was once again glad it hadn't been him she had to face this night. Raine's role in this battle had been a success. No one could question her rule.

Now the primary goal was dealing with the horde of possessed water users, including ten frost drakes and hundreds of armored soldiers. She waited for Mist to finish blowing a thick fog into a group of oncoming soldiers. Then she hopped up onto her dragon, pulled into the saddle, and put on her flight mask. Mist greeted her bond-mate with a thought.

"Glad you're well, little one. Shall we get started?"

Raine nodded. "I've no other plans."

The new Winter Queen leaned forward as her white dragon leaped into the sky.

***

Claire and Raine had worked out the plan with several contingencies. Jack knew that despite the ten furious frost drakes that would be there in seconds, there was a plan for them, too.

The biggest issue with a flock of insane frost drakes wouldn't be winning.

Depth alone would likely be able to handle them all. No, the problem was the collateral damage. One blast of frost fire into the crowd would easily kill dozens of people.

Mist was here with an extremely important role; she was the only one who could purify large groups and the drakes. Raine could do it, but not at the scale needed tonight. That left Depth, Maeve, Puddle, and maybe 'Frost Man?'

No, that was stupid. Jack had never come up with a good name.

Hundreds of soldiers were here and helping with the possessed, but they had little protection against Winter's own defenders. Jack was now running through the throngs of soldiers and bystanders, putting up walls as he went.

He formed a maze of ice all through the battlefield, separating corrupted troops from untainted citizens. He put up protective domes over the unarmed to shield them from attack.

Then Jack saw what they'd most feared: three possessed soldiers had overwhelmed a fourth. As the man was held down, one of his opponents leaned over him and a stream of black ooze dripped onto the man's face. He convulsed only twice before he stood and joined his new allies in spreading the corruption to another soldier.

In time they would be able to grow their numbers faster than Mist could cleanse them. Jack dashed to the four men and locked them to the ground with a thick layer of ice. He formed another dome over a group of ladies-in-waiting for one of the council members. Jack was going through power quickly, but this too was an issue Claire had planned for.

As he ran, a mangy warg worked beside him. His right hand settled on Maeve's scruffy head; he drew raw energy from the orb in her throat. Power flowed into him and he filled the stores of his core and both elemental power stones in his hands. Jack would need that energy.

The frost drakes had arrived.

***

Depth had always enjoyed being a dragon. He knew how dragons fought and how they would think. He very much wanted to save the drakes. There were too few dragons in this world as it was, and killing these would leave it even more empty.

The irony of the situation is that it was his job to keep them alive while still subduing them. As strong as he was, one Pressure blast would pulverize any drakes it hit and might kill those who were even remotely close. He'd have to simply distract his opponents.

His kind were beings of power and, like most of the dragons in Fairie, these were long ago bred for offense. They would converge on the most significant threats first, divide, and conquer. No one on the battlefield looked more threatening than the massive sea dragon.

Depth took no chances. The leviathan took a deep breath and let out a thunderous roar of challenge. If they'd questioned his power before, they had no doubts now. Of the ten frost drakes of Winter, seven chose to attack the enormous intruder.

Not one of these enemies was any match for him. His dimensions only hinted at his power. It only took about twenty years after his Naming for him to reach this size. He'd had many centuries to build the spirit of water that sustained him. In a way, that power made this more difficult.

As they came at him, Depth backed into the water. He had wanted them to see his vast bulk, but now the exposure of so much of his body would make him easy to hit. Any drake that missed a target his size couldn't hit water if they fell from a boat. Now only the arch of his neck and the top of his back were exposed. The rest was shielded by the dark water of Loch Mozeg.

The assault began with multiple streams of frost fire. He weaved through the assault as best he could, but still suffered several hits. The intense cold hurt, but his power and the water worked to counteract the effects even as he was blasted.

If the drakes hadn't stayed with him as he went into the water, he'd have had a hard time fighting back at all. He couldn't fly and was slow and clumsy on land. They did follow, though, and Depth used the same method of attack every child in a bathtub would. He splashed.

Usually, a spray of water would only annoy a frost drake. After all, they were creatures of the water realm. It was a different story when those splashes could knock down the thick walls of the Black Citadel.

A flipper swung and a column of dense water hit a drake head-on. The blast of frost fire managed to freeze some of the liquid just before it hit him, only making the impact more devastating. Another came at him from behind, readying an attack on his unprotected back, only to slam into a wall of dark water lifted by his powerful tail.

Once the drakes entered the loch, Depth made sure they weren't able to crawl out. Less than a minute after the fight had started, only two of the drakes remained in the air. They seemed to realize they were outclassed and moved to shore to seek easier prey.

Depth let them go, keeping the five he'd doused stuck help-lessly trying to swim. His wide smile of triangle teeth was one of satisfaction as he spoke to his great spirit.

"You said I could only hold three."

Fluvial's voice trickled into his mind. "I admit, you impress. Try not to squish my little queen, though."

Depth continued to dunk and splash the five trapped in the dark water. Every time one thought it was going to reach the edge of the ice or the rocky shore, he pulled them back into the dark waters. He was saving their lives with his efforts.

The drakes trying frantically to swim away admittedly didn't see it that way.

\*\*\*

Maeve ran alongside Her Boy. The happy hound knew there was a fight going on, but she had her pack. She would die to protect Her Boy and the other members of her family if needed.

There were many needing help right now, but the hound only had eyes for the large crystal blue dragon that had spotted Jack putting ice walls everywhere.

Maeve had seen one of these hurt her boy, almost kill him, and make him slow for centuries... or minutes. Dogs have a weak concept of time. Either way it wasn't going to happen again.

As the large creature picked out the man who was rapidly altering the field of battle, it began a dive to gather power for the frost fire that would stop him. It had dismissed the warg. The brutish creatures were of some concern in a large pack, but this one was alone and looked like it hadn't eaten in weeks.

Maeve had started gathering mass the moment she saw the drake. Usually, she wouldn't attack unless given the signal. Good girl Maeve got treats. At this moment, Maeve was in a rare state of mind that didn't care about treats. She would protect her boy. Also, maybe still get treats.

The drake had just begun to release the deadly blast of cold flame when a stone hound that was almost twice its size slammed into its side. The icy rock she'd taken to increase her mass made her look like a true horror of Winter. Maeve saw Jack give her the signal to hold and, though she wanted to kill the dragon, she obeyed.

Jack began to form the prison of ice that would trap the drake. Thick bands of water formed as he summoned the power through the stone in his left hand. Her Boy took all the heat from the water and clear ice remained.

It only took a few seconds to imprison the enemy. As Maeve lifted her massive stone head, the final band locked the drake's mouth shut. No more frost fire would pass its jaws until it had been freed.

Maeve looked up to see another drake coming to help its companion. Jack was already moving. His giant stone hound followed.

A huge tail of earth and rock wagged as she aimed her leap.

***

Puddle was a unique being. Many spirit powers had been used to hatch dragons on various worlds. Depth had explained that there was a time in his home world when he'd seen a dragon of similar form and power to Mist.

Though Bloom was an oddity as well, she had a basic structure and function in common with both death and frost drakes. Those were also quite common in other worlds. A strong, agile dragon with an excellent offensive breath was a common deterrent and protection for the realms that sustained them.

Unlike other dragons, Puddle had been born of a scarce type of water spirit that didn't exist in this world, though that might not always be the case. On top of that, he'd gotten a taste of another spirit when the first had run out. Pressure.

The combination allowed him to manipulate his form into any stage and form of water. In truth, had he not been Named it might have kept him from growing. The power required to move quickly from snow to steam was immense.

During his long hours of training, Depth had shared his own energy with his bonded disciple in the world of fast time. Magic was weaker there and his training used a good deal of it.

He thought of it as training, but in truth it was trial and error, with the sea dragon trying to guess what he was doing wrong. Fortunately, the power itself guided him in many ways.

Had he fed exclusively on the spirit of Pressure that Depth had offered, he'd have genuinely been a dangerous foe. Now he was still quite lethal, but his defensive capabilities were terrific. How do you stab flowing water? How do you attack snow? What defense do you have against the steam roasting you inside your armor?

Of all the opponents Puddle could face, a drake of water with no other weapon than a cold burp was laughable. When his mentor had called seven of the drakes, he'd almost been disappointed. His own roar of challenge was able to attract two of them, and they flanked him from either side.

Twin spouts of frost fire streamed at him. They flowed through a cloud of thick fog that phased into a ball of ice before crashing into the closest drake.

The impact stunned the dragon, and as it began to fall, a tail of water wrapped around its neck as a stream of Puddle's mass shot out and grabbed the other. The two drakes were pulled together by the larger fluid form. The water constricted as they collided. The whole mass of the three dragons slammed into the frozen earth. Puddle held them with a force that allowed them just enough room to breathe, but much less than would be required for frost fire.

His head reformed and looked out at Mist as she blew purifying fog onto a drake that was frozen to the ground. Raine kept watch over the skies around them. That one plus his two made three. Depth's words came into his mind.

"I have five of our enemy locked down; two are coming your way. They seem to have decided I was too much dragon!"

Puddle looked over to see Maeve pouncing one of the drakes. His azure eyes scanned the sky and he felt ice run through his spine.

The remaining drake was diving straight for his sister. Mist was occupied with purifying the dragon she was standing over and Raine hadn't seen the attacker yet. Puddle sent the message to his brood-mate.

"Mist, above you!"

The white dragon looked up just in time to sidestep a blast of cold flame. The ground crackled and popped where she'd stood an instant before. All the defenders were either dealing with other drakes or too far away. Some of the possessed soldiers were gathering around Mist. Puddle was tangled with the two dragons still wrapped in his watery grip.

Claire had made it clear that once Mist had revealed her power, she'd become the primary target for the enemy. Now Puddle knew the Autumn Queen was right. The drake landed hard only a few feet away from Mist.

His sibling had already gathered her power, but if Mist had to trade blows, the frost fire would likely damage her enough that she wouldn't be able to fly. She'd quickly be overrun by the possessed soldiers.

Puddle hadn't practiced this technique much, but whatever happened this night, he wouldn't see his only sister die. He gathered his essence, forming a ball of mist. He applied pressure to the gas, and it shrank to a shot of dense water.

The water shifted to ice and then he released the pressure on only one side. The explosion launched the compact half ball of ice at astounding speed. His aim was a bit off. His jaw clenched as he hoped it was enough.

"Be careful, sister."

\*\*\*

Raine heard the words Puddle sent to Mist and her dragon acted before she could even register them. Mist pushed hard to her left and the blast hit the ground harmlessly where they'd been only moments before. She turned as the frost drake landed atop the bitterly cold ground, eyes solid black.

Raine felt the words leave her lips in a whisper.

"Oh Brook, what has become of you?"

Brook was a drake favored by her family. Myrin had often spent time with her. Now the dragon's eyes were like a new moon sky.

The frost drake had flecks of icy froth at the corners of her mouth and was breathing hard. Spots of slick ice were cracking along one side of her jaw. Depth had lost control of a couple of the drakes over the loch. She was one of those.

Raine could already feel the power building in her bond-mate. Mist meant to cleanse this drake. The Winter Queen knew there wouldn't be time. The next blast of frost fire wouldn't miss at this distance.

Soldiers were gathering around them. Mist needed to get into the air soon, or they would be overrun by sheer numbers. They wouldn't survive this.

Just as the blast was about to release, the possessed drake Brook shuddered to one side, and her left front leg gave out. A small ball of ice exploded into the joint. The pain and shock caused a moment's gasp. The blast would have still come a couple seconds later, but Mist needed only one.

The cleansing cloud launched right into the frost drake's face. Brook's eyes went milky and she hacked for a moment before the black ooze began to leak from her nose. Brook slumped onto the other drake that Mist had cleansed, the two of them in a heap.

Raine parried a thrust from a climbing soldier. "Mist! To the sky!"

The white dragon didn't hesitate or even look to see the threat. Powerful snowy wings flapped once as her rear legs pushed out. They were in the air. Two soldiers jumped to grab on and they too were lifted up.

Both men had weapons, but it was all they could do to keep from falling. Raine pointed to the drakes Puddle had locked in place.

"Land there, we need Puddle free!"

Mist landed hard, sliding to a stop. Raine jumped off to deal with the stowaways. She parried the attack of the closest possessed soldier while the other seemed to be stabbing Mist in the leg with a bronze sword.

"Don't worry, my queen. It will be hours before he draws blood."

Raine ignored him, parrying a spear swing with the broken Frostbite. She rolled in close, a move Jack had used on her so many times. She grabbed the man by the throat and poured a wave of Purification into his core. His inky eyes rolled back and went milky as the man collapsed, retching thick ooze on the ground.

Mist poured the fog of her cleansing breath onto the two drakes Puddle held as Raine looked up to see Jack running toward her. They were near where the fight with Myrin had taken place only minutes before.

Jack looked ragged, his clothes torn. Half his tunic was missing and he had scrapes and bruises all down one side. She'd never seen him happier. He looked up and gave her half a smile.

"The rest of the drakes are either iced to the ground or in the loch with Depth. Puddle can fish them out and Mist can cleanse them. It's time to play our final card."

Raine nodded and had Depth slap his tail down one more time. The blast of water sent droplets flying all over the battlefield. Before the signal could trigger the secret weapon, Raine saw a possibility they hadn't planned for.

Mist had been pouring her cleansing power into both those of the water aspect and the drakes. Each time there was an expulsion of black ooze. Raine had thought it was the beaten corruption leaving the body.

Now she realized that it had only retreated from a husk it could no longer inhabit. In the clearing, the ooze was gathering, slowly forming into a shape resembling a man. The form seemed to harden, creating fine details. Then, to her shock, it looked right at her and spoke.

"This one must not stand in our way. This one must die."

Raine could see that most of the fighting had halted. Most of the soldiers who had clashed against the corrupting influence now watched as the true Bitter Challenge began. Jack put a hand on her shoulder.

"This is your fight. Against this enemy, no one is as powerful as you."

She felt him draw from her power. Jack pulled it into an orb in each of his hands. He mixed her energy with a stream of water to form weapons. One hand held a short sword, the other a long dagger. He handed them to her and began the work only he could do.

In the ground near their feet appeared two portals. Both were dark blue, but one had the sheen of crystal and the other was dark and splotched with greasy blackness. She recognized them. Each opened to the center of the heart-dew of a great water spirit.

The bedrock of a realm was its storehouse of energy, shared to maintain the balance of all who stood on it. Mist finished working on the other drakes that Puddle had pulled in and stood over Jack. The dragon of flowing water nodded to her as he moved to take his place to guard the prince in his vital task.

The shadow let out a keeling screech as it realized what the prince was doing. Jack put a hand in each portal, one onto the heart of Winter's power and the other to the core of Fluvial. He began to draw the corrupted energy.

The prince was able to pull evil intent out of magic, but this wasn't intent; it was not just raw power. This was manifest destruction, hunger made real. It wasn't something Jack could cleanse and he needed to feed it into Fluvial's core clean. Mist had drawn her own power and began to release it slowly.

Dragon breath was a blast of power by default. It had taken weeks of study with Depth for her to learn how to maintain a steady flow of Purification. It was what Jack would need for this task.

The stream of fog was lean and concentrated, flowing right onto Jack's neck and back. As he pulled the power from the corrupted great spirit of Winter, the weave of Mist's Purification was absorbed into him and used to wash the energy on its way to Fluvial.

Raine had no idea how much energy Fluvial had left. She lived on borrowed power in this land. Already she could feel an increase in her own energy. As the shadow rushed Jack, it wasn't Puddle who intercepted him, but Winter's Queen.

She lashed out with her longer blade and the creature howled. The edge of purifying ice cut into his form. Foaming, hissing, damaged ooze dripped from the wound. It turned on her and attacked, her own weapons a blur before her. There was no way to know how long Jack would take.

Before, a smaller amount had taken him nearly half an hour, but he had to convert the energy's aspect from change to water. This needed to be cleansed, but he had Mist for that. However long it took, the prince couldn't stop until the task was complete. She would give him that time.

Raine dodged and countered the man of shadow several times. Each hit left a foaming mass of ooze. Given time, the damaged slime would be expelled and the thing would be whole once again.

Again and again she hurt the creature. Her form was refined and the weapons made from her own power served her well. As Raine fought, she began to focus more of her spirit into each blade to keep the potency high.

The entity was merely a brute, caring only about stopping the prince. It could feel the power being stolen and reacted as if being bled of its life force. Raine made sure turning its back on her was too expensive, ripping and tearing every time it did so.

Then it seemed to shift the focus to her. The queen realized as she fought on that it wasn't getting weaker, but stronger. Though it lost mass every time it expelled the damaged part of itself, it was still getting larger. Her focus had been so intent on her opponent that she hadn't realized it never stopped forming.

Tendrils of the ooze were moving on the ground even now, leading to the feet of the shadow thing. She fought on, desperately trying to think her way out of the situation while fighting an ever-stronger opponent. How much of the ooze had been expelled?

The drake Brook had seemed to wretch up buckets of the stuff. There were ten drakes and hundreds of people. The part in front of her could only be a small part of all that was out there.

Her heart sank as she slashed with her dagger and then stabbed and twisted with her sword. Despite her accuracy, the mass was now well over a head taller than her. The shadow expelled the damaged tissue and shuddered.

To Raine's horror, the form split into two beings, each as large as the one she'd started with. They both spoke to her as if vessels for a voice coming from somewhere else.

"This one can hurt us. This one must die."

# CHAPTER 16

Gray could feel his stomach twisting into knots. He'd carried Myrin immediately to Bloom, leaving the piece of Frostbite behind but keeping Caledfwlch in its sheath. The scabbard was the only thing keeping this woman alive.

Myrin hadn't been able to speak the whole time he'd carried her. Once the dragon had hit her with a blast of green-tinged fog, she'd started to cough and looked up at him in panicked anger.

"What do you think you're doing laying hands on a queen? I'll have you flogged! Guards, seize him!"

Gray looked around, annoyed that he was standing with this spoiled wretch while her sister fought for Winter. He knew she'd been consumed by the corruption, but he was still angry that he wasn't fighting alongside his friends. The young woman then seemed to notice she was outside in a strange place. Dark blue eyes stared daggers into him.

"You dare to kidnap a royal daughter of Winter? You'll die for your insolence!"

She raised a hand, building up Frost Fire. Gray didn't have the patience for it. Dense air wrapped around her wrists and pulled them behind her back. He reached over and took the scabbard that was still touching the skin of her back.

He started to ask Bloom to watch over her, but the dragon was linked with Joobel, her eyes glassy as she watched the battle through her bond-mate's eyes. Harvest too was in a trance, though all knew that the death drake's guard was never too far down.

Gray decided to show the annoying woman what her selfishness had gained. The distance to reach Bloom was a decent walk and some time had passed since he'd left to carry Myrin to the healing drake. Gray walked back through the halls of the Keep with a magically shackled woman, who it must be said wasn't smelling great right then.

Myrin still wore the stained gown under the carelessly donned armor. Her hair was greasy, and the woman looked like she hadn't had a good meal or full night's sleep in weeks. Her bloodshot eyes still darted around, but now out of confusion instead of madness.

Guards stopped to stare as he walked through, but none made a move to stop him. Whether it was fear of him, or respect of Claire's orders, he neither knew nor cared. In a few minutes, he stepped back into the workshop. Upon the wall was the viewing portal.

The figures below moved as if in thick syrup, time moving at only a fraction of what they experienced. Myrin stared in awe at the scene below.

Jack was working to advance the energy from Winter's corrupted great spirit to Fluvial. Mist was giving a stream of purification to him to counter the tainted spirit of the core. Puddle was standing guard over them both, though Gray could see his agitation at letting someone else do the fighting. Depth was channeling his power through Fluvial into Mist, to keep the white drake's power stable.

Looking over the scene, he could see many soldiers still fighting, but now most were in combat with some kind of shadows. In the center of it all was Raine.

His friend was standing alone, fighting two of the black forms. Just up the hill, four more were forming. She was going to be overrun. Gray turned to the others.

"I need to go. Now!"

Myrin seemed to realize that this was all taking place in front of her home. She failed to read the room, shock evident in her voice.

"Raine is alive!"

Gray could have slapped the woman. It would've been a first for him, and he'd have beat himself up for it later. Joobel had no such concerns. It wasn't a first for her and she probably wouldn't even remember having done it. The clap of gnome hand to royal cheek brought silence to the room.

Joobel was crying. So were Claire and Issabol. All had played a role in the night's success or failure. Standing by was taking its toll on all of them. The gnome was just the one the most afraid.

Her fear and helplessness had found a target in the selfish Winter royal. Joobel's voice now high and angry, she delivered the criticism the wretched woman so desperately needed to hear.

"Raine is alive because you failed to kill her! She's been pushing herself for years to try to save the kingdom you'd let rot. Can you not see she's outnumbered and overwhelmed?"

Joobel stomped a foot, her tears dripping to the floor.

"We couldn't go to help because of you, because Winter would reject her if someone else helped. You tried to kill her! You got Jack hurt, and now you have the nerve to act like her being alive is some insult to...."

Joobel had been so fired up, she hadn't seen the expression on Myrin's face. The former queen was shocked, that was true, but she was also crying. Gray still didn't know how much she could remember, but Myrin had thought her sister dead. She was now dealing with the revelation that Raine lived.

Myrin put a hand to her chest. "I thought... I'd killed her. I just knew once I was a queen, I could fix everything. I was so angry... always so angry. The people loved her, I was so jealous. I wanted them to see me that way. I'd do anything to help Winter."

Gray latched onto that. He looked down at the sword in his hand. He looked at Raine, slowly fighting off two shadows, and being stalked by four more. Then he looked back to Myrin, his dark eyes narrowing as an idea formed.

"Anything?"

\*\*\*

Raine was failing. Twice now, she'd taken hits from the shadows. They'd stabbed with some sort of spear and pushed the corruption inside of her. Her power was fighting it off quickly, but she couldn't keep this up much longer.

The shadow on her left struck but left an opening as she blocked. She countered with an upward flick and tore a gash up its side. The other lashed out and she parried it with her sword's momentum.

The other limb hit her in the stomach. More of the ooze sank in and her head swam. She could quickly cleanse any one hit, but the constant attacks and her near-empty core were showing. She fell to one knee as each opponent readied another shadow spear.

They didn't get to use them. One moment there were two shadows, dripping black ooze. A blur moved past and slime flew in all directions. Maeve, currently the size of a large horse, had saved her.

The hound was wearing a larger version of the warg disguise and would probably get a treat for doing so. Raine was growing fond of the strange creature who rarely left Jack's side. The queen was worried for her, though.

The creatures seemed to learn that Raine was immune to their form. Any time one of them had touched her, she'd pushed out with her power and they'd burned. At least, that's the word she used in her mind.

Only she and Mist had that advantage. Depth was just extremely powerful and could counter through sheer supremacy. All others were vulnerable.

Maeve was ripping and snarling at the ooze, but though she bit and tore the ground where it landed, the hound couldn't hurt it. Now it began to flow all around her, pushing into her ears and nose. A great gout of it went into her mouth. Raine gasped in horror as... Maeve seemed super annoyed.

Her great stone head shook and she rolled around. Then she sneezed and barked. Maeve couldn't hurt the ooze, but neither could it hurt her. The information was filed away as Raine looked up to see four more of the shadows approaching.

She'd burned through most of the corruption she had been hit with, but was still exhausted. Raine drew a steady flow of power from the jewel in her breastbone, Fluvial's energy a constant stream into her core.

Raine cleared her head. The odds of holding out against two were low; six was certainly too much. Then a crossbow bolt struck one shadow in the head. It turned to see a large man in ornate armor bearing down on it with a sword. The blade caught it in the shoulder and sliced down into the lower abdomen. He slid out the blade and stepped back, drawing its attention.

Raine knew the man. He was a Commander in the Winter army. Something... Kenn. She had to let the thought go as the three remaining shadows closed on her. The voice from over her shoulder was the last she'd thought she would hear this night.

"Did you save us any?"

Raine turned to see her sister standing with Gray. At least she thought it was Gray. The large figure was wearing a flight mask. Her sister was holding the sword Caledfwlch in its sheath. Myrin held out the sword.

Her sister forced a smile. "Care to trade?"

Raine looked from Caledfwlch to her sister, then to the approaching shadow. She ran her power into the blades to top them off and then took the scabbard. Myrin whipped her new sword in a long arch and readied her forms.

"This isn't over, sister. You and I still have business to discuss."

Raine winced, then looked over to the large man. She smiled and pushed her hair behind her ear.

"I thought we said this had to be Winter's fight."

The figure merely shrugged. "I'm told the aspect of air is welcome in Winter."

The queen wanted to explore the gesture, but Gray had pulled up a semi-circle of opaque air behind them to let them fight in one direction. Raine once more put her hand on the hilt of the humming blade. The blood-song filled her ears.

Raine had spent most of her time wielding the blade holding back, spending most of her effort controlling the lust for battle. She'd had to if there was to be any chance of sparing her sister's life. Now she fought an enemy that she had no intention of sparing.

The shadows were on them. Gray spent most of his time supporting the two women. He stabbed with a blade of air a few times, but it did little more than slow them down.

Soon the three fell into a rhythm. Both women had learned from the same teachers and the forms were similar enough that soon they were in sync. Gray used small quick shields to absorb the spears of corruption, tossing the dense air away before his own power was tainted.

With the boost to defense, the two women were able to work much more aggressively. Raine learned in moments that Caledfwlch had an even better effect than the swords with her power blended into them. The blade seemed to cut the bonds animating the ooze.

Even with all of them working together, even with all the uncorrupted soldiers of Winter's army, and the newly cleansed joining the fight, the ooze was gaining ground. Wherever a spear of the slime hit, a fighter fell and rose to join the corrupted. Raine heard the words coming from behind her.

"It's like fighting zombies; the fallen become more soldiers for the other side," Gray said, voice quavering.

Time passed. More and more fell. The shields Gray used were barely fast enough to stop the attacks coming at the women. More shadows formed and joined the fight against them. There were too many!

Perhaps if they'd gotten there a week before, or even a day, things would be different. The Black March had just gained too much ground. It was so effective at getting around her Purification.

Suddenly, all grew silent.

Raine heard Mist roar behind her and Jack approached to stand at her side. His words confused her for a moment. In his hand, he held a small blue orb of dense water energy. It moved on its own, like a snake coiled into a ball.

Jack's face was a mask of grief. "The old great spirit was too far gone; her mind was slipping. Her last wish was for the rightful queen to have this. Do you accept this power?"

Raine didn't realize what he meant at first. Her eyes grew wide; what he held in his hand was a core spirit. Once a great spirit of Winter, now no more powerful than herself or Myrin. She didn't know what this spirit was. To ascend to become a great spirit, one need only have attained a certain level of skill and power. It took countless lifetimes to gather so much.

Then she looked out to the oozing shadows that were attacking her people. She didn't weep or run.

There was no more plotting and trying to gather allies. Power was something she desperately needed. Something her kingdom needed. She wouldn't turn it down when offered.

Raine nodded, her face solemn. "I accept."

The prince didn't hesitate further. He pulled her close and slammed his palm just below her neck. The power pushed into her core.

The spirit was powerful but exhausted, like an old stag who had ruled the forest for his time. It began to stretch, prodding her own spirit, as if wary of another power being so close. Raine accepted it.

Her own spirit swirled around this one and then she felt the power of Flood. She faintly remembered having the power as a young girl. She'd used this ability to save a village from drought and helped to drive away an invading army.

The memories of that woman were fading, but now Raine's body remembered how to wield the skill. Her core remembered how to command the water in the ground, the air, and, in this case, the massive contents of Loch Mozeg sitting only twenty paces away.

Not the meager power of a basic water spirit, but the supremacy of its namesake. Flood. This spirit wanted to fight back.

Mist was free of her task. Puddle no longer needed to guard Jack in his duty and Depth was once again free to help in the fight. Winter had a new great spirit and she'd held off this corruption once before. Raine's eyes began to emit a pale blue light as she held out a hand to the water behind her.

A stream of liquid came to her as if it were a trained serpent. As it touched her hand, she infused her other power. The water wasn't just crystal clear and clean, it carried the properties of Purification. She launched the stream high into the air, dumping in her power as she went.

All around, the fighting soldiers were hit with the cleansing rain. Its thick drops of water glowed a pale white in the dusk of a Winter day. Then came the screams.

Some were the screams of men; their skin hissed and burned as the cleansing rain tore the ooze from them. Others were the inhuman screams of the shadows. It sounded almost sweet.

The foam that once formed when Raine scored a hit with her sword now appeared everywhere a drop landed. The young queen began to stumble, but then she felt energy flow into her. Jack had one hand on her neck, feeding her the gifted power of the water realm fast enough it burned within the spirit paths of her body. She'd have all she needed.

The shadows gathered all the ooze the soldiers were expelling. All at once, the inky forms began to move together; the mass merged and shifted. After only moments it was clear what was forming. A huge black dragon.

It was larger than the flying dragons that stood with Raine and her party. Other than eyes that were as black as the rest of the form, it had an uncanny resemblance to Harvest. The dragon reared back and opened its mouth as if to roar, but all that came out was a keeling whine.

It was looking straight at Raine. The massive form took two huge steps and leaped at her. She lowered the stream of water to hit the approaching form. The mass foamed and hissed, but it was too big to stop outright. For an instant it seemed all was lost.

A tidal wave of sapphire hit the ebony form.

\*\*\*

Depth's disciple was a fun-loving sort. He'd formed a rather odd bond with a dark-skinned man named Gray. The man had come to him when he was only a couple of months old. The human was carrying a stack of parchment that listed off several ideas to help the strange drake best utilize his unique form.

Puddle's abilities fascinated the man. The shot of ice that helped save Mist had been Gray's idea, as had the snow that could scout for the group, and switching to ice mid-air to make a solid impact.

These were all effective and quite fun for Puddle. He hadn't used half the tricks they'd worked out, but there was one he had been looking forward to.

As soon as Jack had finished, Puddle asked his sister for a bit of her power. Mist let loose a vast cloud of the cleansing fog and Puddle whipped his form into vapor, incorporating the energy into himself. As he landed in his solid form, he leaped forward to see the black thing that was no dragon. This corrupt imposter was attacking his family.

Many dragons fought with overwhelming power and ferocity. Had he done so, he would've been formidable. The man had taught him that a little power can do amazing things if applied in the right way. Puddle knew that a lot of power used in the right way was even better, and often entertaining.

As his bulk slammed into the ooze, he didn't take on the form of ice, or mist. He molded himself into a bubble of dense water that was infused with Mist's spirit. Puddle hadn't gotten much of Depth's spirit in the hatching. He couldn't breathe a fog of devastating pressure. There was only one real way he could use the spirit of the old sea dragon.

His water wrapped around the dragon-shaped ooze. As soon as the dense liquid had fully encased it, the bubble constricted. Grey foam hissed and passed through the dark blue shell of water.

The ooze tried to do the same, but Puddle wouldn't allow it. All night long, the strange drake had held back, hoping the shadows would gather. If the ooze had dispersed, they'd have had no chance of getting all of it. Now he had the enemy in his grasp.

The ooze fought back. Tiny spears shot out of all sides of the corruption. Those attacks drained his sister's power from him, but he continued his assault. The ooze was packed into a tighter and tighter sphere.

The power of Mist protected him for crucial seconds, but the mass of dark power soon overwhelmed the energy she'd gifted him. The tainted spirit began to infest his own. He didn't let up, even when he felt his mind starting to slip.

Then he felt new sources of power infuse him. Jack was powering Raine, who poured her Purification into him. A great blast of identical magic came through the white breath of Mist. Maeve barked and ran in small circles in case that was useful somehow. It wasn't, but her enthusiasm was always uplifting.

His form was now poison to the ooze. It turned in on itself, shielding a core of corruption with the refuse of the purified layers of mass. It was well-protected inside, shielded from his assault.

Then Depth finally waddled to him, but not to provide the Purification like the others. His mentor's gift of power fed the

Pressure he was already putting on the ooze. The black sphere got smaller and smaller.

Layers of foaming black began to filter through Puddle's bubble of force. Finally, the core of the sphere gave out, the last of the ooze crushed and cleansed by pure overwhelming force.

Raine sighed, a wide smile spreading across her face. Gray groaned, the sound clear even through the mask. The big man found everyone looking at him in surprise.

He merely shrugged. "I wanted to get a sample. We could test it and find more ways to fight it."

Jack stopped petting his mangy warg and reached into a pocket, pulling out a large vial. Instead of glass, it was made of a light purple crystal. Clearly Issabol had made it. The prince handed the flask to Gray.

"Claire said you'd want this. I took it straight from the source while I was moving energy."

Gray clapped the prince on the back as he pocketed his prize.

***

Raine could hardly believe they'd done it. Her land was saved, at least for now. She was still shaking from weariness and adrenaline as Myrin walked to stand next to her. The woman looked sad and exhausted; her words quavered.

"I guess you're the queen now."

Raine narrowed her eyes at the sister she still loved, but couldn't trust. She pushed her hair behind one ear as her jaw clenched.

"It was Mom's decision. I'll not back down."

Myrin shook her head. Looking down, she seemed to notice her filthy clothes for the first time.

"You won't have to. I thought I was worthy, that I could fix everything. I'm sorry, Raine. I am so sorry. I... I couldn't control... I failed Winter."

Raine just nodded. Myrin's selfish attitude had cost lives. The corruption wasn't her fault, but her actions had made it so much harder to fight.

"I forgive you. But I'll not give back the throne."

Now it was Myrin's turn to nod. She wiped a tear from her pale cheek.

"You shouldn't. You'll be the best queen this land has ever seen. Many will fight you, though. As long as there's another heir, Winter will have no peace. You're the queen Winter needs." She gave a sad smile. "Perhaps I was what it deserved."

Raine was surprised to hear the words, truly grateful for the help in battle, and glad her sister lived. But Myrin wasn't done.

"You're not queen yet though, sister. We stand on the field of battle and my spirit remains."

Raine almost took a fighting pose, but Myrin only hugged her little sister tight. Spirits, the woman really needed a bath. Myrin's next words were only a whisper.

*"Maiden becomes mother, as mother becomes crone.*
*I bequeath you my burden and my heart.*
*May you protect your protector, and provide for your provider.*
*Until the circle is complete."*

Caught so off-guard, Raine didn't realize what was being said until her sister had finished. Myrin kissed Raine on the cheek, then collapsed to the ground. The spirit that held her sister's life force flowed into Raine.

Myrin lay gasping on the frozen dirt.

\*\*\*

Jack had channeled power into Raine and still stood close as Myrin moved to speak to her. He heard those softly whispered words. He hadn't been good at paying attention when his tutors instructed him in the old traditions and the magic that held them. The only reason he knew those words was because Claire had explained to him how his own mother had died. Jack had the words etched on his heart. Hearing them brought back old pain.

How he wished there had been something he could have done for his mother. In that land, only a spirit of change could have saved her, the area so infused with miasma that it was the only way a person could breathe.

Myrin wasn't his favorite person, but she'd risked her life in the fight and now had given that same life to secure the throne for her sister.

She'd sacrificed herself to ensure peace for her kingdom. It was out of character for the selfish woman. Perhaps she'd grown; maybe she deserved another chance.

The only way to save someone who had no spirit was to replace it. That was usually not an option, as getting a new spirit would require taking someone's life. You'd just be trading one for another. Jack almost considered taking one of Raine's spirits.

Myrin was right, though; as long as she held the aspect of water, she was a candidate for the throne. Normally it wouldn't matter, but the accusations against Raine and the disarray in the kingdom would make things complicated.

The families of Winter would try to put a puppet in control, and those who respected the law would fight back. It would mean a civil war. He knew well that many would come to hate Raine and her future edicts in the coming months.

There was one being present with a spirit that really had no purpose. Before Myrin finished speaking, he put his hand on Maeve's head and searched for the spirit of earth he'd put there years earlier. It was nestled deep inside the orb that stored Maeve's extra energy.

The magic brought back memories of the fat man who'd tried to kill him. Anwir's spirit had a taste like bitter metal. Jack pulled the power into a ball in his hand. If he had to handle these things anymore, he was going to learn to juggle them.

As Myrin fell to the ground, Jack caught a glimpse of the horror on Raine's face before he slammed his palm to Myrin's chest, just below the base of her neck.

The prince held the contact as he pushed the power into her core, making sure it settled inside and kept her life flowing. It took several seconds, but both the spirit and her core were desperate for connection. He only needed to bring them together.

Myrin gasped once without getting a breath, then she inhaled loudly. She brought in as much air as she could. Her pale face began to return to normal, as if she'd been underwater longer than was safe.

Jack moved as Raine pounced on her older sister. They both hugged and cried. Myrin got slapped again but there was love in the gesture. Jack let them have a moment.

The prince looked up to see a Commander of Winter's army was approaching, no doubt to request instructions from the new queen. Jack gave the man a half-smile as he winked with a bright yellow eye. Suddenly the man seemed to have urgent business elsewhere. The prince deserved a little fun.

No one would believe the guy anyway.

# CHAPTER 17

G ray still wasn't sure how he'd ended up in charge of organizing the relocation of the trolls. He could've sworn this whole thing had been entirely Joobel's idea. If not for the help that Norim had provided with forming lines and keeping records of everyone, he'd have long since given up and retreated.

The Stone Spear tribe had been somewhere around three hundred people if he wasn't mistaken. That was around how many he'd seen in the time he'd spent there. As it happens, the tribe was spread out across a large portion of the southern half of the Mountain Wyld.

Now he looked upon thousands of tall, lean trolls. Bright paint stood out on the dark green skin of the many individuals that would soon pass into the open fields of northwestern Autumn.

It wasn't just the trolls. Family groups of brownies and scattered sprites, as well as a small group of pixies, were ready with signed copies of Joobel's immigration treaty. Some of those waiting even turned out to be residents of Summer who feared the whims of the ruling classes.

Gray quickly realized that the changes in Autumn had long-reaching effects. He had to postpone his trials in the realm of Dawn until they could resettle the many groups moving into his new kingdom.

Still, he was proud to be a part of a change for the better in this world. Crowds walked past him into the portals that would safely carry young and old alike to the temporary camps that would serve as a safe home. The young trolls greeted him as 'Wind Walker.'

Deep down, Gray was ashamed of his outburst in the troll camp. Of course, he'd thought Joobel was in danger and they had more or less shot them both out of the sky. Yet the trolls seemed to respect the power that would help protect them in their new home.

One of Autumn's soldiers came to report that they had more refugees than space in the prepared camps. Gray sighed as he thought of how this would cause further stress to his queen.

Claire had seemed only a little relieved at their victory in the attack on Winter. After a couple of hours of modest celebration, she was back to work on the logistics of her office. The picture of her bent over her ledgers and maps, tapping a quill against her lips, made him feel wistful.

He'd admitted to being in love with her and she seemed to have similar feelings for him. Yet she'd pulled away after she was found to have the corruption of the Black March deep in her spirit. She'd struck him that night, the blow laughable for someone his size, but she seemed to see it as an unforgivable action.

For a man who seemed to have more ideas than time to explain them, he had no clue how to be with the woman he loved. His hand moved to shield the light of the sun. The tall man altered course for some of those moving past.

It only took a few minutes to redirect some of the refugees to the capital. The school facilities were newly finished and they could use the space to house some of the people until new towns could be established. The guard went to arrange the lines to lead the people to the proper destination.

Gray turned around and found he was looking into the face, well more the chest, of Rakash. He glanced up in order to meet the troll's dark eyes. The chieftain looked both happy and stressed. His large three-fingered hand clasped Gray's shoulder tightly as he addressed him. Again, Gray was impressed at how well he spoke despite the tusks in his lower jaw.

"My people are excited at the prospect of a new beginning. I want to thank you again for this opportunity."

Gray smiled, holding back a wince from the grip on his shoulder.

"Your thanks are for my small friend; it was she who arranged your welcome into Autumn."

The troll's laugh was deep and seemed to lisp slightly around his long brown tusks. He smiled long teeth as he clapped Gray's back. Despite the man's thick coat, it knocked some of the air from his lungs. No small feat.

"You must not ignore your influence over my people. You are the Wind Walker. You blew our camp to the sky and defeated many of our better hunters. Your influence helped us reach an accord."

Gray's face went red. "I'm still sorry about the outburst, I—"

Rakash held up his hand, stopping the attempted apology, his words stern.

"You fought for your fellow. Do you think that becoming your ally would not afford us the same? We were a dying people; my hunters would fall to protect your home because it will now be our home as well. We intend to uphold our side of the bargain."

Gray was both touched and intimidated. He held no doubt the chieftain meant those words. He held out his hand. After a moment, the troll seemed to understand his gesture. Gray's large, dark-skinned hand was dwarfed by the green three-fingered grip of Rakash. He uttered only two words before allowing the tall figure to join his tribe through the portal.

"Welcome home."

*** 

Raine loved the time in the evening when she got to fly with Mist. Only an hour earlier, while drinking tea in the war room, she'd scolded Claire for not taking enough time to ride with Harvest.

The Winter Queen was in her warm riding furs; the thick white coat made it hard to even see she was riding Mist. The drake's white scales perfectly matched the warm outfit. She had a fitted riding mask that had been a gift from the man she still intended to win over.

If Claire didn't make a move soon, Raine was going to try again. If her age had been an issue for Gray before, she'd closed that gap substantially.

Tonight, she wasn't just joyriding. Mist had a destination and Raine was fighting every moment to refrain from turning her around. They'd won the battle. The Black March had been held off for now and her control over Winter had been solidified.

The method and display she'd used the night of the Bitter Challenge had so overwhelmed both the military and the great families that no one had dared to challenge her rule, at least not yet.

Some were terrified of her power. Purification, Flood, and her sister's Frost Fire all swirled through her core. She had much to learn to properly control them. But most of her people were in love with the woman who'd saved the kingdom.

Many of the people who were injured the night of the Bitter Challenge had been healed. Once the fight was over, Raine announced she'd hired the services of Autumn's now-famous healing dragon. Money well spent.

Green-tinged fog had brought many from the brink of death. Less than a hundred had died in the battle. Between the cleansing of the corruption and the healing from Bloom, the rest made a full recovery.

Only one of the frost drakes had perished. With the return of Sleet and the addition of Mist, Winter still had a formidable flock of protectors. The power this gave her helped in offsetting the backlash of her first decree as queen.

Slavery was now forbidden in Winter; no one could capture, transport, or own another of any of the races of Fairie. This caused all the problems she'd predicted. But her trade agreements and alliance with the growing wealth of Autumn had helped bring many to her side.

The looming threat of Depth kept many others from voicing complaints. Raine decided it was best to rule from the back of something scary. She now understood how vital Harvest was to Claire. It kept things simple.

Mist began her slow spiral to the edge of the ice covering the top half of Loch Mozeg. The large white dragon landed next to her brother of iridescent azure. Puddle stood on the edge of the ice speaking to Depth, his adopted father and master.

Depth had taken several dragons under his flipper, so to speak, but Puddle was his pride. Depth was a citizen of Autumn and so was Puddle. Raine had given both of the water dragons permission to roam the realm of water; they were both bonded to Fluvial, after all.

She greeted the dragons in her mind, pushing the words out through dragon-speak.

"Thank you for being here."

None spoke, but she could feel the pulsing emotion of support. Raine put her hand down on the hilt of Caledfwlch, the blood-song echoing in her mind. She felt the need to draw the blade, to challenge even these powerful beings with its strength. The Winter Queen ignored the call and kept the sword in its scabbard.

She wanted to sit once again with Fluvial. The great spirit of water had used the stolen power and her overwhelming strength to lay claim to the Fairies' realm of water. Raine wanted to hug the jovial spirit of flowing water and thank her for her help, but for a great spirit to take human form they must ignore all they can perceive through the bond with the realm.

Fluvial could afford to meet when she'd only been linked to Depth, who needed little protection and power. Now an entire realm needed her help and guidance. Raine fought her own selfish desire and respected Fluvial's responsibilities.

Raine used her authority as queen to call out to the spirit who'd backed her when she'd had little more than a half-formed plan. Without the great spirit's support, she would've had to watch her home fall into the madness that had taken her mother.

Once again, she heard the blood-song. Her hand slipped to the grip of the sword without thinking. The power she had gained as a vessel of three spirits and as the queen of a mighty land had excited the blade. The blood-song seemed to form words in her mind.

*Take up my power and none shall stand against us.*

Raine shuddered as her own words moved out to the deep waters.

"You've given me many gifts. I owe you my kingdom, my bond-mate, and my life. I haven't the riches to repay you for these, but I will serve this land until the circle is complete. This, however, wasn't a gift but a loan. Some power isn't meant to be kept, only used as needed."

The woman gripped the scabbard, pulled back her arm, and paused. The blade was calling out, even without her contact. It knew she was choosing weakness over power and it seemed offended.

Her arm began to shake, and she felt the tears building in her eyes as she fought to return the burden the blade put on the wielder. For a moment, Raine was afraid she would fail.

Gentle pressure against her left leg told her Mist was with her. Another on her right told her Puddle was there as well. Depth had been practicing restraint on his volume because his words in her head only made her slightly dizzy.

"Letting it go will not leave you alone."

Raine screamed. The sound carried her pain, frustration, and anger. As the cry echoed off the frigid water, the sword flew through the air. She sent the scabbard as well, her gift to the next wielder of the blade. That accessory had saved her sister's life, a good trade in her opinion.

The blade swung end over end as it flew over the water. Just before it would have made a splash, a hand shot up to catch the grip. The sleeve of a blue dress that flowed like water could be seen wrist to elbow. Then the arm slowly sank back into the murky depths.

Raine sighed as she felt the world grow lighter. Over two years she'd shouldered that weight. Now it was lifted. Only in its absence could she feel how much it had affected her. She pushed one last word of thanks from her mind as she hugged Puddle and sort of leaned against Depth.

After a moment, the Queen of Winter climbed back aboard her bond-mate and took off to her home in the Black Citadel.

There was a kingdom to govern and ruling it well would be hard. Raine would do just that.

Even though something else would be far easier.

*** 

The woman stepped into the Swaying Pixie Tavern just as the sun moved below the horizon in the southwestern sky. Long red hair was pulled back in a loose ponytail that swayed against the back of her fitted leather tunic. The deep brown color added modest contrast to her lightly tanned skin.

Tight-fitting pants of the same deep brown ran into the tops of knee-high boots of shiny black. Bracelets of silver and blue hung from her left wrist and a bracer of copper fitted with bright green gemstones clamped upon her right forearm, the guard reaching up to the elbow. A long whip of tan leather hung from her right hip.

She moved slowly into the main room and walked over to sit at the bar. Instantly several men around the room started making eye contact with one another to decide who got the prize of such a shapely woman delivering herself into such a questionable part of town.

It was only a few seconds before the trophy fell to the tall, overweight man sitting in the corner. He wore a large apron over a bare chest, trousers of greasy sackcloth, and worn work boots. He had long hair that hung around his face, though the top of his head was mostly bald.

The man meandered up to loom. He seemed to have a considerable amount of experience looming. Even sitting on the high stool, the woman had to look up at a steep angle as he spoke.

"Me thinks you'd be comfier at me table."

The words seemed to get no response. The sizeable meaty hand put around her arm, however, did. She smiled widely as she was pulled from the bench. Then the woman slammed the heel of one shiny black boot into the bridge of his foot.

The man leaned forward in pain as she wrapped a cord of her whip around his neck and jumped over him. His body followed; she used her hip to flip the man who was around three times her size.

A great whoosh left him as the landing knocked the air from his lungs. Her boot kicked off his chest to land her seated back upon the stool as she leaned to the barkeep.

"Ale... in a *clean* mug."

"What about em?" the barkeep said, nodding to the oaf gasping on the floor.

She gave him a bright smile. "I don't know what he's drinking, but it won't be bought by me. He isn't my type."

The bartender lifted an eyebrow. "What is your type?"

She shrugged. "I have a thing for merchants. Those selling... a particular sort of merchandise."

The barkeep poured the frothy brown liquid in a mug and set the glass in front of her. He leaned in.

"A lot of merchants around. Whatcha looking to buy?"

The woman sniffed the brown liquid. "I was told a man named Lazuli might be able to see my needs are met."

The barkeep's smiled waned. "Who gave you that name?"

She set the mug back on the bar. "A mutual friend. One who drinks alone in the dark."

The barkeep nodded as he stepped into the back. She crossed her legs and waited. The other patrons made great effort to not take in her lithe form.

At least not visibly.

***

The young man slowly moved his foot back and forth on the side of the mangy warg sitting at his feet. He watched as the woman entered and sat. He never moved when the large man tried to pull her away.

Now he waited as the barkeep went into the back. He pulled the broad rim of his hat down slightly as an ancient elf stepped from the swinging door to the kitchen.

Rychell Balcan had appeared no more than twenty autumns when he'd last laid eyes on her. For him that had been over two and a half years ago; for her, it would've been just over seven months.

She'd been arrested for trafficking slaves through Autumn. The punishment had been aging to within one year of her death. Her reddish-blonde hair was now grey that lightened to white.

Her brown skin was waxen and deep wrinkles etched into her features. The wood elf's lean body was bent and stooped. Slender fingers were large at the joints with arthritis. For an elf, the punishment had cost her countless centuries.

She looked out around the room, but she didn't note him. He too had aged, though nothing like she had. He watched as the elf discussed something with the redhaired woman.

His ears weren't good enough to make out the words, but after a few minutes, the woman stood up and followed her guide up to the second story of the tavern. The sound of the ancient elf moving up the stairs seemed painfully slow.

The young man waited patiently for the signal. A clay sphere sat in the front pocket of his tunic. It was hollow; inside was another smaller clay ball. He waited for about fifteen minutes before he felt the smaller ball begin to rattle. Standing slowly, he made his way to the stairs.

No one took note; it was near where the room he rented would be. The warg stretched and followed after him, tail wagging so hard her back end moved with it.

He walked by several doors, but the rattle was most energetic near the end of the hall. The warg sniffed around and pointed her nose at the last door on the left, front left leg lifted to indicate she'd made the scent.

His hand moved to turn the knob, but it was locked. A line of heat formed on the tip of his finger and he sliced the bolt in half. The wisp of smoke from the wooden door jamb was acrid in the air. He pushed with one finger and the door swung slowly open.

The elf was in a corner with a broken table on top of her. Two heavily armed guards were crumpled up on either side of the door. A thin man in bright-colored robes was lying on the floor. He had a blonde beard but little in the way of hair on his head.

The man's face would typically have been quite pale, but it was currently a bright shade of red. The lean woman was sitting on top of him, looking quite relaxed. She seemed very concerned with the condition of one of her nails. She didn't bother looking up to greet him.

"Well Jack, I'm sure glad you came along. I don't know what I would've done without you."

The prince gave her half a smile. "Hello, cousin. Were you able to get the information?"

"Oh, Laz here will tell you whatever you want to know...." She reached down and patted the man on one cheek. "Won't you, sweetie?"

The slaver seemed to fume but nodded that he was an open book. Jack smirked and started to lean down.

Right before he was able to speak to the man, the prince jerked up at the sound of a loud hum coming into the hall from outside. Maeve, who would typically put herself between Jack and danger, moved to the wall and wagged her grey warg tail. She knew that sound.

As the gnome came through the door at full speed, the young man had no time for words. She grabbed him and lifted him to the ceiling, pinning him to the rafters. Her lips met his and the kiss lasted almost a full minute before Joobel pulled her face away. He was still pinned to the ceiling.

Her smile was ear to ear and made her bright blue eyes squint. "Oh, I've waited years for that. Happy eighteenth birthday, my love!"

Jack was stunned. The surprise of seeing her in the odd setting, combined with the kiss that had removed most of his already few words, left him with a dumb look on his face. Myrin managed a response before he did.

"Happy birthday, Jack. Say, do you want to finish talking to this guy, or can Maeve eat him?"

Jack continued to work his mouth like a fish out of water for a long moment. Finally, he kissed Joobel back. Soon she landed, and now it was his turn to hold the surprise.

He knelt down onto the rough boards of the room. The prince reached into a pocket and pulled out a small piece of cloth, opening it to remove a lovely ring. The gem was bright green and the metal was a faint coppery purple. Jack took Joobel's left hand and slid it onto her finger. These words he had practiced.

"You weren't the only one under orders from our queen. I've had this for almost a year. Issabol and Claire both helped me make it, but the power came from me. The gem is a part of the shell from Bloom's egg."

Joobel sniffed, looking at the polished gem. "It's lovely."

"It's one of a kind, not unlike you. I love you more every day. Joobel of the Sept of Fallen Leaves, will you do me the honor of walking through the pumpkins?"

The gnome's high-pitched squeak of excitement would have shattered glass if Myrin hadn't already broken all of it. Despite the noise and excitement, the gnome only said one word.

"Yes!"

Joobel gave Jack another kiss, just as long, and shot out of the room with wings humming. Long silver hair waved behind her as she left.

Myrin looked at her partner in this bust and sighed. She stood and lifted Lazuli up to his feet. The woman righted the broken table as best she could, moved a chair, and made him sit down.

She handed him a stack of parchment and most of an inkwell with a quill that was only slightly bent. Myrin patted his bald head and grinned.

"Just start writing names and locations; if you lie, the warg will bite something off."

The man looked at Maeve, who gave him a wolfish grin. The hound did like to smile. Lazuli began writing furiously.

Jack shook his head at his cousin. She stood and punched his arm hard enough to leave a bruise, then whispered her thoughts in his ear. The half-smile she held wasn't unlike his own.

"It seems the Demon has met his match."

# EPILOGUE

Erysichthon prepared for the cull. The highest honor among the Kalakuta was the ascension to full consciousness. As the horde absorbed more and more worlds, some were filled with races of intellect and skill.

If enough were consumed, then the Kalakuta could also have beings that could think and plan. They could further the empire. Erysichthon had plotted the demise of many worlds. There were a few the horde had encountered that had resisted them, but never one that Erysichthon had been in charge of.

The Kalakuta needed an endless supply of spirit energy to survive. They couldn't collect the power itself, but the energy gained from consuming those who did would fuel both the strength and number of the horde.

This latest world was ripe with it. Few were so saturated with energy and the task of its conquest was a high honor among the Kalakuta. The four who controlled the gift of ascension had a saying.

*'The horde's leader will learn from its first mistake;*
*others will learn from the second.'*

Erysichthon had now failed to claim the ripe world twice.

The plan had been clever. The biggest threat to the Kalakuta was the spirit of power that was most resistant to them.

Erysichthon had subtly attacked the mind of the ruler of that great change spirit.

That queen was strong and did too much too fast. She was exiled for her schemes. Even so, the plan had regained hope when another took both her power and the seeded corruption within her. By that time, the second attack was underway as the younger great spirit to the north had been too weak to resist the Kalakuta. Erysichthon then had not one but two holds on the world.

If only the others had agreed to attack all out, the plan would have succeeded. Now all of the influence that had been gained was lost. The Kalakuta had consumed most of the worlds left that had any hint of power remaining. This one could have sustained the horde for some time. His failure had put them all at risk.

Long limbs carried this failed leader of the horde before the others of its kind. Hisses and snarls of disgust carried from the elevated platforms all around. Four other tall, slender bodies stood just off from the center. They were conversing in the language of the Kalakuta.

The guttural grunts and light hisses carried information back and forth between them. As Erysichthon reached the center, an eerie silence came over the chamber. All four of the others turned as one to meet large shiny black eyes.

Like all of those who had reached ascension, they were tall and thin with large heads. Their eyes were the color of a polished night sky. There was no anger or hatred.

Emotions were discarded as a wasteful and useless byproduct of the intelligence that was stolen from countless worlds. One form spoke; which of the rulers of Kalak didn't matter, they were as one. They were the four. The words were soft and calm yet carried throughout the chamber.

"Twice now, you failed to claim the world of bounty."

"Our laws do not allow a third attempt."

There was no defense, no arguing or resistance. Another of the rulers put a slender black claw onto the shoulder of Erysichthon and then the mass of black ooze no longer had a mind. The physique of corruption was reverted to a pool of ebony slime.

The pool moved to rejoin the collective known as the horde. The discussion among the four continued. Time was growing short and no other worlds had been found that could sustain the Kalakuta for any significant period. Who said what was of no consequence; they were as one.

"There cannot be another failure."

"This world must be claimed."

"Yes, we are already losing mass to the lack of energy."

"One must be chosen who can claim this land and do so quickly."

"The last was without failure before this place."

"Yet we starve."

"There is another who has never failed."

"This one must be given more of our strength."

"All of the previous investment was for nothing."

"Yes, all the mass we sent forth is gone."

"Yet now we have less to feed."

A pause. The other three turned to the ruler who so plainly stated what all were thinking. They continued.

"Our situation is desperate."

"So much time wasted on one world."

"The power that makes it so profitable also makes it strong."

"It is learning how to fight back."

"We teach it how to do so by trying to win with subtlety."

"This is true, so much time spent."

"Time we no longer have."

"We are in agreement then."

"We must begin to push with a full assault."

"Then we will send the one known as Amphiaraus."

"This one will be given the whole might of the horde."

In one voice, they spoke, "It is agreed."

The four rulers then walked from the center of the chamber. Once they had departed, the other ascended began to leave as well. None doubted the wisdom of the four; they had the collected mental abilities of countless minds.

They were the undisputed rulers of the Kalakuta. The race of the horde. They were death.

The destroyer of worlds.

END

Dear reader,

The novel you just read is part of a series. I'm already working hard to get more volumes out and I have over a dozen novels and short stories being revised and edited in this world.

I've decided to work independently of major publishers so I'm able to work toward the story I want to tell as opposed to following trends and taking the risk of stopping before the tale is complete.

When you're finished reading this, please loan it to someone you know who enjoys this type of story. Take a few minutes and leave a review on the vendor you bought it from. A good review on Amazon, Barnes & Noble, Kobo, Google Play, or Apple Books will help me build a reader base that will grow my ability to get more books to market.

Also, taking a moment to log on to a book website and leave a review would do wonders for our small publisher. Goodreads, Library Thing, Book Riot, Bookish, Booklist, Fantasy Book Review, LoveReading, Kirkus, and R/books all have a base of readers who might otherwise never hear about our work.

Finally, visit our publisher website that has previews of current and future books as well as full-color maps. We are working on fan art, character summaries, and accept reader suggestions for future works.

www.decharlathan.com

Thank you again for purchasing this book. Don't miss Autumn's disastrous attempt at education in the short story *First Day*. The main story continues in *Spring's Contest*. Available now.

Jeremy Graves

www.ingramcontent.com/pod-product-compliance
Lightning Source LLC
Chambersburg PA
CBHW031544240626
47153CB00002B/380